FACE OFF

THE BADDEST CHICK

BUY

FOR MELODRAMA

FACE OFF

THE BADDEST CHICK

NISA SANTIAGO

Face Off. Copyright © 2013 by Melodrama Publishing. All rights reserved. Printed in the United States of America. No part of this book may be used or reproduced in any manner whatsoever without written permission except in the case of brief quotations embodied in critical articles or reviews. For information, address Melodrama Publishing, P.O. Box 522, Bellport, NY 11713.

www.melodramapublishing.com

Library of Congress Control Number: 2012949763
ISBN-13: 978-1934157664
ISBN-10: 193415766X
First Edition: April 2013
10 9 8 7 6 5 4 3 2

Interior Design: Candace K. Cottrell
Cover Design: Marion Designs
Model: Vanessa

ALSO BY NISA SANTIAGO

Cartier Cartel (Part 1)

Return of the Cartier Cartel (Part 2)

Bad Apple: The Baddest Chick (Part 1)

Coca Kola: The Baddest Chick (Part 2)

Checkmate: The Baddest Chick (Part 3)

Dirty Money Honey

Guard the Throne

PROLOGUE

The sweltering Houston heat made Apple wish for a New York winter. The humidity was irritating, as the sun hovered over the Southern city with vengeance. The city was so far removed from her world, she didn't know how she stayed or survived away from New York for so long. Houston, the fourth largest city in the country, seemed so small in her eyes. Where she came from, Harlem, New York, far and wide every day was a hustle and bustle. The people in Houston were so outdated, so green. The men weren't ready for her hustling ways.

Apple's plan was to take over Houston—make her money and make a powerhouse move. She needed to lay low for a long while from Harlem, and Houston was just the place. It was far away from home, so she wasn't known in the area. But with Guy Tony by her side, the two dominated the city's underworld with violence, heart, and wit.

Her unexpected relationship with Guy Tony was touchy. It wasn't too long ago that she'd tried to have him killed. She couldn't understand why he rescued her from her harsh captivity.

She was ready to die in Mexico. Shaun had fucked her head up really bad. The rape, the abuse, and the cruel treatment in that sleazy Mexican brothel did something to her that she couldn't comprehend. It changed her. Changed her into something dark and malicious. She felt abandoned and dirty. She felt lost at one point, and she knew there was no turning back for her.

The numerous plastic surgeries on her face took away a few of the scars and gave her back her beauty, to an extent, but the scars she carried inside of her, as well as the hatred, anger, and bitterness—well, it was going to take more than plastic surgery to heal her. Apple felt that the world owed her something, and she was dead set on snatching it with violent force.

Apple still couldn't read Guy Tony. What was his motive? Was he planning on serving revenge on a cold dish? She was grateful that he had come to her rescue when he had, but she couldn't understand why he'd done it after all she'd done to him. It boggled her mind.

Guy Tony treated her like everything was cool between them, and he was willing to continue the friendship/relationship they'd had in Harlem. Was he that naïve, submissive, truly forgiving, or what?

But Apple couldn't dwell on it. She was free from the torture and captivity that Shaun had her under, and now she was back in business through none other than Guy Tony, who had become a major force in Houston. He was the man, a force not to fuck with. How he did it confused Apple, because in Harlem he was only a sidekick and a yes-nigga, taking orders—always the Robin, never the Batman. But now he was running things in Houston like a thorough don. He had a crew of thugs and killers and a reliable drug connect. Apple didn't think Guy Tony had it in him, but he'd proven everyone wrong. It was hard to believe.

Her first few nights in Houston with Guy Tony were awkward and unsettling. She was still a mess from the horrendous experiences in Mexico. Every night there were recurring nightmares, and she would wake up screaming in a cold sweat, feeling like she couldn't breathe. She was sinking in pain and sorrow and paranoid of everything and everyone. But, somehow, Guy Tony coached her through the challenging incident. He was there for her, helping her to heal.

It took her a month to gradually come into her old self again. She was away from the nightmare, but the nightmare was still embedded into her mind, taking over her soul and eating her up from the inside. She hated Shaun with such a strong passion. She knew she wouldn't be able to rest until he was dead. She wanted to see him suffer the way she'd suffered. She wanted him torn apart and his body parts scattered across the country. What he did to her was unforgivable, and he would pay for his sins.

Apple created a list of those who needed to die, and surprisingly, Guy Tony was still on that list. Even though they were together, she still felt seething disgust for him, because she didn't understand him. If the situation were reversed, she wouldn't have helped him. She would have left him there to rot. His kindness had her feeling twisted.

In Houston, he was a murderous, kingpin thug, but with Apple, he was still that love-stricken sweetheart from Harlem.

What the fuck? Apple thought to herself. "Why are you helping me like this?" she had asked him.

"'Cuz you need it," he replied.

She didn't thank him, couldn't thank him, but she could fuck him to show her love and appreciation. Her body was his, and the two had a heated sexual interaction that was so strong, it rocked their souls to the core.

Guy Tony showed his love greatly. What was his in Houston was also hers. At first Apple walked around him on eggshells. He was in control, but in time, she became more comfortable with him again, and it seemed liked he had forgotten that she'd once tried to have him killed. Worried that Guy Tony was waiting to catch her off guard to commit some malicious act against her, that wicked thought would always creep into the back of her mind. But at the moment, she had bigger fish to fry—more enemies to crush in her fist and stomp underneath the heels of her shoes, like the bugs they were.

Houston also became her city, her domain, with her helping to control the drugs, guns, prostitution, and the money. She was living like a queen, and Guy Tony was the king by her side, and together they ruled Houston like Bonnie and Clyde. But when the day came when he decided to show his true colors, she was going to be ready for him.

In her mind, his mistake would be letting her bounce back from her downfall and sharing his world with her. She'd established some dangerous, high-end connections down in Houston and was becoming well-liked and feared at the same time, just like her counterpart.

*

Apple stepped out of the shower and wrapped the towel around her wet video vixen body. Her face was ninety percent healed, and she no longer stared at the grotesque scars that made her close her eyes, shed tears, and shake her head in shame. She was coming back into her beauty, with the help of money and the best doctors across the globe. Of course, her surgeries were expensive, but well worth the money spent. It was great to see beauty again—to almost feel whole again.

Apple readied herself in the large bathroom, lotioning her skin, fixing her hair, and checking her nails. Her customized 7,500-square-foot ranch-style home on the outskirts of Houston epitomized grandeur, coming with a spectacular free-form indoor pool, and a dramatic vaulted entry foyer with a suspended stairway and polished, pillowed French limestone flooring that complemented the elegance of an exceptional great room with a stone fireplace. There was a high-end entertainment center, floor-to-ceiling windows, and formal dining room. This home was a huge step up from the Harlem projects she grew up in, and she only wished that her twin sister Kola and those other haters could see her now.

She exited the bathroom and heard Guy Tony shouting from the other room tucked away in the corner of the house, where he did business with his men, and where sometimes things could get really ugly. It was nicknamed "the dungeon." This evening, things were no different. Guy's voice boomed out like thunder.

As she walked toward the room, her cell phone rang in her hand. She halted her steps and answered the call from an unknown number. "Who's calling?" she answered dryly.

"Apple, we need to talk," the voice said to her.

Apple knew the voice immediately. She felt flushed for a moment; her heart beating like it was a cannon going off in her chest. There was no mistaking it. It was Chico.

"How the fuck did you get my number?" she barked.

"You think I ain't got my ways of finding you?" Chico said coolly.

Apple was dumbfounded for a moment. Ever since that brief meeting with him in the Hamptons, Long Island at Blythe's extravagant birthday party, she'd made it clear to Chico that they were now enemies. He'd tried to reason with her, but she wasn't hearing it, feeling forgotten and used.

"We need to link up and talk about things," Chico continued.

"Talk about what?"

"About us . . . business."

"There is no business between us."

"I know what went down wit' you in Mexico. I know what Shaun did to you down there, and if you want that muthafucka wit' a ribbon, then you'll meet me."

Apple sighed. "Where?"

"Harlem. I need to tell you my side of the story."

"Okay. When?"

"This weekend."

"I'll be there." She hung up.

Apple didn't care for Chico's side of the story. All she understood was that he had forgotten her—left her to rot in a foreign country and replaced her with some new Barbie bitch under his arm. The only thing on her mind was revenge on the people who had wronged her.

Apple walked toward the corner room, the dungeon on the lower floor, where she heard Guy Tony shouting from. The door was shut, but it wasn't locked. She entered the room, but wasn't taken aback by what she saw. The floor to the office-sized room was lined with plastic, and Guy Tony stood over two bound and gagged men. They were on their knees, hands tied behind them and whimpering. Guy Tony gripped a 9 mm in his hand and ranted. There were two other thugs in the room with Guy, both looking detached from what was taking place.

Apple stood at the doorway wrapped in her towel and didn't flinch. She didn't care that Guy's men saw her unclothed. This was her world. She was used to seeing the ugly—murder and death, and she accepted her situation like her monthly period.

Guy Tony turned and glared at her. "What you want, Apple?" he growled.

"Handle ya business first, baby, and then we can talk."

Guy smirked and focused his attention back on the two young men on their knees and at his mercy. They could be heard whimpering and pleading for their lives under the duct tape over their mouths.

"Shut the fuck up, snitches!" Guy Tony exclaimed from behind his first victim. He raised the pistol to the back of the man's head and squeezed. *Pop!*

The man folded over and collapsed facedown against the plastic, contorted in death, as crimson blood began pooling beneath him.

Guy positioned himself behind the second man. He raised the 9 mm and repeated the same action. *Pop!*

And he fell to his death too, lying next to his cohort.

Guy Tony looked relieved. He gazed down at his wicked deed. "Fuck wit' me!" He handed the smoking gun to one of his goons. "Take care of this. Wrap 'em up, bury 'em, and make 'em disappear."

The goon nodded, removing the pistol from his boss's hand.

Guy then turned his attention back to Apple. He walked over and made his exit, closing the door to the room and leaving his men to clean up the mess and the bodies.

"Now, what you wanna talk about?" he asked.

"Chico just called me."

"And?"

"I want him dead."

Guy Tony smiled. "That's my bitch."

ONE

Lyondell's on Frederick Douglass Boulevard in the uptown Manhattan community of Harlem was teeming with patrons this balmy Friday evening. The chic restaurant was the hot spot in Harlem, with its polished décor in caramel hues and warm earth tones, and the dimly lit chandeliers setting a sensual mood. The music was jazz, and the crowd was posh.

Apple strutted into the place clad in a miniskirt, exposing her meaty thighs and fresh tattoos, and a tight, tiny metallic halter top with a plunging neckline that showed enough cleavage to make the room feel almost X-rated. She was accompanied by a young goon when she spotted Chico at the bar, downing a drink. He was all thug and all riches, his jewelry decorating him like ornaments on a Christmas tree. He wore his Yankees fitted tilted on his head, Timberland boots, and appeared to be alone.

"Fall back," Apple told her bodyguard. "I wanna talk to him alone."

He nodded and disappeared into the foyer.

Chico turned to see Apple coming. She looked stunning. The two locked eyes. Apple didn't smile. Things had drastically changed between them. Their love was torn apart now.

"You look good, Apple."

"Thank you."

"Have a seat." Chico gestured to the chair next to him. "Let's talk."

Apple, her nerves on fire, took a seat near her ex-lover. With the pistol in her purse and her goons on standby, it was clear she didn't trust him.

"You want a drink?"

"I'm not thirsty. You know why I came. You left me to rot in Mexico."

"Look, to set things straight between you and me, I fuckin' searched for you, turned this city inside out trying to find you, but you just upped and disappeared on a nigga. I hired professionals to find you, and then when I found out about your abduction, I sent the squad to get you back, but you were already gone."

"And I'm supposed to believe that?"

"You fuckin' believe what you want."

"You easily had me replaced with that fuckin' Barbie on your arm, threw her an extravagant birthday party in the Hamptons. That's how you forget about me? By being in some new pussy?"

"You're fuckin' unbelievable. I loved you, Apple."

"Look, cut the bullshit. I came here for one thing and one thing only. Where is he?"

"So this is how it's gonna be between us from now on?"

"I'm about my business. You give me what I want, or I'll just take it."

"I got what you want outside in the trunk."

"How did you find him?"

"Like I told you, I have my ways and resources. The same way I found you is how I found him."

"You expecting some reward for this nigga?"

"After what he did to you, I don't need anything."

Chico stood up, and Apple did the same, and the two made their exit from the restaurant and walked onto the streets of Harlem. It was late, so the block was quiet. The only activity came from the restaurant they'd just left.

When Apple's pricey heels hit the concrete pavement, she was watchful of everything. Chico was dangerous, and she had her eye on him.

"Where?"

Chico pointed to his gleaming black Benz parked across the street. "He's in the trunk, bound and gagged for your pleasure. Just follow me." He started to walk toward his Benz, his keys in his hand. He hit the alarm button.

Apple felt uneasy. Something wasn't right. She started to follow behind Chico but stopped in her tracks.

Chico turned and asked, "You coming or what?"

For Apple, it didn't add up. It seemed too easy. Chico seemed too comfortable. "No," Apple uttered.

"What the fuck you mean, no? You wanted this muthafucka, and now I got him for you, gift-wrapped in the trunk."

"How did you find him? You never explained that to me."

"I told you, I got peoples out there," Chico replied heatedly.

"What peoples, Chico? Guy Tony couldn't find him, so I'm supposed to believe it was that easy for you?"

Chico fell silent, and the two locked eyes.

And then it suddenly happened. Chico's goons came from nowhere, like dark devouring light. It was an ambush.

Apple quickly removed her pistol from between her inner thighs and fired recklessly, trying to survive. She took cover behind a parked car, but not before a bullet ripped through her upper thigh. She fell on her side, cringing.

Chico thought he and his goons had Apple pinned down, but little did he know, she had planned an ambush herself.

A dark van careened the corner, hurried onto the street, and came to an abrupt stop. The side door flew open, and machine gun fire from two Uzis lit up the block.

Tat! Tat! Tat! Tat! Tat! Tat! Tat! Tat! Tat!

The erratic gunfire shot out car windows, shattered glass windows of shops and storefronts, violently pierced a few of Chico's thugs, and sent patrons dining in the nearby restaurant scurrying to the ground for cover like rats. It sounded like a third world war on the streets of Harlem with the screams and all the chaos.

Chico opened fire at the van with his Glock as he stood poised in the middle of the street with the gun in his hand and his arm outstretched. His expression displayed the mind of a lunatic.

"You fuckin' bitch!" he screamed.

Apple's goons had quickly gained the upper hand. Chico's men were outgunned and outnumbered. Chico stumbled back, still firing at the threat. The men in the van were relentless and trying to shred everything in their sights. They made Harlem look like the streets of Mexico—like two cartels at war.

Chico was retreating to his car with bullets whizzing by him, but before he could get inside, a shot tore into his shoulder. He quickly thrust himself into the driver's seat, slamming the door behind him, and sped away. His Benz took the brunt of the gunfire.

Two men helped Apple off the concrete and carried her into the van. Her leg was coated with blood, but she would live.

"Muthafucka!" Apple yelled as the van sped away with her in the back.

Police sirens echoed in the distance. After the smoke had cleared, two lay dead on the street.

TWO

The Miami sun fell on Kola as she cruised through South Beach in her pink Audi R8 Spyder drop-top. The searing sun was little by little casting behind the horizon, and the city gradually began to light up in an array of colors.

With her music bumping and the warm beach air flowing through her hair, Kola was feeling like that bitch. Miami was her playground, and she was living like a superstar, taking the helm of an illicit machine and making millions. She had everything a chick could ask for—money, power, and sex from any man she chose.

She was building her empire, and with her cousin Nikki by her side, and OMG as her drug connect, she was on top of her game. She was climbing rapidly in the city's underworld, where men had traditionally ruled with iron fists. Now she was ruling just as fiercely. She was deadly, smart, and ambitious, and her name was ringing out like Trick Daddy's in "Sugar." She was mingling with all the superstars and athletes—Trina, Pastor Troy, Rick Ross, Gucci Mane, Lil' Wayne, LeBron James, and Dwyane Wade all knew her name and had love and respect for her.

Kola partied with the stars till sunup and dined in only the priciest, cream-of-the-crop restaurants Miami had to offer—establishments the average Joe could only dream of setting foot into. She was able to afford anything and go anywhere, moving throughout Miami with no limitations. A cosign from a powerhouse drug kingpin like OMG, along with her wit and sex appeal had her gaining ground as the queen bee bitch in the South.

Kola navigated her Audi onto Collins Ave. The palm trees that lined the street stood erect and green, framing a tropical bliss. The streets were becoming dense with evening traffic piling up, and the afternoon crowd was steadily making way for the nightlife.

She pulled up to the Grand Beach Hotel and stepped out onto the pavement clad in a luxurious white Ooh! La, La! Couture lace mini-dress featuring a short sleeve silhouette with billowing shoulder panels, and a plunging front bodice that tied around the neck, and Jimmy Choo shoes. She caught the attention of every male in the area.

She handed her keys to the young, pimply-faced valet in the red vest. "Take very good care of my baby," she said to him.

Kola strutted into the four-star beachfront hotel on Millionaire's Row and moved through the lavish lobby toward the row of elevators situated down the hallway, her Jimmy Choo's click-clacking against the polished granite flooring. The place was bustling with tourists as well as management and employees.

She nodded toward Sergio, the concierge, and he immediately got on the telephone to announce her arrival. Kola was now a regular, and the hotel treated her like she owned the place.

She pressed for the elevator and soon got on with an aging couple celebrating their anniversary in Miami. The elderly couple couldn't take their eyes off Kola as the elevator ascended. Her white dress clung to her shapely figure like a show of affection.

"You're beautiful, miss," the wrinkled woman said with a warm smile. "Love your dress."

Kola turned to her and smiled. "Thank you."

The elevator came to a stop on the seventh floor, and the couple stepped off. Kola watched them exit and shook her head, hoping she never got old and wrinkled. The doors shut, and the lift continued upward to the top floor, where Kola got off.

She headed toward the suite located at the end of the hallway of the seventeenth floor. She knocked twice on the door, which was ajar. She pushed it open and stepped into a sumptuous suite that offered accommodation of exceptional grace and comfort, providing a picturesque and panoramic view of sprawling South Beach, from the clear blue ocean and the extravagant yachts that lazed still on the sea to the towering hotels and buildings lining Collins Avenue.

The spacious suite was decorated with all the amenities—large-screen televisions, a kitchen, a pool table, sleek computers, and in the bathroom, a clear standing shower cab, along with a whirlpool tub recessed into its own private nook. Scented oils, baskets of soft towels, and candies were displayed near the queen-size bed.

Kola looked around. OMG was out on the terrace in his white terry robe, a cigar clutched between his fingers, taking in the beautiful day.

"I'm here, baby," she said with a smile.

OMG turned to greet her. He took a pull from his cigar and exhaled, eyeing Kola's luscious attire. His robe was open, showing his drooping pecs and various tattoos, and he wore boxers underneath the robe.

"You lookin' good, Kola," he said, the gold Rolex around his wrist nearly blinding her.

The two were having a secret affair in a private place. OMG was a married man, and his wife was a hard-core, ride-or-die, gangster bitch—an old-school, pit bull-in-a-skirt type of bitch who would give Kola a run for her money.

But Kola didn't care about the bitch. She always went after what she wanted, and OMG was no different. He was the boss of Miami, and she couldn't be with anything less.

OMG would reserve over-the-top suites, and Kola would meet him there for some dick. She couldn't get enough of mixing business with pleasure.

OMG was truly smitten by Kola. The minute he'd laid eyes on her, he knew he had to have her at any cost. She oozed sexiness. Her beauty topped that of any big-booty video vixen in the city, and her street savvy was extraordinary. Men fought to be with her.

But OMG had her on lockdown; she was his unwritten pleasure, his forbidden plaything, and even though he was a married man and Kola still considered herself single, she became off limits to anyone in South Beach. OMG was obsessed with her, and no man dared to put his hands in Kola's cookie jar when OMG was already snacking on the goods.

"Damn! I can never get tired of looking at you," OMG said with a pleased smile.

"You like my new dress? It's expensive, and I wore it just for you."

"I fuckin' love it," OMG said, a little coarseness in his tone. "Now take it off."

"My pleasure."

Kola untied the elfin knot around her neck and slowly began to peel the dress away from her tempting flesh, wiggling her curvy figure out of the material and letting it fall to the floor.

OMG approached her in the room, still puffing the cigar. He couldn't wait to wrap his arms around such perfection. Kola's naked body glistened like crystals, even with the fading sun, and her tits sat up on her chest. Her booty was juicy, and the hair on her pussy was trimmed to precision.

"I fuckin' want you," OMG proclaimed.

Kola responded with a naughty smile.

When OMG neared her, his stout frame engulfed her like a typhoon swallowing up a small boat. His hands roamed freely over her curves, caressing her small waist and sexy bottom. As he held Kola's softness in his arms, he grew harder in his boxers, his steel rod coming to life.

Kola could feel the large bulge pressing hard against her nudeness.

The two kissed passionately, their tongues wrestling with each other's.

OMG cupped her tits, squeezed her succulent ass, and then thrust her upward in his massive arms.

Kola loved it. "Take me out on the balcony," she said. "I wanna fuck under the sky."

OMG loved the idea. She was his little freak. He carried her out onto the extensive terrace and released her from his arms.

When Kola planted her bare feet on the floor, she turned and peered at Miami. The sky was changing, evening was approaching rapidly, and the setting went from a clear blue sky to a dark orange, mystic blaze in the sky.

OMG tossed his robe into the suite, and then removed his boxers, exposing great lengths of hard flesh to Kola. He stroked himself methodically, never taking his eyes off her.

"You know what to do," he said.

Kola dropped to her knees in front of him and gripped his dick in her small fist. She leaned forward and swallowed up the mushroom tip then, sliding her lips farther down his long shaft, deep-throated OMG down to the base, moaning all the while.

OMG started to moan also. He gripped the back of her head and pushed her face into him. "Ooooh shit! Suck that dick!" he grunted as Kola's slurping sounds grew louder. He lifted his chin and closed his eyes, one hand behind her head, the other on his hip.

OMG, his dick wet with saliva, could feel his flood rushing forward. The strong suction from Kola's full lips had him in a haze.

He quickly jerked his dick from her clenching jaws. "Shit! You gonna make me come like that."

Kola looked up at him with a dirty smile, her eyes filled with hunger. She rose up off her knees, and OMG quickly positioned her into a doggy-style posture. She gripped the terrace railing, and spread her long, thick legs, exposing her goodies. She could feel her juices leaking out of her and running down her legs.

OMG grabbed her slim waist and slowly penetrated her heated flesh with his hard dick.

Kola cooed, "Ooooh! Fuck me!"

OMG began to ride that ass, slapping her backside. He squeezed her slender neck and wrapped his fist around her dark, long hair and tugged at it like it was the reins to a horse. Kola liked it rough.

As his big dick thrust in and out of her, Kola moaned, gazing over the terrace, her eyes transfixed on the deep blue sea. The cool, evening breeze brushed by her hard nipples as their sexual rendezvous was exposed to the city of Miami. Being on the seventeenth floor and fucking under the canopy of sunset was exhilarating.

Her pussy pulsed nonstop around the dick, and her beauty sucked the beast into her deeper and deeper.

"Shit!" Kola cried out. "Gotdammit! Fuck me just like that, you big, black, sexy-ass, King Kong-dick muthafucka! Oh shit! Ooooh, baby, that dick is so good! So damn good!"

"Oh yeah! Oh yeah! Oh yeah! Oh yeah!" OMG chanted, shoving his throbbing dick all the way to Kola's core.

OMG felt his balls contract, and he was ready to release his seed deep into her. Her pussy was so good, it was making his balls cave in, and he seemed dumbfounded for a moment. He drooled like a big dog and was unable to pull out. The strong suction and Kola's heated velvet walls were too much and too good.

He kept strong-fucking Kola for a moment, becoming an animal in that tight, wet heaven. He felt the flood rushing to his tip again and snatched his dick from out the pussy. He released his warm, white fluids onto her lower back, gripping her side for stability.

Both of their minds spiraled into bliss as their orgasms rocked them both into screams of more and more.

OMG exclaimed, "Oh shit! Ooooh yeah, that was so fuckin' good."

"You love it, daddy?"

"You know you're my favorite bitch."

Soon, the two were wrapped around each other on the bed. Neither could let go of the other. They lay nestled and fucked again and again until night and stars completely covered the sky.

Kola rested her head against OMG's thick chest. Playtime and pleasure was over with. Now it was business.

"I need a re-up again," she said to him.

"Damn! Already? You a natural-born hustler, Kola."

"I make moves."

"I see. But, yo, I can only get you a half of a ki right now."

"What? I'll go through that within a day, OMG. I need some ki's."

"I know. But the shipment is coming in late. I won't be able to supply you that until next week."

Kola sucked her teeth.

"Look, you the first I'll call when shit touches down, but until then, just take the half of ki and be fuckin' happy, Kola. You lucky you gettin' that for now."

Kola didn't continue to argue. She knew OMG always looked out for her. She was a three-ki-a-week-moving bitch in South Beach, and she had clientele that she needed to feed. Her phone had been ringing constantly like it was the president's, but she had nothing to nourish them with, since work had been dry for her the past few days.

OMG told her, "Come down to my stash house tomorrow evening and come get that."

"A'ight."

Kola looked at the time. It was getting late, and she had other engagements to tend to. Miami kept her busy. She squirmed away from OMG's hold and started to get dressed.

"Why the fuck you leaving so early for?" OMG questioned.

"Business, baby."

"Shit! Bitch, you need to come over here and suck my dick again."

Kola smiled. "I got you spoiled."

"Yeah, you do. Now come spoil me again."

"Next time. I gotta meet wit' someone."

OMG rose up out of bed, glaring at Kola as she put her dress back on and reached for her shoes. "You know I don't fuckin' share you with no one," he spat.

"Stop wit' that jealousy shit, OMG. You know I'm only fuckin' you."

"So where the fuck you going?"

Kola looked at her lover. Her deadly black beast lay naked against white sheets and looked like he was ready to strike if she gave the wrong answer. At times, OMG was a very intimidating figure, acting like he owned her.

"I'm meeting with Nikki. You remember, my fuckin' cousin? We got some money invested in this club on Washington Avenue, and we gotta meet with the contractor to go over some details. Shit, you think drug money is the only money I'm tryin' to get in this town? I'm a businesswoman, OMG. You fuckin' know that."

OMG came down from his perch on the edge of the bed. He smiled. "I know."

"I told you about that, baby. I'm only fuckin' wit' you."

"And I love it like that."

Kola slipped into her shoes and gathered her things. She said goodbye to her man and exited the suite. She hurried outside, snapping orders at a different valet to hurry with her car.

Her pink Audi bended the corner soon after, and the young valet hopped out and held the door open for her. Kola climbed into her car and handed the valet a fifty-dollar tip.

"Thank you, ma'am!"

Kola hissed, "Do I look that old to you?"

"No."

"Then don't fuckin' call me ma'am."

She sped off and made a sharp right at the next light. As she drove through the streets of South Beach, her cell phone rang. It was her mother calling.

Kola rarely spoke to Denise. In her mind, New York was a distant memory. There was nothing left for her in Harlem or anywhere else in the city. She had experienced betrayal and heartbreak there, and she'd barely escaped the city with her life. She had too much going on in Miami now to worry about her mother or anything else. South Beach and all of Miami was home to her now.

The cell phone continued to ring. Kola was reluctant to answer, but she knew her mother. The bitch would keep on calling until someone picked up.

Kola snatched the phone. "What, Ma?" she barked into the phone.

"Bitch, you tryin' to avoid me now?"

"I'm busy. What do you want?"

"Your sister is back home."

"Apple?"

"Bitch, what other sister you got out there? Of course, Apple, and she's raising hell in Harlem again."

"I don't give a fuck what she's doing. That bitch is dead to me. She can have Harlem; I'm making moves elsewhere."

"Her name is ringing out here once again."

"Ma, I told you, I don't give a fuck about her, so don't call me about that bitch again. Fuck her!"

"You're cold, Kola. You need to mend things with your sister. I hate to see my girls actin' like this. Y'all supposed to be family. Y'all are twins."

"Family? Is you fuckin' serious, Ma? You're the one that was playing us, playing both sides, but taking her side more, when you knew she was dead wrong for what she did. So don't fuckin' talk to me about family. We haven't been a fuckin' family in a long time. That bitch can rot in hell for all I care. She should have stayed her ass in Mexico and died there."

Denise sighed heavily. "Where did I go wrong with both of y'all?"

"By giving birth to her."

Kola hung up and continued to her destination without giving her mother's words or Apple a second thought. Nikki was the only family she had love for.

It was about money and respect for Kola, and nothing else mattered, especially any affairs in New York.

THREE

The stash house in Little Havana, which was home to many Cuban immigrants, was one of many pickup and drop-off locations for OMG's operation. The two-story brick home with a stucco rooftop was always occupied with thugs and drugs. Security cameras were situated throughout the house, watching the premises from all angles, and three fierce pit bulls roamed the perimeter as deterrents to would-be stickup crews.

The living room was occupied with a half-dozen loud young thugs seated on a worn couch and playing Xbox, and on the wooden table were guns of all calibers and small vials of crack cocaine.

Kola was the only eye candy in the place. She wore white shorts with a matching top and tennis shoes. She had the young thugs' attention. They stared at her, but none of them dared to be disrespectful to her.

The long, slender man wearing sagging jeans and zigzag cornrows followed OMG's orders and stuffed half a kilo of cocaine into a brown paper bag and handed it to Kola like it was the last of his school lunch. The transaction was smooth. The half-kilo of coke Kola received would be gone in a day or two, tops.

"That's all y'all niggas do, is sit on your asses and play that stupid game," she said roughly to the group.

"Why you care, Kola?" Dino replied, a short, stocky teen with a bad temper. "What? You wanna come sit on my lap and play wit' me?"

Kola rolled her eyes. "Grow up."

"We get money too, yo," Dino replied.

"Uh-huh. Next time, watch your mouth around me."

Dino smirked.

Done with business, Kola pivoted on her clean white tennis shoes and headed toward the doorway. She didn't want to spend one minute longer in a room filled with adolescents pissing the day away. Even though she wasn't that much older than the teen boys, she felt more mature and more grown.

Kola exited the stash house, put the drugs in the trunk of her Audi, and sped away. It was a balmy evening, and her day so far was perfect. Business was good, and her life was great.

The minute she turned away from the property, she got on her cell phone and started making calls, reaching out to those in need of product. She had over twenty missed calls and countless unread voice mails. In Miami, there was always an opportunity to get paid, legal or otherwise, and in Kola's mind, a broke bitch was a lazy, dumb bitch.

Kola and Nikki were working on opening up a nightclub in the South Beach area. Kola had the right connections to make it dynamic and popular. She had already been spreading the word about it, getting a buzz going for her new venture. She had the cash ready for radio spots and ads, promotional materials, and for billboards to be plastered all across the city and near the I-95 and 395 highways. She wanted to become a legitimate businesswoman.

She'd learned a lot while being with OMG and wanted to follow in his footsteps. So in the past few months, she started to launder some of her money into legitimate small businesses, such as party promotion, a boutique on Ocean Drive, and other cash-intensive businesses. She was learning the ropes and educating herself more about Miami and the business world every day.

Kola jumped on the 395 and headed east toward the buzzing part of the city, nodding her head to a Rick Ross CD and doing eighty miles per hour. She had a lead foot, weaving in and out of lanes. But then she had to slow it down suddenly, reminding herself that she had a half-kilo of coke in the trunk. She slowed her Audi down to sixty and stayed in her lane. Sometimes that youth came out of her, and she had to check herself. She was only twenty-years old, and still a party girl—a live wire with so much spark in her, she could catch afire easily.

She turned right on to Exit 2B and drove south. The streets were lined with evening traffic, since the Heat was in the playoffs, and the people and fans on the streets were showing their support with Heat T-shirts and sporting numbered jerseys of their favorite Heat player.

Kola passed the massive American Airlines Arena on her left, where there were thousands of fans lingering outside, ready to attend the playoff game. She drove farther down U.S. Route 41. The gleaming buildings that towered over the road were an indication of the city's wealth and elite population. Downtown Miami was a spectacle of riches and wonder, with the pristine waters glimmering from the sunlight and the lavish yachts and boats decorating the marina.

She turned into the Port of Miami and went to a well known spot called Largo's Bar and Grill, which was packed with people. She strutted into the laid-back fish spot. The wicker couches overlooking the water and flat-screens made it lively and comfortable for those chilling and watching the Heat playoff game.

Kola was there to meet up with her cousin. They had planned to dine on coconut shrimp, nachos, and fried calamari. But when she arrived, her cousin wasn't around yet. Kola sighed, feeling frustrated. She hated when her cousin was late.

Before Kola moved any farther into the place, she removed her phone from her pocket and called Nikki. The phone rang a few times before Nikki answered.

"Bitch, where you at?" Kola spat. "I'm here."

"I'm not gonna be able to make it, Kola. Something came up."

"What? Bitch, what happened? Everything good?"

"This nigga actin' up again."

"What? He tryin' to put his hands on you?"

"Nah, that nigga know better. But I know he fuckin' some next bitch. I found a pair of panties in my fuckin' bedroom that ain't even my size or color, so I'm about ready to fuck this nigga up, Kola."

"Damn! Handle ya business, cousin, and call me back."

"You know I will."

Kola hung up. She sighed. It wasn't fun dining alone. Plus, she had some important business to discuss with Nikki.

She had warned her cousin about Simpson, that two-faced muthafucka. She thought he was an asshole, and she never trusted him. He was a low-life drug dealer trying to come up in Miami, and Kola always felt that he was playing her cousin, only getting with her because of her reputation.

Simpson was many things, but a thorough and real nigga he wasn't. Kola felt he was a fake thug, a wannabe. He was cute and talked a good game, but Kola read his kind like a book. But Nikki proclaimed to be in love with him, saying that the sex was phenomenal. She was blinded by a big dick and a cute face, but love was love, and Kola knew the feeling. So she could only warn and advise her cousin.

Kola turned and made her exit. She wasn't in the mood to eat alone, even though she saw plenty of men giving her hospitable looks. But they weren't her type, and she wasn't there to find a mate.

As she headed back to her car, she thought about calling OMG. It would have been the perfect day for his company and some dick, but she figured he probably was spending time with his wife and family. She strutted to her Audi feeling disappointed. It wasn't the first time Nikki had stood her up over some dick.

Kola jumped into her pink Audi, revved the engine, and pulled out of her parking spot. This time, she was going home. She wanted to change into something skimpier, drink her some Cîroc, and enjoy the remainder of the sun-drenched day lounging on her patio and catching a tan. *Fuck it!*

As Kola navigated her way through downtown Miami, she couldn't shake the feeling of being followed. She glanced in her rearview mirror and noticed a dark sedan three cars behind her. It had been on her since she left the bar.

Is it police? She hoped not.

As she drove, her heart began to pound rapidly like a drum in her chest. She constantly checked her mirrors. When she made a turn, she glanced in her rearview only to see the sedan make a turn too. "Shit!"

The streets of Miami were too crowded to take whoever was following her on a high-speed chase with a half-kilo of cocaine in the trunk. She didn't know who she was dealing with.

Shit! She had to think.

She drove a few more blocks and made a few more turns. She would soon reach I-95. Once she was able to jump on the highway, she would be ghost. But, surprisingly, the sedan was no longer behind her.

She made a few more turns and even slowed down a little just to make sure, but it was gone. She sighed with relief.

"Damn! That's crazy. Get it together, girl. You always been careful. Ain't no one following you," she said to herself.

She cruised down 13th Street feeling more relaxed. The area was light with traffic, and the sun was fading from the sky.

A breeze began circulating with night encroaching, and Kola caught a chill. When she came to a stop at a red light, she decided to put her top up. The roof began to cover the car, but just then the sedan that had been following her earlier came to an abrupt stop in the intersection in front of her, blocking her exit with its blaring lights.

"What the fuck!"

Soon another sedan and a black Yukon came from behind, red and blue lights flashing, blocking her ability to reverse, and suddenly, she found herself surrounded by law enforcement.

Up to a dozen men in dark blue flight and flak jackets with FBI imprinted on the back, badges showing, and guns out, charged at her, screaming, "Get out the car! Get out now!"

Kola's door swung open, and she was instantly dragged out of her car and thrown to the pavement. She felt a man's knee pressing into her back, and her arms being folded behind her. They began reading her Miranda rights as they placed the iron bracelets around her slim wrists. All she saw was boots and movement as she lay still against the pavement.

The feds began going through her vehicle, doing a systematic search of it. They opened the trunk and removed the brown paper bag containing the half-kilo of cocaine.

One of the agents said, "Bingo!"

"We on the money?" another asked.

"It's cash out time in Vegas," he replied.

Two men grabbed Kola by her arms and pulled her up from the pavement. They knew she was dangerous—a killer and a notorious drug dealer in the underworld. They had been performing scrupulous surveillance on her for the past month.

Kola knew to keep her mouth shut. She didn't utter a single word during her arrest. The feds tore her car apart, searching for other incriminating evidence, but there was nothing else.

They shoved her into the backseat of the sedan.

The white boy in the mirrored sunglasses smirked. "We've been waiting for you for a long time, Kola. Gotcha!"

Kola grimaced. She was ready to smack the smile off his face, but she was in no position to fight. The only thing she was concerned about was making her phone call and contacting her cousin and a lawyer. She wondered what other charges the feds were ready to pin on her, because murder, money laundering, and extortion, among other things, were all possibilities.

FOUR

Apple strutted with a slight limp into the towering Trump Plaza. The shot had grazed her leg, and she was treated by a doctor who'd promised to keep the small surgical deed a secret. He was paid handsomely and sent on his way.

Apple felt she belonged in a palace like the Trump Tower, sharing residence with such stars as Beyoncé, Erik Prince, and Bruce Willis. Guy Tony had the money and clout to secure residency in the building. It was costly, but well worth the price they paid because she wanted a secure building while settling old scores in New York. It was so good to be back in New York. The smell of the city brought her to life.

Apple had gotten word that her sister Kola was now in Miami with their cousin Nikki. She would deal with Kola later on. Now her only concern was continuing to build her empire and seek out vengeance on Chico, and with Guy Tony ready and willing to do whatever she asked, she had the goons and killers on standby to seek and destroy.

She rode the elevator to their penthouse suite on the 50th floor. When she entered her suite, it looked like an army base with artillery displayed all over the place. AK-47s, Uzis, and Glocks were scattered across vintage wood tables, and Guy Tony's goons lounged around the penthouse like it was some kind of clubhouse.

Apple glared at the half dozen thugs who'd traveled to New York from Texas with them. It was hell trying to get them to fit into such a posh environment; they had no class and no manners. They were out of place in Trump Towers, like a Muslim at a Klan rally.

The men were pigging out on Chinese food and pizza from Domino's and watching videos and movies in the living room.

"Where's Guy?" Apple asked.

"He in da next room, shawty," one of the thugs responded.

"Don't y'all got anything better to do than just sit around and make a fuckin' mess in such a beautiful room?"

The same goon replied, "Ya got work fo' us, then we gon' do it. I know we ain't come up hurr ta look pretty. Shit, we smuggled all these guns up in da city. I's ready to make use of them."

Apple looked at Crunch, a menace with a strong appetite for murder and violence. He had "Down South Backcountry Boy from Texas" written all over him, from his offbeat wardrobe to his way of speaking. Crunch, with his box braids and gold grill, stood six three and weighed over three hundred pounds. It was his first trip to New York, and he was in awe of the way it moved like a machine, running twenty-four/seven.

"Y'all niggas don't embarrass me in this building," Apple told them.

Crunch laughed. "Ya, shawty, we up hurr ta take care of business, and the quicker we get ta murderin' niggas, da faster we get ta go back home."

Crunch was black, huge, and uneducated—and one of Guy's top enforcers. Apple wasn't fond of him, but he was good at what he did. He knew how to hunt and was powerful with his hands. He could easily snap a man's neck like a twig.

She turned on her heels and went to meet Guy Tony in the next room, but before she could leave, Crunch lifted his right leg from the couch like a dog ready to pee and executed a rippling fart that echoed out and stirred laughter among his peers. Then he smiled and continued eating.

"So fuckin' nasty." Apple held her breath and moved faster from the poisonous stench.

Guy Tony was alone in the adjacent room with the lights dimmed. He stood by the floor-to-ceiling windows and peered out at midtown Manhattan. It had been a while since he'd seen New York as well. He had mixed feelings about being home.

As he gazed at the steel metropolis, he began to think about his past. Growing up had been rough. Supreme had taken him under his wing and schooled him about the streets and business. There was this unsettled feeling stirring inside of Guy. In fact, he still felt some guilt for murdering his mentor. He knew he looked like a fool taking Apple back after the attempt on his life. But look at him now. He was the boss hog, the nigga in charge, and the one able to afford a magnificent penthouse suite in one of the most opulent buildings in Manhattan. Apple had no choice but to respect him, even if she didn't love him. He wanted to show and prove to her and to anyone that doubted him that he could do it bigger and better.

Guy Tony had taken Apple by his side, because she gave him the motivation to succeed. The murder attempt on his life completely changed him. It made him become meaner than a starving junkyard dog. Killing that fool Munchies a while back had fueled the iniquity in him and opened a Pandora's box.

"Baby, what you doin?" Apple asked, coming into the dimly lit room.

Guy turned to face his woman. "Thinking," he replied softly.

Seeing him standing by the window like a boss, shirtless with tattoos decorating his skin, and his physique filling out like an NBA athlete did something to Apple. She had never seen this man look so good. There was a definite change in him.

Apple approached her lover and embraced him. "What's wrong, baby? What you thinkin' about?"

"You don't need to know," he replied coldly.

Apple didn't push it. She and Guy had their special and not-so-special moments together. This was one of their not-so-special moments. Guy Tony averted his look from Apple and gazed back at the city. Apple took a step back and looked at him for a moment. It was clear to her that he didn't want to be bothered. "Whatever," she said and left the room.

She had her own troubles. The demons were swimming around inside of her. She was still pissed that they'd missed their opportunity to murder Chico. But what pissed off her even more was, Blythe, Chico's bitch, was walking around in her shoes. It still bothered Apple greatly that she had been replaced. Chico had been her love.

While she was a sex slave in Mexico, she'd dreamed about him night and day. But it seemed that he was living it up in New York without a care in the world. And to make matters worse, he'd tried to murder her, so any remnants of feelings she still had for him dissipated on the night of the shootout.

Apple removed herself from the room, giving Guy Tony his privacy. He was never her heart, but only a convenience for her. Guy had the army she needed. She fucked and sucked him passionately, and she poured everything she had into her relationship with him, but no matter how high the throne he positioned himself on, she still felt she had dominance over him. He put on an excellent show for her, but once she got what she needed, she was ready to cut him off quickly. She had some respect for his come-up, but he would never be like Chico, no matter how heartless, rich, and powerful he became.

Apple settled into one of the many bedrooms of the penthouse. Her room had a breathtaking panoramic view of midtown. She shut the door and sat in one of the many relaxing chairs in the bedroom. She kicked off her shoes, inched her satin dress up her thigh a little, and stared at the bullet wound in her leg—a welcome home gift from Chico. She picked at the scarring tissue in her leg and began to fume. It was war. She then stood up and peeled away the dress and went into the bathroom to shower.

Apple had a devious scheme that she was ready to implement. She wanted to hit Chico where it would hurt him the most. Getting at Blythe would be like taking candy from a baby.

*

The pearl-white Bentley that Apple drove was a New York gift from Guy Tony. His lady needed to move around a city like New York in style. And it was Apple's kind of car to cruise on the New York streets and hit up all the well-known nightclubs from downtown to uptown.

She drove north on Park Avenue toward a club called Dynex, a posh uptown venue that catered to some of the city's elite. Located on 79th Street, the 10,000-square-foot space hosted some of the hottest R&B and pop acts, like Justin Timberlake, Mary J. Blige, Britney Spears, and Anthony Hamilton. And the VIPs flocked to the glass-enclosed lounge, the dimly lit chandeliers setting a sensual tone.

Apple pulled up to the spot in her flashy ride, and it immediately turned heads out front. There was a long line outside, and the bouncers were brawny black men who looked like they didn't take any shit from anyone. Apple stepped out the car, placing her black slingbacks onto the pavement and looking stunning in a fitted one-sleeve ruched mini-dress.

Apple was accompanied by one of her Texas goons, Terri—six four, muscular, with long dreads stretching down to his back. His platinum grill and dark, onyx eyes complemented his threatening demeanor.

She bypassed the long line by giving the main bouncer a three-hundred-dollar incentive to let her through. When she stepped into the club, it was lively and swarming with well-dressed revelers jamming to a Kanye West track. But Apple didn't come to party. She came for a reason and was steadfast on implementing her scheme. She scanned the large crowd, searching for Blythe, knowing it was one of her favorite places to party.

She and Terri went into one of the private sections of the club, where it cost $1,500 for bottle service. She had no problem putting up the money for two bottles of Cîroc and Cristal, and Terri kept her company, giving the impression they were a couple, when he was really her goon on standby. Naturally, he caught looks from ladies in the spot.

The night ensued with Apple getting a little tipsy from the Cîroc. Terri watched everything like a hawk as he sat stone-faced in VIP the entire night, intimidating the crowd.

Apple's plan on running into Blythe to develop a confrontation was a disappointment. She spent three hours among the partygoers, but Blythe was a no-show. She picked herself up and left Dynex, with Terri following right behind her.

*

The next evening, Apple was at Q-spot in downtown, and the evening after that, Cheetahs in midtown, and then Club Brand in uptown. Day and night, she was at every hot spot in the city searching for Blythe.

Two weeks went by, and she started to become a well-known figure in some of these clubs, where she spent money like it was water and caught attention like she was an A-list celebrity.

After weeks of searching, Apple finally got what she was looking for at Club Brand. Club Brand was a lively spot with a popular DJ and mixed crowd. It was after the midnight hour when Blythe strutted into the 96th Street nightclub with her female entourage. Blythe walked into the place like she was the first lady. Clad in a black ultra low-cut halter dress with a plunging neckline, and long, flowing black hair, she became the center of attention and turned heads with her daring attire. She was with three other girls, each of them following her lead while in the club.

Blythe was escorted to the VIP area by one of the club workers, and soon a waitress in skimpy attire hurriedly navigated her way through the thick crowd and toward Blythe's area holding two sparkling champagne bottles in the air.

Apple, leaning against the railing on the next level that suspended above the revelers downstairs, watched Blythe from above with Terri standing close by, ready to commit anything. Terri was a heartless thug, and if Apple had told him to shoot into the crowd and murder whomever, he wouldn't give it a second thought. His stoic persona made him hard to read, which was scary.

Apple watched Blythe flaunt her wealth—or Chico's wealth. Expensive champagne bottles flooded the table. Her entourage surrounded and praised the long-legged beauty like she was priceless. It was obvious that Blythe was a regular in the club. And she ate up the attention.

"This fuckin' Brooklyn bitch," Apple said through clenched teeth. "She come uptown to Harlem and think she the bitch runnin' shit. I got somethin' for her Brooklyn ass."

"Ya need me to do somethin'?" Terri asked quietly.

"Not now, Terri. We're just here to watch the show."

Terri nodded.

Apple focused her attention back on Blythe. There was a private party in her VIP area, where the girls downed the bubbly, laughed, danced, and took pleasure in the attention they were getting from the men and some females. The ladies all looked delicious in their club attire, each dress or skirt shorter than the next, revealing more flesh and booty.

Apple hated a Brooklyn bitch, especially one who took away her man and thought she was the queen bee bitch on her turf. Blythe wasn't running shit; she was only leaching off Chico. Apple was ready to cut the bitch's throat, throw her in the trunk, and drop the body off somewhere for the rats to feed on.

Apple scowled. She had seen enough. She needed to make her presence known. She spun on her long heels and moved through the party crowd and walked down the stairs like a bitch on a mission, Terri right behind her like her shadow. She rushed toward the VIP area where Blythe and her bitches partied, dancing in their stilettos and flirting with the cute men. They had their own personal security, but that didn't stop Apple from approaching the lively group of fake, whack bitches.

When she came near, a beefy guard in black tried to stop her from approaching any farther, extending his hand to push her back.

"Sorry, this is a private party," he said.

"I don't give a fuck what it is. I need to have a few words wit' that bitch right there."

"Well, if you ain't invited in, then you ain't getting past me."

"Excuse me?"

"Shorty, just turn around and go that way. I'm trying to be nice here."

"Fuck you! You know who the fuck I am?"

"I don't give a fuck if you're the damn pope; I'm just doing my job, and right now, step off!"

"Watch ya fuckin' mouth when you talk to her." Terri's fists were clenched, and he was ready to connect some hard blows against the man's cheekbone and face. Fortunately his pistols were in the car, because he was the type of goon to shoot first, and fuck any questions later.

Blythe fixed her attention on the drama ensuing by the entrance to her little party. She noticed a nicely dressed woman that looked familiar.

"What the hell is going on over there?" one of Blythe's friends asked.

"It looks like some stupid and jealous bitch trying to act up and throw some salt on my private party," Blythe said. "Let me go handle this bitch." She walked over to where the argument was happening.

Apple, scowling, locked eyes with Blythe.

"Bitch, you know me?" Blythe asked sharply.

Apple returned with attitude, "You know who I am, right?"

"No! Why should I?"

"Bitch, you need to tell Chico he a foul muthafucka, and I'm gonna come for him and you, bitch!" Apple said. "I'm his fuckin' ex that the nigga left abandoned in Mexico for a dumb, whack bitch like you! But it's all good, 'cuz I'm back home now, and things gonna definitely fuckin' change around here."

Suddenly, Blythe's hardcore demeanor changed. She had heard about Apple through the grapevine and knew she was not a bitch to fuck with. Her reputation was fierce, and even gangsters knew to tread lightly around her. The bitch had been through it all. She'd lost her little sister to a violent death, was at war with her twin sister, had acid thrown in her face, and was kidnapped and forced to turn tricks in a Mexican brothel. The bitch had endured all that, and was still standing and healed almost immaculately.

Apple shouted, "Yeah, bitch! Look at me! You know the fuckin' name."

By now, Blythe could hardly look into Apple's black eyes. Her mere presence sent chills down her spine. Blythe could feel her heart palpitate more and more, knowing Apple was one unpredictable bitch. And with stone-faced Terri standing right behind Apple, Blythe's festive night could easily end up being on the evening news the next day.

"I don't want any problems with you," Blythe said softly.

"Bitch, you got a problem with me when you started fuckin' my man, and thinkin' you can replace me!"

Blythe's girlfriends stood up behind their friend, like they had her back if anything jumped off. But, honestly, they weren't ready to go against Apple and become targets on her radar. They were mostly around because Blythe showed them a good time.

"Bitch, what? You ready to step?" Apple shouted.

"I don't want any problems wit' you," Blythe repeated.

"Bitch, you are a fuckin' problem."

Blythe was ready to get on the horn and call Chico. The lump in her throat was heavy. She didn't want to look scared in front of her peoples, but she was put into a predicament she clearly wasn't ready for. Blythe might have been a Brooklyn bitch, who' had seen her share of fights, but Apple was a whole different ball game—murders, kidnappings, extortion, and the list went on and on.

Security was on the scene, ready to defuse the tense situation. Apple had busted up Blythe's little VIP party. The look in Blythe's wide eyes told Apple that she had put some fear in her heart. She gave Blythe a warning and walked away with her one-man shadow, leaving Blythe petrified.

The minute Apple was gone, Blythe was on her phone calling Chico to come get her. She was too scared to leave the club. Even though she was with friends, they were no good to her when it came to the danger she was facing.

Blythe screamed into her phone, "Chico, this bitch had the audacity to show up and threaten me. Come get me, Chico. I need you to come get me now!"

"I'll be there in a few," Chico replied.

By the time Chico arrived, Apple and her goon were long gone.

Apple was ready to play cat-and-mouse with the couple, and once they were in her claws, she was going to shred them apart like the poor little creatures they were. It was going to be painful and bloody.

FIVE

Kola sat in her small cell and gazed at the traffic zooming by on the Dolphin Expressway. It seemed cruel to put her cell window right next to the highway, where she was able to watch the traffic flow freely while she was detained on drug charges at the Women's Detention Center on 7th Avenue. She had been there for several days now, and everything seemed hopeless for her. She couldn't get in contact with her cousin Nikki to let her know she had gotten jammed up, she didn't have a lawyer on retainer, and the connects in Miami—her get-out-of-jail-free card—were nowhere to be found. She tried contacting OMG to no avail. All his numbers were disconnected.

Kola sat hopelessly in the cramped 8 x 10 jail cell, her mind spinning and the worries overwhelming her. She couldn't help but think about how she had gotten caught up. She had always been careful, or so she thought. She didn't do too much talking of personal and illicit business over any phones. But in Miami anything was possible. It was the feds that came for her, not any locals like Miami-Dade or the state.

When Kola saw the insignia across their jackets the day she was arrested, feelings of panic shot through her. There was no escaping the feds or a federal indictment. They played ball hard and fast, and when they came for you, they already had concrete evidence for an arrest and conviction.

The agents interrogated Kola for hours in a small, white, windowless room, trying to get her to talk about her network. They wanted OMG and his underlings. But Kola wasn't a snitch. She cursed the feds out, and kept her mouth shut. She wasn't about to become anyone's pawn. The feds came at her with the threat of a long prison sentence if she refused to cooperate, but Kola stood strong and silent, angering the federal agents. They knew Kola had strong ties with OMG, and if they could flip her, then they had a solid chance at an arrest and conviction for OMG.

*

The one good thing Kola had about being locked up in the Women's Detention Center was meeting Sassy. The two had met while being arraigned and processed. Sassy, who had caught a gun charge on the humble, was a gangsta bitch from the Pork & Beans Projects in Liberty City.

At first, Kola was on some bitch shit. She didn't feel like talking to anyone. She had no desire to make any friends on the inside, and with her notoriety on the streets, none of the bitches in lockup wanted to fuck with her.

But Sassy was different. She was a beautiful Cuban and black woman who didn't take shit from anyone. When Kola locked eyes with her as they both waited for their arraignment, she thought Sassy was going to be a problem. Her mouth was rude and foul like Kola's, and they both were fierce in Miami, so it seemed like it was just a matter of time before the two bumped heads.

The first day inside, Sassy was already the alpha and omega, and proving how hard her character was to any bitch who doubted her. Two girls from West Little Havana had approached her in the cell with the intention of slicing her face open with a concealed razor blade that was somehow smuggled into the holding cell. She'd had a previous beef with the girls on the streets and had shot one of their cousins. The bitch lived but ended up with a permanent limp. Now the girl's older cousins saw the perfect opportunity to exact revenge.

Sassy saw the plot against her unfolding and was ready for anything. Kola sat in the short gap between them and also noticed the drama unfolding, but it wasn't her business to get involved. As long as they weren't fuckin' with her, she was cool.

Sassy stood up with her fists clenched and her face in a scowl. The small crowd of females in the cell had parted like the Red Sea, giving the girls an opening to fight and cut each other open. Though it was two against one, Sassy wasn't going to back down from any fight.

"What, bitch?" Sassy shouted.

"You a foul bitch, Sassy," one of the girls shouted back, ready to strike with the small razor in her hand. "Why you do my cousin like that?"

"Fuck you, bitch! Ya cousin was a fuckin' bitch. But if ya gonna leap, then leap, bitch. I ain't about dat talk. Y'all bitches know what I'm about!"

But the screaming echoing from the ladies' cell caught the attention of a few correction officers, who charged into the jail cell and roughly subdued the girl carrying the razor blade. She was dragged out the cell, placed in isolation, and had extra charges added to her file.

"I don't give a fuck!" Sassy said.

Sassy was that bitch ready to go out and die for hers. Don't let the pretty face fool you; she was a piranha. She may have been small, but she carried one hell of a bite.

She took her seat back on the hard wooden bench that was joined to the wall and kept silent. There was something about her that Kola liked and respected. She reminded Kola of herself.

Hours passed as the girls continued to wait for their arraignment in their own private worlds. It felt like doomsday for all the young girls waiting, though the majority of them had been through the judicial system numerous times.

Kola sat calm and quiet as the cell was gradually clearing, as case after case was being called, some of the girls having their own legal representation, others a court-appointed lawyer.

On the inside, the charges the feds had pending against her were making Kola's stomach do flips. It was hard to be cool with a federal case looming. It was chess time, and Kola didn't know a thing about the game. She was still a young girl, no matter how harsh her deeds were on the streets, and now she was thrown into the lion's den—where the big boys in suits and ties played brutally in the courtrooms, making deals for your life, and where the prosecutor came gunning for you with charge after charge.

Maybe you could take a plea, take a lesser charge, if they were willing to play ball, or perhaps you chance it, fight the charges in a trial, pray for a sympathetic judge and jury, and receive a not guilty verdict. But, at the end of the day, all the risks in doing so fell on the defendant.

Kola and Sassy had sat near each other, both quiet, awaiting their fate. And with the noises of the detention center all around, there was no peace of mind, only inmates coming and going, correction officers screaming, bitches yelling, and the lingering stench of other bitches hitting their nostrils.

Kola felt the place was disgusting. She yearned to be in her lavish condo and stretch out across her soft bed.

"I know you," Sassy said, disturbing the silence between them.

Kola was somewhat distrustful. "Where you know me from?"

"You fucks wit' my people, right? Rash, Nikki, and Dante?"

"Yeah, them my peoples too. Nikki's my cousin."

"Nikki's my bitch. We go way back," Sassy said.

"I don't ever see you around."

"'Cuz I'm always up in this bitch." Sassy gestured at the cell bars that contained them. "I stay catchin' charges 'cuz I'm a bitch about my paper, an' I stay bussin' my gun."

Kola nodded. "I see you be holdin' ya own."

"Fuck them two hatin'-ass bitches. You think I'm supposed to back down 'cuz the bitch pulled out a razor? She muthafuckin' lucky da C.O.s came in when they did, 'cuz I was about to be that bitch to snatch that shit away from her an' catch extra charges when I cut her fuckin' face open." Sassy flared her nostrils. "They some dumb bitches."

Kola chuckled.

"But, yeah, Nikki and I used to be up in Miami an' tossin' shit up in this fuckin' bitch. When ya see her, ask about me. Sassy dat muthafuckin' bitch that run wild wit' the pistols an' everythang! These bitches ain't fuckin' wit' me, feel me? Shit! An' when I gets out, I'ma see what's up wit' a couple of other bitches an' hoes!" Sassy was still heated.

Kola liked her. She was a real bitch. "You gotta handle yours."

"That's muthafuckin' right. And I heard about you, you a bitch that can definitely handle yours." Sassy had said. "Where ya from?"

"New York."

"Never been up dat way, but I heard ya get it poppin' up there."

"And you?"

"Pork & Beans, where we stay real all day, every fuckin' day. But they got me on some humble . . . a gun charge. Ain't no thang, tho'."

"I caught a fed case."

"Fuck the feds! Asshole, tight-suit-wearin' muthafuckas!" Sassy screamed. "They got my cousin hemmed up on some stupid charges. Ya know what the feds stands fo'?"

"What?"

"Faggots 'n' easy dick-suckers!"

Kola laughed. Sassy was a trip, and she loved it.

"Yeah, they stay suckin' our dicks and shit. Fuck 'em! Let me take my dick out and piss on a federal fuckin' agent. They don't fuckin' scare me. Niggas out thur snitchin' cuz they scared of the feds. Faggot-ass muthafuckas!"

"I like you." Kola smiled.

The two began to bond. As they waited to see the judge, they talked and talked. Sassy informed Kola of the way things worked down in Miami. She had been through the system so many times, it was like second nature to her.

When Kola told Sassy that she had gotten hemmed up by the feds, she tried to advise her on what to do. But Kola already knew the number one golden rule—Always keep your mouth shut—You don't say shit. And she needed a very good attorney.

"Shit, you gotta see a judge for ya fuckin' arraignment in like twenty-four to forty-eight hours after ya arrest. See, these muthafuckas be tryin' to have ya wait all week and shit, like we ignorant. Dey fucked up down hurr and shit."

"I see that," Kola replied.

"But anyway, you gonna be a'ight."

They continued to talk, getting to know more about each other as the hours continued to pass.

Finally, Sassy was called by the C.O. to see the judge. But before she was escorted from her cell, she gave Kola her number and said, "Yo, if you in da area, come see me, Kola. I'm in da Pork & Beans, North West Sixty-Second Street. Chain' up wit' me, ya hurr?"

"I'm gonna do that, Sassy. Keep ya head up," Kola replied.

"You too."

Kola watched them take Sassy away, and she suddenly felt alone. She knew Sassy was a real bitch, and that there wasn't anything fake about her. She was going to make it her business to check Sassy and link up with her after her own release.

*

A week had passed, and Kola was heartbroken. Her session with the judge didn't go too well. The feds were pounding on her hard for that half-kilo they'd found in her trunk.

Kola was remanded back to the county to await her bond hearing in thirty days. *Thirty fuckin' days in this bitch*, she thought. Being caught up in Miami was the worst. It felt like hell. Suddenly, she was missing New York.

SIX

Apple's moans echoed throughout the bedroom as her butt cheeks clenched uncontrollably and her hands tightly grasped the bedroom sheets. She felt his long tongue dipping intensely into her pulsating pussy, and his lips sucking on her clit like it was delicate fruit. Naked and vulnerable in his strong hold, she entangled her legs around his masculine frame, squirming. His well-defined arms raised her long legs into the air, exposing her dripping wetness even more, and he went to work on her pussy like it was a full meal, his tongue lapping up the juices.

Apple closed her eyes in the dark room and enjoyed her pussy being sucked dry by this scandalous slice of a thug. The more he ate her out, the wetter she became. His tongue game was brutal; the oral sex performed on her, damn near mind-blowing. The only sound in the room was the slurping of her sweet juices between her legs, her flavor being tasted and swallowed. It felt almost unreal to her.

The passionate oral then stopped, and Apple found her legs being spread wider, giving her lover ample opportunity to take her honey pot any way he wanted. He leaned forward against Apple, positioning himself between her thick, shapely legs.

The thrust was powerful, like a big rig barreling through a tight tunnel, causing her to gasp. His body pressed down on top of hers, making her feel like she was between a hot iron and the ironing board.

Her manicured nails slightly tore into dark sections of flesh, scraping deeply down his back, drawing some blood from the miniature wounds she created. "Fuck me!" she found herself crying out. "Fuck me!"

The sex was concentrated, and the dick tunneling inside of her made her want to melt.

But then, suddenly, the mood changed. She opened her eyes and found his hands wrapped around her neck, and his squeezing against her windpipe grew tighter and tighter. It was hard to breathe.

He continued to fuck her, but it was more forceful—turning into rape. She felt his dick growing more and more inside of her, like a thick bubble expanding.

What the fuck! Apple thought. The mood in the room was spinning out of control.

She looked up at Chico. At first he looked the same, handsome and gifted like always. But then the luxury of the room she was in began to unexpectedly change, transforming into the hell she once found herself captive in—the Mexican brothel.

Chico's features went from handsome to demonic within the blink of an eye. "You fuckin' bitch!" his voice boomed.

The rape became more wild and evil. Apple felt herself being pinned down by many arms all of a sudden, and she couldn't move an inch. The force against her was so strong, she felt like she had become a paraplegic with her naked body glued to the stained, thin mattress.

Suddenly blood was coming from her vagina, and quite a few men stood around watching and laughing.

"Get off me!" Apple screamed. "Get the fuck off me!"

But her screams fell on deaf ears. Chico's demonic soul continued to torture her in the polluted room connected to the dark brothel. His hands morphed into razor-like claws and started to shred her skin, peeling away flesh and bone.

Apple felt herself being literally torn apart. The eyes in the room were far from welcoming, more like sadistic and evil. The more she screamed, the more they smiled and laughed.

Then Shaun appeared in the middle of the rape, becoming the focal point of it all. He seemed to have grown stronger and far more vicious than he was before. Once Chico was finished with her, Shaun savagely attacked her.

Apple screamed. This was not happening. Not again, and not now. She had grown powerful herself, but in the presence of Shaun, she was a tiny fly tangled in steel-like web. The more she struggled, the tighter she felt trapped, and the more it hurt.

Shaun's wicked apparition was burning heavily into her flesh. "I told you, you fuckin' bitch, there is no escape from me. From this!"

Shaun's breath felt like fire, and his stench was overwhelming.

Apple screamed, "Noooo!" Then her voice was suddenly muted. Her pussy was being stretched from her wildly, like a rubber band stretching to its limit and ready to snap.

Her nipples started to melt from the heat of Shaun's fiery breath, and her looks began to change dramatically. The plastic surgery she had performed on her face over the months began to thaw out. The acid was eating away at her skin again, and the disfigured Apple once again started to break the surface. But this time, it just wasn't one side of her face that was disfigured. It was spreading fast, and soon her entire face was being eaten away by the acid. Then her body began to mutilate and become contorted with boils and scars.

"You ugly bitch! This is your life from now on! You ugly bitch, there's no escape! There's no escape! There's no escape!" Shaun chanted.

Apple struggled once more, but the more she fought, the uglier she was becoming. She found a mirror, and what she saw staring back at her shook her sanity from its core. Her face looked like a land field, and her body was covered with sores and boils. It hurt, and it was nasty.

"I can't! Noooo! Noooo! Get off me! Get off me! NOOOOOOOOOOO!"

The nightmare jolted Apple awake in the middle of the night in a cold sweat and shivering. The room was still, but her cries boomed out like thunder in the sky, and she was breathing heavily. The sheets were wet from a puddle of sweat she'd created.

Apple's eyes darted around the empty bedroom. She sighed with relief, realizing it was only a nightmare. She removed herself from the bed, her sweat making her skin glisten in the night. She looked at the time.

Apple walked toward the bedroom window and gazed at midtown Manhattan lit up like a Christmas tree. It was three a.m., and the city was still going strong, still alive, unlike Houston, where everything would shut down at a certain hour, and the place would look like a ghost town on some nights.

"It was only a bad dream," she said to herself, standing by the window naked.

But the nightmare fueled Apple's anger against Shaun even more. That muthafucka was in her head so much, it was becoming hard for her to sleep. She couldn't think of anything else but revenge. She had created a hit list, and Shaun was at the very top of it.

Apple went into her handbag and removed a pack of Newports. She lit up a cigarette and took a much-needed drag. She looked at herself in the full body mirror and she was the same. Her figure was still shapely and attractive, and her face normal again from the surgery. She would never be that same-looking Apple when she was a hundred percent, but what she paid for, the transformation, was well worth it. She was able to look at her reflection again and not cringe. The doctors had performed a miracle.

Apple remained awake and stood poised by the floor-to-ceiling windows watching the morning sun gradually come over the city, smoking

Newport after Newport. And as the sun invaded the bedroom, bringing about a glorious spring morning, Apple's mind bore no light, and no sunny days in her head. Only darkness, hate, and the thirst to see blood spill lived within her.

Later in the day, Apple took the Bentley and went shopping on Fifth and Lexington Avenues, and throughout the midtown area. She went ham with her spending, buying Gucci, Prada, and Chanel outfits, shoes, jewelry, and makeup. The shopping spree bill totaled $15,000, and everything was paid for in cash.

When she was done with shopping, she traveled across the Hudson to the other side, taking the Lincoln Tunnel into New Jersey, to a very important meeting with someone. She sat back in the luxurious vehicle as it sailed through the tunnel and into Union City.

Terri was her companion; he was becoming her number one shadow. He was like the hawk soaring through the skies watching everything. The day was fading fast, and rush-hour traffic into New Jersey was always a bitch, but they pushed through it and headed toward Newark. Terri cruised into Newark while Apple was on the phone talking business.

Newark was trying to come alive with new businesses that were trying to replace some of the fading ones. The city was hit hard by the recession. Many jobs were lost, and unemployment had soared. Certain gangs had taken over blocks, drugs were always rampant, and towering buildings that were once homes to many residents sat vacant and lifeless, like a decaying corpse, indicating the hard times the city had endured. The locals were lingering on street corners, some enjoying the beautiful spring evening, others conducting their illicit business. Graffiti adorned the walls in the neighborhood and the front of many businesses, and young men were scattered about with their sagging jeans and gang colors.

Terri was familiar with the city. He had cousins in Newark that ran with some of the most vicious gangsters around. Though it had been years since he'd been back, he didn't miss the city at all. Houston had become more of a financial windfall for him. Dealing with Guy Tony, he was making money in abundance. Newark to him was always going to be a memory. But he didn't have a problem chauffeuring Apple around the city. She sat in the backseat of the Bentley looking and feeling like a boss bitch. She gazed at the city behind the tinted window on the vehicle. It was easy to see out, but hard to see in. Apple watched as the car turned heads, some looking in awe at the Bentley cruising through their impoverished neighborhood.

Terri made a few turns and traveled a few miles, and then the car came to a stop in front of a two-story condo on Clinton Avenue. While most of the homes on the dilapidated street looked run-down and old, the condo looked brand-new. It was part of the city's gentrification agenda to help rebuild the community, starting with the restoration of run-down urban areas, and trying to bring back many jobs and more middle- and upper-class residents.

Apple stared at the condo from the backseat of the vehicle.

Terri shut off the car and craned his neck to fix his eyes on Apple. "This is it," he said to her.

Apple nodded.

Terri stepped out and opened the back door for his employer. Apple stepped out of the car clad in a pair of white Diesel jeans, wedge heels, and a sexy, beige off-shoulder net top.

She gazed up at the condo. "This is it, huh?"

Terri nodded.

"Get the bag out the trunk, and let's take care of business."

Terri nodded and walked to the trunk. He opened the back and removed a small, black Nike duffel bag. He closed the trunk and moved toward the condo with Apple following behind him.

The two weren't worried about trouble. Terri, in his white button-down shirt underneath a grey wool suit, along with his habitual stone-cold demeanor, concealed a holstered Glock 17 under his attire. He was surgical with any pistol in his hand—a sharp shooter, a killing machine.

When they got to the door, Terri pushed the intercom and waited.

A short moment later, there was a reply. "Who this?"

"We here to see Jet," Terry announced.

"We as in *who*?" the voice behind the intercom asked.

"Apple and Terri."

"Hold on."

The two waited patiently. Terri noticed the small, black bubble-shaped camera watching them from above. There were bars on all the windows, no cars in the driveway, and the door seemed thick, with an iron gate out front.

A short moment later, there was a buzz, and the door was unlocked. Terri swung it open and guided Apple inside. They stepped into the confined foyer, and before they reached the stairs, an armed soldier came trotting down, the 9 mm visible in his hand, but pointed toward the ground. He wore fatigues, dark shades, and army boots. And his image and attitude spelled ex-soldier.

He and Terri locked eyes. "You here to see Jet, right?" the man asked.

"For a business proposition," Apple chimed.

The soldier was ready to search them both, but Terri wasn't having it.

Before the soldier could place hands on Terri, he uttered, "I'm already carryin', playboy, and we're only here for business, not looking for any trouble." Terri swung open the flap of his suit jacket, revealing the holstered pistol on his side.

The soldier paused and looked at him. "Jet doesn't see anyone that's armed. It's protocol."

"Well, it's my protocol to protect this woman here, so I guess we're in a little dilemma here, huh?" Terri never took his eyes off the man.

"I guess so."

"Look, we came too far to get into this bullshit. I can go alone, Terri, and you stay down here and wait for me."

Terri looked at Apple with uncertainty. "You sure?"

"I'm a big girl, Terri."

Terri nodded.

"You okay with that reasoning, soldier?" Apple asked.

The man nodded.

Terri handed Apple the duffel bag and remained in the foyer while she followed the man up the stairs. Terri kept his eyes on them until they rounded the corner at the top of the stairs and disappeared into a side room.

Apple didn't know what to expect when she saw the man called Jet. The only thing she knew about him was, he was an ex-marine turned mercenary, a highly decorated soldier with a dishonorable discharge from the Marine Corps because of wicked acts of violence he'd committed overseas.

During his second tour in Afghanistan, he took aggression toward his enemies, including al-Qaeda and rival soldiers, to a completely twisted and sadistic level. Jet would cut the head off of an al-Qaeda man, chop off his dick, and stuff it into his own rectum. Jet would gouge out these men's eyes and cut out their tongues.

This sadistic action went on for months, until he was finally reported by one of his own men. The military did an investigation and found Jet guilty of war crimes. Jet was the best soldier in his unit, and he was good at tracking down his foes and killing. He thought it was a plus to his country, getting rid of evil, and doing onto them as they were doing onto us, but the Marines thought differently. He was deemed no longer fit to serve his country and was charged with crimes against humanity. It angered Jet, feeling his country and his unit had turned their backs on him—betrayed him.

Jet ended up doing some time in Leavenworth, and when he was released, he vowed to continue putting his deadly skills to use and became a mercenary. He would get paid for his adept services—like the A-Team, just deadlier and more vicious.

Apple entered the room behind the man, and it was like she'd stepped through a portal and entered an arsenal filled with weapons of all kinds. The room was painted black, had military insignias decorating the walls, and displayed prominently was the Eagle, Globe, and Anchor. Written in red and blue bold letters on the opposite side of the Marine insignia was "Peace is for bitches. Only men respect War!"

Apple saw arms and ammunition of all kinds displayed across numerous stainless steel tables in the room—assault rifles, AK-47s, M-16s, grenades and grenades launchers, rocket launchers, Glocks of all calibers, .45s, 9 mms. This man and his team were ready for any kind of war that came their way. And the surveillance was high-tech, with monitors watching every corner of the building, motion lights for the dark, and the steel doors secured with a magnetic lock.

It seemed like Jet was paranoid about something.

And a room like this, filled with high-tech military weapons in the middle of the ghettos of Newark, seemed far-fetched.

Jet stepped out of a back room, and Apple fixed her eyes on his powerful structure. He stood six three and was framed with muscles from head to toe. His arms were well-defined—biceps and triceps expanding—and his chest protruded like two large lumps. He was shirtless and swathed with tattoos and scars. It looked like he could crush anything with his bare hands. His eyes were dark—like onyx embedded into his skull. His bald head gleamed, and his chocolate-covered skin made him almost lickable in Apple's eyes. It was easy to see why they called him Jet.

"I heard you have some business for me," Jet said to Apple, his voice raspy and stern.

"Yes, I do."

"Have a seat. Let's talk." Jet gestured to the black leather couches cattycornered in the room.

Apple took a seat, and Jet followed behind her. They sat opposite each other. Jet leaned back into the cushion, spreading both his arms behind him, and across the back of the couch and gazed at Apple with intensity.

"I need someone found and taken care of immediately," Apple said.

"I like that, straight to business. Who is this person you need to be found?"

"His name is Shaun, and the last I heard, he was living in Mexico. I hear you're the best in tracking people down, no matter where or how far they run."

"I am. I have a team of killers that are thirsty for the hunt," Jet stated with smugness.

"Well, I need for your dogs to hunt. And I'm willing to pay handsomely." She pushed the duffel bag near Jet, who leaned forward and unzipped the bag and stared at the stacks of bills bonded together inside.

"That's a hundred thousand in payment for your services to be rendered."

Jet smiled. "Nice. And how do you want me and my men to bring him back to you?"

"I want him brought back to me piece by piece. And I want his head separately and last."

"And so you will have it that way."

"How long?"

"Depends on how far we track him. I'll send out the bloodhounds, try to get his scent, and then we'll work our skill from there."

"Oh, and I want him to suffer. I want this muthafucka to be tortured, and I want it on film. I want him to cry out so bad, he'll be yearning for death."

"Possible, but that will cost you another fifty thousand."

"Done."

Jet nodded. He saw Apple as a vicious and strong woman. He loved her. She was about her business and obviously had much of it, from what she was paying him.

When they were done talking, Apple stood up, Jet did also. They shook hands. And Apple turned to leave the room.

Jet said, "You know, we could use a woman like you on our team."

"Oh, really?" Apple was somewhat flattered. "And why's that? From what I heard, you don't view women as reliable soldiers."

Jet chuckled. "From what I've seen and heard of you so far, you're a cold and smart female. You've done your homework on me, and I've done my homework on you."

"I see. Well, Jet, I'm about my business. I'm a businesswoman, and I'll leave getting dirty in the trenches to you and your men. I'm a Park Avenue bitch right now—love makin' money and having the finer things in life."

"As do I," Jet replied with a smug grin. "And killing is one of the finer things to do in life."

"Just get me what I asked for, and we'll continue a good business relationship in the future. I have a feelin' that you won't disappoint me."

"I never do."

Apple left the room. Terri was still waiting for her at the bottom of the stairway in the foyer.

"Everything okay?" Terri asked.

Apple nodded.

Terri opened the door for Apple, and she walked out. Before Terri made his exit, he looked up and noticed Jet watching them leave from the top of the stairway, his eyes lingering on Apple as he pulled on a cigar.

For a moment, the two locked eyes. Terri grimaced at the man. But Jet only smiled and then turned and disappeared into the next room.

SEVEN

The Women's Detention Center in Miami was no place for Kola to be locked up in. She stared out of her cell window at the beautiful, warm spring day with the traffic on 395 flowing freely like the wind. But there was nothing beautiful about her day. She missed her lifestyle greatly. She found herself consumed in regret and anger. Life was moving slow for her on the inside, and she was forced to wear the tacky bright orange jumpsuit that swallowed up her petite, curvy frame day after day.

But Kola had no reason to show off for any of the other girls in the detention center. Some of the girls were like predators in the wild, sodomizing other inmates after dark. Some had connections with the prison guards, and were able to receive smuggled goods from the outside—cell phones, cigarettes, iPods, and even drugs.

Kola was new to this world, but she wasn't afraid of it. Her name rang out from her connections with OMG and Nikki. Everyone knew who she was and what she was about. She walked around fearlessly, knowing if any bitch tried her or attempted to put their hands on her, then they would have a problem. Being linked to a vicious drug organization had its benefits. She moved around the jail with ease and was able to make her phone calls without being extorted or harassed.

Two weeks into lockup, Kola hadn't had one incident with any of the female inmates yet. They gave her hard, foul looks, but slick remarks about her were kept to themselves. They didn't like that she was from New York. In fact, the detainees had a sour attitude toward anyone outside of Miami getting money; especially the way Kola was getting money. But Kola made it known throughout Miami that she wasn't the bitch to be fucked with.

In the Miami jail, the Haitians hated the Cubans, and the Cubans hated the Haitians. The females were like cats, steadily scratching at each other, and fighting all the time. The guards had to constantly tear them off each other.

The day was passing slowly like always. Kola exited her pod and walked down the grated walkway toward the phones, her mind filled with so many worries. In the past two weeks, she hadn't been able to contact Nikki. She needed to get the rundown on what was going on the streets, find out what was being said, or who was snitching. She needed her own lawyer, and she needed to get out, on bond or whatever. The judge in her second court hearing was more lenient this time and set her bail at $250,000. It was high, but Kola was confident that she could get it paid.

Kola picked up the phone in the circular room, where a total of five working phones were in use. She glanced around her and noticed another woman, a Haitian, also in the room with her. Dark-skinned with tight cornrows and very young in the face, almost the same age as Kola, she barely spoke English. She began speaking Creole into the phone receiver, and then Kola noticed the tears streaming down the girl's cheeks as she spoke.

This place was breaking the young Haitian woman down. It was almost heart wrenching to watch. Kola watched the girl speak for a moment, not understanding what she was saying, but knowing it was family she was speaking to, from her manner.

Kola shrugged off the feeling and decided to mind her business, like she'd been doing from the first day she'd arrived. Now wasn't the time or place for her to start feeling sympathetic toward anyone. She dialed Nikki's number again collect, praying she would reach her cousin this go-around.

"Damn, bitch! Where the fuck was you this whole time?"

"Shit is bad out here, Kola."

"Well, fuck that! You know I'm jammed up."

"I heard."

"I need to get the fuck outta here, Nikki, like ASAP. I need you to get my bond paid. I need for you to put up that money, and I need to get a lawyer. I wanna see the outside again."

Nikki didn't respond right away.

"Nikki, you still there?"

"Wit' what, Kola?"

"What the fuck you mean, wit' what? I'm talkin' 'bout puttin' up some cash to get me the fuck outta here, Nikki. I mean, I ain't scared up in here, I'm holdin' shit down, but I can't fuck wit' these bitches in this fuckin' place."

"Kola, I don't know what to do. Since you been locked down, shit done got tight out here."

"Nikki, we both got enough cash to pay this bail. Shit, bitch! If you don't wanna tie-up that much paper, then put ya house up as collateral or somethin'. I don't give a fuck, I'll buy you a new house. Once I touch ground again, you know I'm gonna hit you off. But I'm dead in the water sittin' in this fuckin' bitch."

"Kola, you don't fuckin' get it—The feds raided the crib too and took everything."

"What?"

"They had a warrant and ran into our shit and snatched up the cash, book statements, and guns. It's lookin' bad right now, cousin."

"And where the fuck was you?"

"I wasn't around. I drove by and seen them comin' out my place wit' boxes of evidence."

Kola sighed heavily. This wasn't happening. It had to be a nightmare. How was she caught up like this?

"Well, we got peoples in this city, Nikki. Reach out to someone and make it happen. Since I been down in Miami, we helped out a lot of muthafuckas—a lot of important people. Shit, now it's time for them to return the favor."

"They scared, Kola. Ain't no one tryin' to fuck wit' you right now because the feds are on you heavily, and they don't wanna get dragged into that web."

"What the fuck ya mean, they scared? As much money we put out there, as many fuckin' favors as I done for muthafuckas, and you tryin' to say they ready to have me take the weight of all this, and abandoned me like I ain't shit?"

Nikki was silent.

"Fuck 'em! I swear to you, they better not do me like this. And you mean to tell me that our crib was the only crib they raided?"

"I don't know the details of—"

"Well, fuckin' find out then, Nikki!" Kola screamed.

"A'ight, Kola."

"I can't be sittin' in here like some ass and feelin' vulnerable out there. What about OMG? Have you been in touch wit' him yet?"

"No."

"Why not? Yo, reach out to him and have him put up the money for my bail. He knows I'm good for it."

"I don't think that's gonna be a good idea."

"What the fuck you talkin' 'bout, Nikki?"

"Look, word is you might be on ya own on this one. And if I was you, keep ya mouth shut 'bout everything 'cuz you know if niggas have the slightest inkling that you might be snitchin', then they gonna come for you, and they can get you touched inside too, Kola."

Kola shouted, "Bitch, what? I'm being threatened? I ain't a fuckin' snitch!"

"I'm just sayin', Kola, ya hot right now. OMG ain't gonna want to have shit to do wit' you right now. Everything we do, every move we make, might tie into a conspiracy case against us all."

"So I'm left out there to fend for myself—That's what you tellin' me?"

"Look, I'm gonna work on finding you a good lawyer to represent you and get you outta there. I got ya back, cousin."

"You got my back?" Kola returned dryly. "It sure don't feel like it. All I keep hearing from you is fuckin' excuses."

"Kola, don't even—"

The phone line suddenly went dead. There was no warning, just the rude shutdown while in the middle of their conversation.

Kola sighed heavily and hung up. She was left out in the cold to freeze. She lingered by the phones for a moment, and the cold look on her face made it known she wasn't going to go down without a fight. She felt that something was not right at all. How was it that she was the only one caught up and the only person sitting behind bars with a pending fed case against her? There had to be a snitch involved somewhere.

How was her cousin a free woman if the feds kicked in her door and they found cash and guns in the place? Why wasn't she locked down too? They were partners in a lucrative drug organization in Miami, and like sisters they went everywhere together and did everything together. It wasn't adding up.

The female guard came into the room to escort Kola back into her pod once her phone privileges were over. The day was fading fast, and the loud shouts and rants from other incarcerated females confined in their pods could be heard throughout as Kola was guided to her cell. Some were acting like animals behind the thick steel doors.

She walked up the grated walkway in a foul mood, but she kept her head up and tried not to show any emotions. She would beat this minor setback. She was from Harlem, and Miami was just the suburbs to her. She wasn't a snitch, and this wasn't going to break her.

But she felt mistrust around the people she had once associated herself with. She realized that in this business, there was no such thing as friends, or trust.

The pod door slid shut to her cell, confining Kola to her small world—a small cot, steel walls, and the furnishing and fixtures being anchored to the walls and the floors. The only access Kola had to the outside world was looking through her narrow, rectangular shaped window that gave her a view of the highway.

Kola took a seat on the thin cot and slouched against the wall. She propped one leg up on the cot, while stretching out the other, and stared aimlessly at the wall in front of her. A few tears streamed down her soft, light brown cheeks. She remained that way for hours, tuning out everything around her. For the first time, she felt vulnerable. The young girl in her had surfaced, and she couldn't help but be afraid.

She wiped the tears away with the back of her hand. Her next move was reaching out to New York and getting in contact with her mother, and if she had to put her pride aside, maybe even Apple. Kola didn't want to revert to relying on family. Nikki was family too, and look where it got her.

But desperation started to settle in with Kola, and she needed a way out. She still had great animosity toward her sister, whom she hadn't seen or heard from in a long while. But Kola still felt unforgiving toward that bitch. It made her cringe to think that she might have to reach out to her for help.

*

Kola, dressed in the unzipped orange jumpsuit, the arms tied around her waist, sat at the metal table with four other women in the three-sided concrete room. The other girls were gossiping about their lifestyle, telling the horrors they'd been through—the drug use, prostitution, gangs, fights, and what landed them behind bars. Other inmates talked about the glitz and glamour of their lives in Miami—the partying, the money, the sex, and the cars. Two separate accounts being told by two different groups of ladies—glitter and prominence versus sorrow and heartache—but they all ended in the same situation. No matter what side of the tracks they came from, each account finished with them being locked down at the Women's Detention Center in the heart of Miami.

Kola didn't want to share her tale, so she remained quiet. Everyone was trying to outdo the other with their stories, but Kola didn't like to run her mouth. She didn't want anyone to know her situation, even though her reputation had preceded her.

"What's up wit' you, Kola?" Danielle asked. "Why you so quiet?"

"I'm good," Kola replied evenly.

"You sure?"

Kola nodded.

Danielle stared at Kola. There wasn't any tension between them. Danielle just cared about a few of the girls in the jail, and sometimes acted like a surrogate mother for some of the younger ladies. She was in her late twenties and was a prostitute on the streets of Miami, working underneath a gorilla pimp named Ice. She made hundreds of thousands of dollars while working for her pimp and lived a life of luxury by spreading her legs on a regular, or working on her knees and widening her jaw.

Danielle was from Houston and had come to Miami wanting to live a better life. She was nineteen when she'd left Houston, and the minute she touched down in Miami, she met Ice.

At first, Ice showed her love and the finer things in the glitzy city. He even gave her a place to stay. Danielle fell in love with Ice. He was tall, handsome, charming and established, having his own home, two nice vehicles, and money that seemed limitless.

But the fairytale only lasted a few weeks. Once Danielle became comfortable, Ice turned violent and ugly. Knowing she had no one in Miami, neither family nor friends, Ice gave her a cruel choice—to either pay him back for his kindness or become homeless. Danielle, being scared and alone, chose to pay him back, which meant turning tricks in Miami, escorting, and doing anything and everything he asked or demanded of her. When she became reluctant, the beatings followed—either with his fist, a gun, or any inanimate object he picked up in his hands.

Ice had other girls under his control and turning tricks for him. He made a fortune in the city, raking in tens of thousands of dollars a day. But Ice was selfish, cruel, and treated his hoes like property. If a ho didn't make her quota, talked back, or broke any of his rules on the streets, she was beaten, and sometimes gang raped for hours by a few of his friends.

Danielle decided that she'd had enough of the beatings, the rapes, and the humiliation. Even though she wore the best clothes, rode around in luxuriant cars, and lived in a nice home, she still felt a dog had a better life than her. Her freedom was gone, and her dignity swallowed up by the mistreatment. Her face would remain beautiful, but her body suffered bruises and burns from Ice's hands.

Late one night, while Ice slept, Danielle and her young companion stabbed him multiple times in the throat and face and then burned his body, in the process causing the whole house to catch afire and burn down. They were later caught and both took a plea from the prosecution, receiving the maximum twenty-five to life in a state prison.

Funny thing for Danielle, even though she would spend the rest of her life behind bars, she'd never felt freer. She was never afraid to tell her story, and when she told it, the female inmates would always listen. She was a very beautiful woman with hazel eyes, caramel skin, and long hair that she styled into two long braided pigtails that fell down to her shoulders. Men would pay handsomely just to be with her, but now the women in the prison were willing to be with her too. She was like Helen of Troy.

Kola and Danielle developed a friendship somewhat. They'd both come from a different city to escape something. They both were beautiful women, motivated by wealth, but caught up in the system. And they both were killers.

Danielle was one of the few ladies Kola would actually talk to, and share her story with. She tried to school Kola on the way things worked inside the jail, and the way things worked in Miami. Kola had called it home for only a few weeks, but Danielle had called it home for ten years.

"Kola, you better put that pride to the side. Go speak to your family, and let them know you need help down here with your bail and a lawyer," Danielle advised.

"Fuck my family!"

"Your sister can't be that cold-blooded."

"You don't know that bitch."

"And your moms?"

Kola fell silent. The memory of her little sister Nichols was always so painful to share with anyone. Nichols was the best thing in their family. She was such a sweetheart, a wonderful person, and smart.

Kola surprisingly shared the memories of her murdered sister with Danielle. In fact, Danielle was the only person Kola talked to about Nichols. That part of Kola's life had died years ago, but now, it was starting to resurface. When Nichols died, so many other things died in the family too—sisterhood, trust, loyalty.

"I feel you can have a second chance, Kola. I mean, just reach out and try somethin'. You would rather be stuck in here and die than to reconcile with your peoples in New York?"

Kola sighed.

"Zip up!" the male guard yelled as the door opened.

The ladies pulled their jumpers over their shoulders and followed the guard outside for their recreation time in an enclosed gravel yard. The ladies lined up single file as they streamed leisurely into the yard.

Kola followed behind Danielle, and the two continued to talk as they circled the yard, minding their business, feeling the hard gravel under their feet.

"So what you gonna do, Kola?" Danielle pressed.

"I don't know."

"Time is running out, girl. You wanna be stuck in this bitch?"

Kola didn't, but reaching out to New York would have its cost.

"All I'm sayin', sometimes you gotta bend the knees and humble yourself if you wanna advance and do you. Shit, we're the same, Kola. You're a damn hustler—a fuckin' go-getter. We get ours, and right now, you ain't gettin' shit being stuck in here behind these walls. Reach out to your peoples, get what you can from them, and once you got yourself goin' again, fuck 'em!"

Kola smiled.

Danielle was right. She was a sitting duck behind prison walls. She felt like a bird without wings; a fish that couldn't swim. It was time to take action.

The two ladies continued to talk until their time in the enclosed courtyard came to an end. The inmates were escorted back inside for the evening; they walked into the jail in one long line, heavily watched by the guards and checked for weapons or contraband.

Being in that courtyard gave Kola a little bit of hope. The sun beaming down on her from high above reminded her of some really better days.

Kola went to use the phone. She called home to New York collect to speak to her mother, hoping it wasn't a mistake. She didn't want to seem desperate to her moms. It was destroying her that Apple was back in Harlem and getting rich, while she was suffering locked up in Miami. Her situation needed to change right away.

The phone rang a few times in Denise's ear, and she picked up aware that it was a collect call from her daughter in a Miami detention center. She immediately accepted the call.

"Kola," Denise cried out.

"Ma, we need to talk," Kola replied in a child-like voice. She felt her voice cracking as she became emotional.

"Now you wanna talk?" Denise returned sharply.

"It's not the time to hear your damn mouth, Ma. I'm in trouble."

"What kind of trouble?"

"I fucked up, and I might need to get in contact wit' Apple."

"Apple hasn't been around since she came back. But I'm gonna reach out to her. I'll see what I can do."

Kola sighed heavily. "Thank you, Ma," she said humbly.

Kola felt that her sister, of all people, probably wouldn't want to see her locked down. Despite their bitterness toward each other, they were still blood.

Kola continued to inform her mother about the situation she was in. They talked for a moment, and for once, Denise was finally acting like a mother to her child. The fret in Denise's voice displayed the concern she had for Kola. And, for Kola, hearing someone from home trying to comfort her brought about more than a slight ease to her. She held back the tears that started to well up in her eyes and just confessed to her moms like she was under oath.

EIGHT

Denise threw the dick down her throat like it was a tasty meal. Her full lips wrapped around the nine-inch monster with goodwill, its mushroom tip ramming the back of her throat. The moans from the room grew louder and louder. Denise cupped the young stud's nuts and sucked and jerked him off simultaneously, her saliva wetting every inch of his privates.

He grabbed the back of her head, and his fingers clung to her long braids as her deep-throat actions traveled farther south on his long, stiff shaft. "Oooh, shit!" he moaned. "Suck that dick, baby. Oooh, feels so good!"

Denise quickly got naked and was ready to play with Raymond for the whole evening. Raymond was a local hustler trying to come up in Harlem. Twenty-two years old, he had the body of a gladiator, with his thick arms and powerful chest, his tight cornrows extending down to his back, and his body swathed with tattoos and battle scars.

Denise loved her young thugs. Fifteen years his senior, she was yearning to feel his hard dick curve inside of her.

Raymond coiled Denise over the leather couch, spreading her legs, arching her back, her luscious tits dangling like juicy fruits ready to be picked from a tall tree. He vigorously slid himself into her sweet, creamy hole, and she released a howl, feeling the rigid penetration slam into her.

She tightened her grip around the couch. "Ooooh shit, daddy," she cooed. "Throw that dick into me."

Raymond's hand pushed down on the small of her back, and with the other hand, he reached around and cupped her tits as he fucked her from the back.

The dick inside of her felt like cement expanding between her pink walls, as it tunneled inside of her with the intent to please every border of her flesh. "Fuck me, Raymond! Damn, your dick is so big!"

As the two were lost in the moment of passion and lust, Denise's cell phone began to buzz on the glass countertop. She chose to ignore it. She was ready to come.

The ringing stopped.

Denise threw her phat, round ass back into the man's pelvis, taking his entire monstrous dick inside of her like a porn star. She closed her eyes and continued to howl as Raymond went to work on the pussy.

They went from fucking doggy-style, to Denise on her back, her legs vertical in the air, and her knees almost touching her ears as Raymond was perched over her, slamming his hard dick into that pussy like a sledgehammer. Denise proved her flexibility, contorted crossways across the leather couch, the dick burrowing into her like a drill.

Her phone rang again.

Denise gazed up at Raymond, who was spread out on top of her and handling his business like a thorough muthafucka is supposed to. He didn't let anything distract him. He was focused like an A student.

"Just fuck me, baby!" Denise cried out.

This time, Denise took the dick while lying on her stomach—froggy-style, her butt cheeks spread open, her sweet sap continually dripping between her thighs, as Raymond pressed against her, snaking his nine inches of solid length into her.

Her pussy was contracting around his girth. She felt herself about to come. But the abrupt, hard knocking at her apartment door threw her for a loop. She wasn't expecting any company.

Raymond raised himself up and stared at the door, his body glistening with sweat. Confused, he turned to look at Denise for answers, but she didn't have anything to say to him. She shrugged.

The banging at the door continued and echoed throughout the apartment.

Raymond stood to his feet and reached for his jeans. He was thinking it was a jealous boyfriend, maybe an ex-lover coming by to pay Denise an unexpected visit. He hurried to put on his jeans and grabbed his pistol. If an ex-boyfriend or a current boyfriend wanted to charge into the apartment and start acting up, then he was ready to put a few hot ones into his chest and keep it moving.

Denise donned a long robe and went to the door, her face in a heated scowl as she tied her robe. She looked through the peephole while Raymond stood in the living room shirtless, pistol in hand and held down by his side.

"What the fuck!"

"What's wrong, ma?"

Denise quickly unlocked the door and swung it open. "Apple!"

"Hey, Denise," Apple returned dryly.

"Oh my God! Look at you." Denise was shocked to see Apple's face looking almost brand-new.

"Can I come in?" Apple asked. "I tried to call, but you ain't answering ya damn phone."

Behind Apple stood Terri, her shadow and protector. He stared at Denise with his usual stoic expression.

"Of course, you can come in, baby." Denise stepped to the side and allowed for the two to enter her apartment.

Apple walked in and locked her eyes on the young man who stood in the center of her mother's living room with the pistol in his hand. She didn't flinch, but kept her cool, as did Terri, when they noticed Raymond.

Apple shot a look at her moms, saying with her eyes, *You still haven't changed at all, have you?*

Denise read Apple's look. "Bitch, don't come in here and start judging me. I wasn't expecting to have any company over this evening."

"I just came to talk"—She looked at Raymond—"in private."

"Raymond, baby, leave us for a minute."

"You sure?"

"Yes. I need to have a serious talk with my daughter."

Raymond nodded. Then he collected his things and walked toward the door. Denise followed behind him, and before he made his exit, the two kissed fervently while Apple and Terri watched.

"To be continued," Denise whispered in Raymond's ear, causing him to smile.

"Most definite, ma. I was enjoying that pussy."

"And I was enjoying that dick too. Sorry we had to be interrupted, but I gotta take care of family issues."

"I understand."

"But you know my pussy ain't goin' nowhere."

Raymond smiled again, and they locked tongues once more.

"Denise, I don't have all fuckin' day," Apple chimed.

Denise released an irate sigh and slammed the door behind Raymond. She spun around to face her daughter. "Bitch, you in my home now, so be fuckin' respectful. I didn't know you was coming."

"Just be happy I came to see you at all, after everything you put me through."

Denise quickly took in Apple's wardrobe and knew her daughter had come up once more. Her jeans hugged her curves, her top was definitely from Fifth Avenue, her shoes were stunning, and her diamond earrings were the size of blueberries.

But the biggest shock was Apple's face. It was a miracle that she almost looked like her old beautiful self.

Denise went toward her daughter and slowly reached out to try and touch where her burns used to cover parts of her skin. Apple stepped back, preventing her mother from placing any hands on her.

"How?" Denise inquired.

"Money, and some great fuckin' doctors."

"You look good, Apple. I'm glad to see you again. And who's your friend?"

"Someone you don't need to concern yourself with right now."

Denise sighed.

"Why come to my home wit' this hostility toward me? Was I that bad to you, Apple?"

"You wasn't that good."

Denise huffed and reached for her pack of Newports that was lying on the dining room table. She removed a cigarette and quickly lit it. She took a deep drag and exhaled the smoke from her nose like steam coming from a locomotive.

She then fixed her eyes back onto her daughter. "Look at you. I hear you tryin' to become the queen of Harlem or somethin'."

"I'm just trying to take back what is rightfully mines."

Denise chuckled. "And what is rightfully yours?"

"My respect out here, and then my revenge."

"You ain't gonna never learn, Apple."

"I've been learning and getting better at it."

"You came here to gloat, huh, Apple? You came to show someone that you're better than your mother, ya own flesh and blood? You're still that little girl, but so angry inside."

"I'm no longer that little girl, Denise. Look at me. I have everything that you ever dreamed of, plus more, and I did this on my own."

"And soon you're gonna be where your sister is right now, if you keep the way ya goin'. She's locked down in Miami. I heard the feds finally came for her."

"Fuck Kola!"

"She's your sister, Apple. You would let her rot away in a Florida prison?"

"We ain't been sisters in a long time, Denise, and you haven't been a mother to me in a long time too."

"Apple, baby, listen. You can't take on the world by yourself. Now Kola is still family, despite what you think."

"I don't need any fuckin' family. The only family I have in my life right now is those that are ready to kill for me and help me take out my revenge." Apple motioned her head toward Terri, who stood silently with his arms folded in front of him.

"We are your family," Denise shouted.

"If you was family and loved me like you claimed, then why no one came lookin' for me while I was being held hostage, raped, and tortured in that Mexican brothel? Huh? Where was my family then? Why didn't Kola come lookin' for me? Y'all really think I just picked up and left on my own?"

Her mother fell silent for a moment. She felt sorry for her daughter's misfortune. She had heard the stories about Apple and Mexico.

"Let's just talk, Apple, you and me, mother and daughter. No one else around."

"We have nothing to talk about."

"Yes, we do. I have plenty to tell you."

Apple felt reluctant. She had the urge to just leave, but she hesitated. She turned to look at Terri, who was silent and waiting for her instructions.

"Wait outside for a minute, Terri. I need to have a private talk with my mother." Terri nodded and left the apartment.

Denise shut the door behind him then pivoted on her feet and gazed at Apple. "I knew somethin' had happened to you. It just wasn't like you to up and disappear like that. I wanted to look for you. We all did, but where was I to start?"

"That's only an excuse, Denise."

"Look, we all made mistakes."

"Fuck that! While I was rotting away in that place, being raped every day, and crying, everybody was getting rich and living a good life, forgetting about me. I was dying over there. And you expect me to just come home, sweep all that shit under the rug like it was nothing, and be fuckin' forgiving? Are you serious? People must pay for what happened to me."

"At what cost, Apple? Look at you. You're strong. After all that, you came back from that, and you came up. I look at you, and it didn't break you. I see you're a wealthy woman again."

"And don't expect a fuckin' dime from me, Denise. I did for you once, and I'm not goin' to do for you again."

"I don't want shit from you, but peace of mind."

Apple sighed. "Whatever. Seeing blood spill from those that did me wrong will give me my peace of mind. I fell and was vulnerable once, but I guarantee I won't fall, become vulnerable, or be humiliated ever again."

"And are you ready to spill your sister's blood too?"

"That bitch gets in my way, I'll gut her like a fuckin' pig too."

"Apple, what is wrong with you?"

"Look at me, Denise—I'm not a bitch to fuck with."

Denise shook her head. "Of course, you're not. But let me tell you something, Apple, you and Kola will one day need each other again, believe in that. I warned Kola about Miami, but she didn't wanna fuckin' listen. Now she's fuckin' caught up wit' the feds down there, and that cousin Nikki, I don't trust her. Your sister doesn't have a lawyer or money for bail."

"What that got to do wit' me?"

"In all y'all years of hustling, neither one of y'all got knocked. But things will change for you, Apple, faster than you know it."

"You threatening me, Denise?"

"This is not a threat, it's a prediction."

Apple laughed it off.

Denise knew she couldn't talk any sense into her daughter, who was steadfast in causing her own destruction. The hatred and bitterness was set deep into Apple's eyes, and there was no changing her mind or her ways anytime soon.

Denise took a few more pulls from her cigarette as she continued to give Apple the 4-1-1 on her sister's dire situation. About Nikki, Denise said, "That bitch can't be trusted. She's my niece, but she ain't family."

"No one can be trusted," Apple spat.

Apple was barely listening. Her heart was black like tar and cold like ice. She only wanted revenge. And she was ready to shake the hood to its core to fuck up those who'd done her dirty.

Apple left her mother's apartment with no kind of change in her. Denise could only watch her daughter leave and know it was about to get a lot worse.

NINE

The streets of Harlem were quiet for the moment. The stillness in the air was like a dead calm from block to block. The sun had faded a short moment ago, and the dusk was balmy. The local residents in the project buildings on 115th Street in East Harlem were enjoying the spring sunset, but they were worried about the escalating violence in the area. There was a war going on in Harlem, and certain blocks felt like Baghdad. There was a shooting almost every night, or every other night, even though the cops were doing their regular patrol, driving around in marked cruisers, and walking the beat, moving through the projects and making their presence known.

But a different breed of killers seemed to be lurking about. They had no respect for the NYPD at all, and they had no respect for life. These killers only knew how to do one thing, and that was murder. This out-of-town team of killers would gun down their enemies in public in broad daylight, in front of schools. And there was also kidnappings and torture. Harlem was relapsing—becoming what it was in the eighties again. Civilians were afraid to come out after a certain hour because of heavily armed gangs.

From 115th Street to 145th Street, East Harlem was becoming a nightmare of a place to live. And there was one name behind it all— Apple. She had come back to her hometown with a fiery desire to destroy everything and anything that had done her wrong, and she didn't care who or what got in her way. Once she set the wolves loose to hunt, it seemed like they were devouring everything in their paths.

There was a task force set out to capture criminals, and the NYPD would make arrests, but it wasn't enough. These soldiers from the South and a few from the Mexican cartels didn't give a fuck about police. They would rush into homes and kill families, cutting off arms, heads, and fingers as a warning to others. These killers would shoot up a city block and set fire to homes, trying to eradicate everything. There was no denying it—Harlem was becoming a war zone, like a small Mexican town.

*

Apple sat in the backseat of the gleaming black Tahoe and watched two men walk into the towering project building on 115th Street. The outside to the project lobby was occupied with local Blood members with their sagging jeans, red bandannas, and beads, and gambling in the pathway to the building, as they smoked and drank. She took a few pulls from the cigarette burning between her lips and watched the area like a hawk, her back window tinted and rolled down only a quarter.

The truck sat parked a few cars away on the city block and was tucked away between cars. Terri and Chicano sat in the front seat. Chicano was from a small Mexican town that bordered the United States. He used to run with a ruthless cartel called Los Zetas, and had been a killer since the age of fourteen. His eyes had seen wars and horrors from the time he was a youth. In fact, the only thing Chicano knew and understood since he was a child was death. His father was a killer too, but he was shot dead and decapitated in front of Chicano's eyes when he was ten, and his prostitute mother was butchered by a serial killer when he was eight.

His transition into adulthood was rough. He had been shot several times, kidnapped, and tortured. He had gotten into shootouts with local authorities and had been imprisoned at the age of twelve. By the time Chicano was nineteen, he was a ruthless, stone-cold killer with no morals and no value for human life. Five nine with short hair and brown skin, he was a lean, mean, killing machine for Apple and Guy Tony.

The trio sat parked and waited for several moments. The men who went into the building were Chico's handlers, and they went into an apartment to retrieve product. Apple knew they were armed and dangerous, but so were her two goons. Terri was handling a Glock 17, and Chicano wielded a Ruger pistol and a machete.

The projects were swarming with locals on this warm spring night. The playground was teeming with young children and parents at the early evening hour. But the serenity and enjoyment in the courtyards, playground, and other areas didn't make a difference to Apple. She didn't care about anything but taking care of business.

Apple took one last pull from the Newport and flung it out the window. She said to her thugs, "Y'all know what to do. When they exit, make a scene for these muthafuckas to remember."

Terri and Chicano nodded. Chicano grinned a menacing grin. He didn't speak a word back, but his mind was already set on unspeakable carnage for his enemies. The boss lady wanted to make a gruesome statement, and it would be done.

A few minutes later, Chico's two handlers exited the building lobby and said a few words to the Blood members lingering out front. Then there was short laughter coming from everyone.

Terri was the first to exit the Tahoe, followed by Chicano. The two men seemed to float across the street without detection in their dark T-shirts and jeans. Chicano had on a red ball cap, the Ruger gripped in one hand, and the machete in the next.

Terri marched forward, raising the pistol at the two men, and Chicano did the same. Chico's men suddenly widened their eyes when they saw the danger.

Bam! Bam! Bam! Bam!

The gunshots echoed throughout the projects, sending fright and panic to those in close proximity.

The first shot hit one thug in the chest, and the second shot hit him in his neck. Blood squirted. Then he lurched forward and collapsed on the concrete.

The second victim tried to run, but Chicano fired rapidly, hitting the man multiple times in the back. He dropped to his knees and stumbled against the iron railing in the pathway, screaming in pain.

Chicano ran up and stood over him, his gun trained on the back of his head. Then he decided a quick death was too easy. So he raised the machete over his head, gripping the handle tight, and came down forcefully with the sharp tool and plunged the blade into the man's skull. Blood spewed out around the machete, which was rooted in his skull. Chicano pulled out the blade and went to hacking again, shredding the victim's face apart like it was clay, leaving behind a bloody and contorted mess.

There were loud screams as many people stared at the horrific act.

Chicano grinned, his machete coated with blood, the body beneath his feet almost hacked to pieces.

Chicano and Terri hurried back to the truck. Chicano tossed the blood-drenched machete into the back, and they sped away, leaving behind a gruesome crime scene that would forever haunt those who had witnessed it.

TEN

Chico sat slouched in the striped slipper chair, like the kingpin he was, and watched the big-booty stripper with her tattooed back bend over and spread her ample butt cheeks wide open on the stage. Her goodies exposed, she aimed her smile at Chico. She took the stripper pole like a professional, twirling around it with her legs spread and her heavy tits flopping about. Chico, clutching a wad of Ben Franklins in his hand, took a sip of Grey Goose. The clear, smooth liquid glided down his throat, while his eyes stayed glued to the stripper dancing seductively to Drake and The Weeknd's "Crew Love" blaring in the dimly lit club.

Chico, flanked by his street goons, Rome, Bad, and Torrez, tossed a few hundreds at her and made it sprinkle on the dark-skinned beauty. Then his goons followed him and tossed a wad of money at the girls.

It was all fun and smiles for the moment, but every man knew, in the back of his mind, that a serious threat was looming. Harlem was drowning in violence and bloodshed. Apple was on the warpath and gunning for all of her enemies, trying to wipe them out like a Category 5 hurricane.

Chico's shoulder still ached slightly from the gunshot wound he'd suffered during the shootout with Apple a few weeks earlier. He'd barely escaped with his life. He didn't understand where he went wrong with her, and why Apple suddenly hated him so much. The bitch couldn't get it through her thick, ignorant skull that he had nothing to do with her kidnapping and suffering.

But since Apple wanted a war, Chico was determined to bring it to her at full throttle. She was fucking with the wrong man, and the girl he used to love would die by his hands, in agony too, if it came to it.

However, tonight was his night to enjoy, and he didn't want to think about his troubles. It was his twenty-seventh birthday, and he wanted to spend it with his peoples, along with beautiful big-butt, freaky strippers ready to fuck and suck him and his crew, and buying out the bar and getting tipsy from six-hundred-dollar bottles of champagne and liquor.

The strip club popped off with lively revelers from wall to wall, and the heavy bass from the half dozen speakers rattled the walls and the stage.

The DJ continuously gave Chico love and respect, shouting out over the mic, "I want to wish a happy birthday to my dude, Chico. We love you, my dude! This is your day. Let's do it right tonight!"

Chico nodded and smiled at DJ Havoc. He raised the Grey Goose bottle he was drinking from in the air as a sign of respect and love for those around him. He took a swig from the bottle and pulled one of the naked strippers lingering around the crew into his lap. She chuckled and smiled.

Chico started to fondle between her meaty thighs, feeling her pleasures and taking in the warmth of her scent. "What's ya name, ma?" he asked.

"Coco." She chuckled.

"*Coco*. I like that. You know it's my birthday today, right?"

"I know," she said with a flirtatious smile. "You made your birthday wish yet?"

"Nah, not yet. Why? You gonna help make it come true for me, ma?"

"I don't know. Depends on what you wishin' for."

Chico smiled. He continued to rub the inside of her thick, brown thighs. The way her naked ass sat on his lap was just ideal, with the friction and sexual gyration against him adding to the delight. Her tits were perky, her chocolate-covered nipples hard like small pebbles, and her brown bubble-ass was causing an erection in his jeans.

"Damn, you fine, love," Chico complimented, sliding his hand farther between her legs. He fondled her clit and massaged her walls, setting off Coco to squirm in his lap and moan a little.

"You like that?"

She cooed, "Yeah, daddy."

The soft penetration between her pink walls made her juices drip.

"I would love to unwrap you, but you already naked and shit."

"So let me unwrap you."

"Ummm, I like that."

Coco was ready to please the tall, fine birthday boy by any means, her hazel eyes peering intensely at him.

Chico moved his hands gingerly around her curves, admiring her shape—an hourglass figure with a luscious teardrop booty that was so soft to the touch.

"Shit, love, let's do this. Let me get my birthday gift from you."

"Definitely." Coco rose up from his lap and stood erect in her six-inch red stilettos.

Chico did the same, the Grey Goose bottle clutched in his grip, holding it down by his side and spilling some of the clear fluid onto the floor. He didn't care. He was mesmerized at the moment and couldn't keep his eyes off Coco.

He said bluntly, "I wanna fuck you in all three holes."

Coco chuckled. "Damn! I see you's a freak."

"You don't even know the half of it, Coco." Chico slid his arm around Coco's slim waist.

Coco reached down and grabbed his crotch, feeling the family jewels he was working with. She was ready to do as told. Her pussy was throbbing for some dick action, and she was ready to wrap her full, sensual lips around that hard piece of dick when she removed it from his jeans.

The two began to take steps to one of the VIP rooms located in the back of the club.

"You good, Chico?" Torrez asked.

Chico nodded, but before he could have his fun with the leggy, brown-skinned beauty, Rome got the call on his cell phone. The look on his face said it was urgent. He couldn't believe it. Not today, not on Chico's birthday. He hung up the call and approached Chico with the news.

"Yo, Chico," he called out.

Chico turned, his arms still around Coco. "What up?"

"We gotta talk," Rome said bleakly.

Rome's look already expressed to Chico that the news wasn't good. He pushed Coco off to the side with no words toward her, and went to Rome, leaving her standing there looking dumbfounded, anxious to fuck the birthday boy.

"It's that bitch again, right?" Chico asked.

He and Rome went into a private corner, and Rome said into his ear, "One Hundred and Fifteenth Street . . . I heard it's really ugly over there. They got Sheeba."

Chico's heart sank into his stomach. Sheeba was his first cousin on his mother's side. He had put Sheeba on the money a year ago with something light and not too much of a risk for him, but now the decision seemed to have backfired.

Rome continued with, "They butchered the kid with a machete . . . tore into his face." Then he added, "We on it."

"Fuck that shit, Rome!" Chico screamed. "I want that bitch's head on my lap by week's end. I'ma fuck that bitch up!"

Chico drew attention to himself in the club, startling a few strippers. He tossed the bottle in his hand, smashing it against the wall, and he and his goons stormed out of the club ready to take revenge on behalf of the fallen.

As Chico and his thugs spilled into the Escalade, Bad said in Chico's ear, "I'm telling you, Chico, that bitch came back wit' some muscle. She tryin' to take shit over, and if you tryin' to keep what's yours, then let's hunt that fuckin' bitch and her family down and fuck that bitch's world up."

And the Escalade sped away into the darkness.

ELEVEN

The days dragged by for Kola as she sat in the detention center, where she'd made few friends and some enemies. She started going over certain events in her head. She thought about Nikki, and her story just didn't add up. Something wasn't right with that girl.

And then OMG came to mind. Was everything a setup for her to take the fall? Was OMG fucking her cousin too? And where was she? She didn't come to visit, and whenever Kola called her phone, there was never any answer. Her cousin had completely vanished.

Kola knew she was set up, though. She thought about her sudden arrest every day, her mistakes, how she got knocked. How was she the only one in this predicament? Were Nikki and OMG both plotting on her?

While sitting in the dayroom, she suddenly heard she had a visitor. The guard approached her with the news and was there to escort her into the visitation room. Kola felt relieved to finally have somebody come see her. She thought it was Nikki finally pulling through for her.

She stood up and followed the guard to get processed for her visit. She remained expressionless, even though she was curious about the visitor. If it was her cousin, Kola had a few choice words to say to her. It had to be Nikki; no one else would come and show their face.

Half an hour later, Kola entered the no-contact visiting room, a long, stale-smelling room with mostly family and loved ones of the female inmates, who were seated on the long, hard benches that stretched down on both ends of the room. Visitors sat at a granite counter that was split in half by a large Plexiglas partition. On either side were short stalls with a telephone attached on both ends of the partition.

The guard directed Kola to where her visitor was seated on the other side of the Plexiglas. "Booth six," he said.

Curious, Kola moved slowly down the narrow corridor to booth six and peered at the face behind the Plexiglas. She didn't recognize the handsome young black man at all.

He had no facial hair, and he had chiseled features. His cornrows were neatly done, falling past his shoulders like thin ropes hanging from him. His arms were muscular, he looked fit and healthy, and he carried an aggressive street image, with tattoos covering from his hands to his neck. He wore a Dwyane Wade Miami Heat jersey.

Kola took a seat on the bench, never taking her eyes away from him. She figured he was a representative of OMG who had come to the detention center to speak on his behalf; maybe give her a direct warning to keep her mouth shut while in custody.

The man gestured for her to pick up the phone hanging on the stall, and she did so.

"Do I know you?" she asked with scowl.

"Nah, you don't. But I know you, or heard about you."

"From where?" Kola asked roughly.

He cracked a little smile, showing the gold and diamond grill in his mouth. "Sassy sent me."

Hearing her name brought some kind of relief to Kola. But why would Sassy send someone to visit her? Kola was even more confused. "Sassy?"

"Yeah, that's my cousin. She had some good things ta say about you."

"And what brings you here . . . this visit?"

"She's worried about you and would have come herself, but she ain't too fond of coming back to this place. I don't blame her. I don't do jail myself. But she wanted ta reach out to you, let you know you have a friend down here."

Kola remained quiet.

"We asked around 'bout you, and Sassy says you good peoples. You 'bout ya business."

"I am," Kola replied coolly.

He nodded. "Good to hear."

Kola was still confused about his visit. "How is she?"

"She's good."

Kola nodded.

"But listen . . . we know 'bout ya bail, and we gon' make it work out for you."

"How?"

"We got peoples dat matter. Dat's all you need ta know."

Kola felt strange about the outside help. Even though she and Sassy hit it off, nothing came free. There was always a cost. And Kola was always skeptical about bringing new faces into her world.

Kola said, "I never got your name."

"They call me Copper."

"Copper, huh? You got bank like that? Two hundred and fifty stacks is a lot of money to put up."

"Don't worry 'bout it."

"And what do I owe this favor?"

"No favor. Sassy vouches for you, and we get it done."

Kola was still skeptical. She locked eyes with Copper, and he didn't flinch. He talked with confidence. He sat erect and kept constant eye contact with her. He had the posture of a boss figure and the words of a sharp individual. Kola needed the help, no matter where it came from. If

Sassy had the connections to get her bail paid and get her a good lawyer to represent her, then so be it. She wasn't going to be a fool and turn it down. She continued to look at Copper.

"Then get it done."

Copper nodded.

Kola stood up and turned to make her exit. Sassy was cool, but Copper had shifty eyes and a sly smile. It was hard to trust a man with his demeanor, but Kola didn't have any choice. If they decided to help her, it was a win for her. If not, then she would find other means to find her freedom once more. She walked back into lockup and never looked back.

* *

Several days passed after Kola's talk with Copper. She needed to know a little more about him and Sassy, and the only person she felt she could go to was Danielle, who'd been around long enough to know the players in Miami. She had been in the game for ten years, and South Beach, where she turned tricks and fucked many high-end players, was her playground.

Kola asked Danielle, "You know Sassy?"

"Sassy, yeah, I heard of the name, but vaguely though."

"What she about?"

"She's serious out there in the streets. Heard young girl don't play any games. Deadly, her and her cousin."

"Then why would she want to bail me out? I mean, we talked when I first got here, but ain't nothin' more than that."

Danielle shrugged.

"You think she got serious paper like that, Danielle? I mean, two hundred and fifty K ain't nothin' to sneeze at."

"I know."

"And I ain't a stupid bitch. You puttin' up money like that for my bail, then someone gonna want somethin' else in return."

"I know that too."

Kola wracked her brain, trying to find the angle, but it just didn't add up. "I ain't turning tricks."

Danielle chuckled. "You don't look like the type to take it lying down."

"Fuck that! I'm a boss bitch, Danielle, and if they try and make me someone's bitch, then it's gonna be on and poppin' down here. Real talk."

"Just be calm, Kola."

"What you think I should do then?"

"You want out, don't you?"

Kola nodded.

"Then get yourself outta here. If she's reachin', take her hand and find out why later. But the most important thing is you outta here. That's step one. And then, step two, you'll find out once you get on the other side of these walls."

"You right, Danielle."

"But be careful. If you don't take the bail, stay in your cell and keep a shank on you at all times."

"Why?"

"Word is, you might have a contract out on your head. I just got that kite today."

"What?" Kola asked, shocked. "By who?"

"It's through the wire. Someone put the green light on ya head, so if I was you, I'd watch my back. The bounty is twenty thousand to have you killed."

"Twenty stacks?"

Danielle nodded.

Kola couldn't help but feel scared, but she didn't show it. She was still determined to move around like she was the baddest bitch in Miami, but she only had her reputation going for her in the detention center. OMG and Nikki were her security on the outside. Even though she had proven herself countless times in the streets, without any support, any muscles, or a strong word from OMG to the savages in Miami that she was still his number one bitch, then she was vulnerable just like any other inmate. With her connections from OMG and Nikki fading, the wolves inside began sniffing around, circling their prey, ready to tear into some New York flesh.

"Here, take this."

Danielle discreetly handed Kola a homemade shank. The short, wiry piece of metal had its tip sharpened on the concrete floor to plunge into skin easily, and the handle was wrapped with upholstery thread to make it secure and easy to conceal.

Kola took the weapon and slid it into the sleeve of her jumpsuit, and she and Danielle went their separate ways. Kola was more alert than ever. Everyone was a suspect, and if any bitch tried her, then they were about to get a handful.

*

As the days moved on, Kola was keeping in constant contact with Sassy. And whenever she called collect, Sassy made sure to answer. They were having lengthy conversations, finding more about each other every day. Sassy assured her that her bail was about to be paid, that she would be a free woman again.

"Why are you doin' this?" Kola asked.

Sassy simply replied, "We'll talk when you get free."

It was obvious that Sassy didn't want to reveal any information via the prison phones or through any letters. Everyone was always watching and listening. Kola understood. Sassy was becoming the kind of ally Kola truly needed at the moment.

*

Sassy had come through for Kola, who couldn't wait to leave the detention center. It had been three months since her arrest, and now she would become a free woman. She'd worry about the cost of her freedom later on.

The day was just starting, and Kola wanted to take a fresh shower and clear her head, but inside, there was no such thing as clearing your head. There was always someone lurking, watching and ready to try you in your weakest moment.

Along with the other inmates, Kola walked into the prison shower wrapped in a white towel. The shower was a spacious, white-tiled room with eight high showerheads lining the wall. Five ladies entered the showers and hung their towels on the towel racks near the exit and began to wash themselves.

The showers were noisy, with each showerhead running simultaneously. Kola took the last showerhead at the end of the room, wanting to be far away from the others. A female guard stood watching the door. Kola, two showerheads down from the nearest girl, quickly began to lather her body with the issued soap.

The water cascaded off her brown skin. She washed with her eyes open, and wanted to be in and out. Her release was in a few hours, and the farther she was away from this place, the better.

One by one, the girls started exiting the bathroom when they were done. Only three girls remained, one of them a butch named Meeka.

Kola turned off the shower and moved toward the door then Meeka followed. Kola soon noticed the female guard wasn't posted by the door, but she didn't think anything of it.

Before Kola could exit the shower room, she suddenly felt a piercing pain shoot into her lower back. Meeka had shoved a shank into her. Kola jerked from the attack, and she felt it again and again. It happened so fast, Kola wasn't able to defend herself.

Of the three girls remaining, a second girl left the bathroom fast, leaving Meeka alone to finish up the job.

Kola knew she'd fucked up. She'd let down her guard and left herself open for the attack.

"Fuckin' bitch!" Meeka exclaimed.

Meeka was a hard-core butch, standing five ten with a shaved head, and had the body of a linebacker, with cold eyes and rough, manly features. Soon to be sentenced for first-degree murder, she was feared in the prison.

Kola stumbled against the walls, her blood spilling. Her body was going into shock. Her blood-coated hands stained the white-tiled walls as she struggled to walk and support herself. Then she collapsed on her side in a thud, Meeka towering over her with the bloody shank still in her hand.

Is this it? Is this my last breath? Kola thought.

Kola squirmed, the blood spilling from her body like water pouring from a garden hose. She tried to keep her eyes open, but she felt weak and cold, like her soul was parting from her body.

"You ain't invincible, bitch!" Meeka shouted.

Kola felt paralyzed, and her breathing was becoming shallow. She wondered who paid for the hit against her. She had lots of enemies, so it could've been Eduardo, Cross, Chico, OMG, or some other forgotten enemy from her past.

Right before Kola lost consciousness, she heard the words, "That's from Apple, bitch!"

TWELVE

Blythe stepped out of the shower feeling a little bit refreshed. She tied a large blue towel around her naked, wet figure. The shower was somewhat of a comfort to her from the problems surfacing in her life.

She stared at her image in the large bathroom mirror and sighed heavily, her mind heavy from so many worries and her nerves shot. She didn't know what to think. Her hubby was at war with a psychotic bitch. And the bitch was unpredictable. She had gotten the news of Sheeba's gruesome murder—the way he was hacked with a machete. It made her cringe in fear for her own safety.

Blythe no longer felt secure in their fifteenth-floor home, tucked away and guarded across the Hudson in New Jersey, though security in the building was high-end and tight—cameras, a doorman, and guns. She couldn't even go out anymore without a bodyguard to protect her, so she mostly stayed indoors, out of the clubs, and especially away from anything uptown. Anything connected to Chico was a target for destruction.

But the sad thing about her man being at war on the streets was that she was alone most of the time. It had been three weeks since she'd last had sex, or any quality time with Chico, who was too focused on fighting a war with Apple. It made Blythe a little jealous. His ex still had most of her man's time. Ironic. She still came in second when it came to Apple, and she couldn't help but feel some kind of way.

Blythe lingered in the shower for a moment, until she heard movement in the living room. She heard loud talking, the voices deep and harsh. She figured it was Chico coming home.

She stepped out the bathroom and entered the living room still wrapped in her towel. Chico had just walked in the door, but he wasn't alone. He had a few goons with him—his street lieutenants. They looked perturbed.

He didn't even see Blythe as she stood in the hallway out of their view and watched the men turn her luxury penthouse home into some kind of tactical war base.

Chico was clad in black fatigues, a black tank top, and wore a bandanna tied around his head like a headband. He looked more like a soldier at war than a kingpin, or her hubby.

His three goons were also dressed in all black. One carried a duffel bag that seemed to be weighed down by its heavy contents. He placed the duffel bag on her round mahogany dining table and started to unzip it.

Blythe only stared on, as the tall goon in the black shirt began removing an arsenal of guns from the bag—Uzis, MAC-10 machine guns, Glocks, and other high-caliber pistols.

*

"We gonna fuck that bitch up, Chico," Torrez exclaimed with a scowl, a Desert Eagle in his hand.

Chico walked over and picked up a black Uzi, its clip protruding. He examined the weapon, unhooked the long clip, and checked the ammunition. He nodded. He put the weapon back on the table and picked up two twin 9 mms. He outstretched his arms with the guns and aimed at the wall, looking like some kind of dark action figure or a deadly hit man. He smirked as he pictured staring down at Apple and drowning his ex-bitch and her thugs with heavy gunfire. It was a pleasing thought.

"Yeah, these will do, fo' real," he said.

Rome nodded.

"We good then?" Bad chimed.

"Yeah," Chico replied.

Bad started to cram a few guns back into the duffel bag, leaving out the twin 9 mms, the Uzi, and the Desert Eagle. Those were going to be Chico's personal weapons.

The men talked recklessly about the streets, the murders, the death of their cohorts, and how they were going to retaliate.

Torrez began rolling up a blunt, and Bad and Rome tried to counsel Chico about their next move. Nobody would be untouchable. It had to be ugly and calculated, and they had to hit hard and fast.

"An eye for an eye, Chico," Bad stated. "She got at your cousin, so then you go after her family too."

"What family?" Chico said. "That bitch ain't got family she loves like that."

"What about her moms?" Bad asked.

"Like I said, that bitch ain't got family she loves like that."

Bad said, "I don't give a fuck, Chico! Love her or not, we still get at that bitch, and leave a message for her, prove our point. She still in the projects, right? Left wide open to be got."

Chico lit a cigarette and took a long drag. He walked over to the windows, where he had a picturesque view of the New York City skyline. He was able to see where they were rebuilding the towers at Ground Zero. The new Freedom Tower, still in its skeleton form, was starting to dominate the downtown area of Manhattan. It towered over the other buildings as it stretched into the blue sky, making New York City look whole again.

Chico kept his gaze on the soaring tower being built and took another pull from the Newport between his lips. He couldn't believe that it had to come to this—bloodshed and war with his ex-girlfriend. The woman he'd once loved. He didn't do anything wrong, but Apple had to find some kind of fault with everyone. She'd blamed him for not rescuing her, and then all of Harlem for the torture she had experienced while being held captive and made a whore in Mexico.

He'd tried to talk some sense to her, but she wasn't trying to listen to anyone, so he had to resort to violence. She was being pig-headed and ugly. Her mind was possessed with revenge at any cost.

"I wanna fuck that bitch up, and everything that belongs to her, Chico," Bad said.

"You and me both."

"I can have ten goons in her projects ASAP, and they can kick in that bitch's door and do her dirty," Bad stated. "Maybe get her to talk and give up her fuckin' daughter."

Chico didn't reply right away. He only continued to stare at the city, admiring how beautiful it was. It was the concrete jungle where dreams were made, and also destroyed.

"She don't know where that bitch is," Chico said gruffly.

"You sure about that?"

"Nigga, I'm sure. Apple ain't stupid."

"Don't matter," Bad said. "We still need to prove our point."

Chico knew Bad was right. He couldn't look weak, not right now, and not because of some bitch. Especially his ex-bitch. He had to make a statement—not just to Apple, but to all of Harlem.

Chico took one last pull from his Newport, snuffed it in the ashtray next to him, and turned to face his lieutenants. "You do what you need to do, Bad. Fuck it! Make it happen."

Bad nodded and smirked. He was ready to fuck shit up. "That's what I'm talking about."

Chico finally noticed Blythe, quiet like a mouse, standing in the shadows of the hallway. He frowned at her for listening in on his meeting with his lieutenants.

"What the fuck you standing there for, and listening to business that you don't need to listen to?"

"Can we talk, Chico?" Blythe asked.

"Can't you see I'm fuckin' busy here? I'm at war right now, Blythe."

"I know, and I just need a minute of your time. You seem to have time for everything else, except for me, playing with your guns and always worrying about that bitch."

"Bitch, who the fuck you talkin' to like that?"

"I'm sorry. I just need some time alone with you, Chico . . . some time alone with my man."

Chico sighed. He looked at his lieutenants. "Y'all niggas, get the fuck out, and let me talk to my lady for a moment."

"A'ight!" the men said in unison.

They gathered their things and walked out the penthouse.

When the door shut behind the last man, Blythe walked into the well-furnished living room and closer to Chico. She only wanted to wrap her arms around him and feel his thick frame against hers. But Chico looked reluctant to have any womanly comfort at the moment.

He took a step back from Blythe's grasp, screwing his face at her. It wasn't the time for any affection. His mind was racing with so many things, thinking about different ways to strike and kill his ex-bitch.

"So, this is how it's gonna be, Chico? You step away from me like I'm some plague? I'm trying to show you some love, and I can't even get a fuckin' hug from you?"

Chico yelled, "I got other things goin' on right now, Blythe! You fuckin' know this!"

"Chico, what about me? I'm scared. I'm lonely. I'm horny. And I need comfort. And you out there playin' soldier games with your ex-bitch. How you think that fuckin' makes me feel? We haven't had sex in three weeks."

"Fuck you, Blythe! I'm worrying about my business and reputation, staying alive, and I ain't got time to give a fuck about how you feel. If we dead, then you ain't gonna be able to feel shit."

Blythe glared at Chico. She was ready to smack him, but she didn't dare. Her eyes became glazed. Her tears wanted to fall. She took a deep breath.

"Baby, I love you so much, I don't want to see anything happen to you. I want us to be whole again, have things normal like the way it was before this bitch came back to Harlem."

"With this bitch around, Blythe, things will never be the way they were. She's out for my head and yours too. You understand that? With her out for revenge, it ain't safe to be how we was."

"I just want this fuckin' war over with."

"You and me both."

Blythe sighed heavily. "Are you really going to kill her moms?"

"I told you—Stay the fuck out my business, Blythe!"

"I'm not trying to be in your business. I was just asking a question."

"The less you know, the fuckin' better."

Blythe didn't push it.

Chico pushed past her and went into the next room, slamming the door behind him and leaving her standing in the plush living room an emotional wreck. The tears started to fall.

She could hear Chico's phone ringing behind the shut door. He immediately picked up and started talking.

Blythe slowly walked toward the door, tempted to knock and finish their argument.

But when she heard Chico say, "Jason, what's good?" she knew to move on.

When Chico was on the phone with Jason, she knew not to interrupt him.

Blythe went into her bedroom teary-eyed and feeling hopeless. She shut her door, her mind whirling with so many worries. Every day was a threat to her existence, not knowing if her man would survive this vicious war, or whether he would be incarcerated for his violent actions, and running a drug empire. She didn't want to be alone, but the way things were happening, their future together looked uncertain.

*

Chico pulled up to the curb of Warinanco Park in Elizabeth, New Jersey, and stepped out of the truck flanked by Bad and Torrez. Across the street from the park were two-story middle-class apartment complexes. With working families and soccer moms, the area was quiet and far removed from the ghettos and slums of Harlem.

Chico sighed as he stared at the trees filling the park on the warm, clear evening. He noticed a few kids lingering at the entrance.

"Y'all stay here," Chico told his two lieutenants. "I'll meet wit' him alone."

"You sure, boss?" Torrez asked.

"Nigga, I'm sure. This nigga is like a brother to me."

The men nodded.

Chico walked off, fading down the paved trail that led into the park before emerging in the track and field area. The track was sprinkled with a few joggers and some walkers, trying to keep fit under the fading sun with their iPods and smart phones plugged into their ears, tuning out the world while moving around the Tartan track.

Chico looked around for Jason and soon spotted him in a white tracksuit with black edging. He was alone and walking slowly around the bends, but Chico knew Jason's goons were always watching.

He waited for Jason to reach him as he leisurely walked in the center lane and a few runners sprinted by him. When Jason circled the track, he joined him in their easy walk.

"Chico, glad you could meet up with me," Jason said coolly.

"Always. But you said there was something important you had to tell me."

Jason, with his pale bronze skin, didn't even break a sweat in his tracksuit as he walked. He barely looked at Chico, keeping his eyes forward, focused on his walk. He looked more like a handsome and fit suburban dad out for an evening walk than a drug kingpin having a meeting with another drug kingpin from Harlem.

Chico was wearing beige cargo shorts and a T-shirt, along with white Nike's and dark shades. The two looked like good friends talking, enjoying the summer days.

Jason spoke in a low whisper as they walked closely. "You got problems," he said.

"Who don't?" Chico replied nonchalantly.

"First, this psychotic bitch you're at war with, you gotta put her down."

"What you think I'm tryin' to do?"

"She's bad for business."

"You think I don't know that?"

"Listen, the bodies piling up in Harlem are bringing you unwanted attention . . . first, from the local police, the mayor, the congressmen, and the community. And then that shit brings about the feds to come sniffing around in your ass. And when the feds start sniffing, they ain't gonna leave your ass until they catch shit on you."

"I fuckin' know that too."

"Well, know this—You fuckin' up, Chico!"

"What you mean?"

"You remember a few months back I told you about Two-Face? Told you to keep it clean, not to have anything come back to you."

"Yeah."

"It's coming back on you."

Chico looked confused.

"Word is, his uncle—You know Roman, that crazy muthafucka you met with down in Texas who's running a cartel down in Mexico?—he's coming for you."

"For what?"

"His nephew. Word got back to him that you're responsible for what happened to Two-Face. I told you to keep it away from you, and point it in the direction of Cross and his peoples."

"And I did."

"Then why does he think you have something to do with his murder?"

Chico was lost.

"You have a leak in your camp then. Somebody's snitching, reporting to you, but telling your business to other people. Fuck, Chico, the shit is piling up on you hard and fast! Handle it."

"Don't worry about me, Jason. I will handle it."

"You better, because I can't always be there watching your back. I do what I can."

"I got my own back, Jason. I'm a fuckin' problem to anyone that thinks they can fuck wit' me. I'ma kill 'em all."

"Then be that problem and handle your business. But, until you do, this is gonna be our last meet. I'm gonna have to part ways from you until shit cools down with you."

"So you just gonna turn your back on me?"

"It's just business, Chico. I have my business, my damn interest to protect, and you have yours. I don't need to get entangled in webs thick like yours. But my gift to you to handle your growing problem is Ion."

"You givin' me Ion?"

"You're gonna need his help."

Chico smiled.

"He'll be in town next week. I'll set it up for you, but he's not cheap."

"I know."

"Don't fuck this up, Chico. Ion's coming to town to clean house for you. He does that, and then it's back to business like normal. But until your world cools down, and Ion does what he does best, I'm gone—no contact, no numbers from me. I'm ghost."

Hearing that Ion was coming to New York made Chico feel better about his problems with Apple.

Harlem wasn't ready for a killer like Ion, a killing machine, and ex-Navy SEAL who had become a hit man. It was more profitable and more fun for him to kill for money than for his country. Fifteen years of killing, from the Seals to the streets, had made him the most proficient and adept killer around. He was strong and patient, but most of all, he was discreet at his job. A sharpshooter, good with a blade, any knife, and excellent at hand-to-hand combat, he could either shoot you between the eyes from a distance, or snap your neck up close.

"You take care of my man, Chico."

"He's gonna be put to good use. Believe me, he's gonna have a lot of work on his hands."

"Fifty thousand up front, cash money for his services."

"Done."

"Don't fuck this up, Chico. You know Ion's picky with his services. He's doing this only because I asked him to."

"And I appreciate that. So let the games begin," Chico replied with a smirk.

The two men continued their brief meeting while walking the track. The sun was slowly fading behind the horizon, and the other joggers and walkers on the track were thinning out, giving the men even more privacy.

Jason and Chico shook hands and went their separate ways. Chico walked back to his truck, where his two goons were still posted up, smoking cigarettes, and talking shit.

They noticed Chico approaching.

"We good, Chico?" Torrez asked.

"Yeah, we definitely good."

All three piled into the truck and drove away. Chico knew that the storm was about to become a lot worse in Harlem. Ion was about to tear the city apart with his bare hands. Apple and her Down South crew weren't ready for a killer like Ion. Shit, all of New York wasn't ready for the shit storm heading their way.

THIRTEEN

The sweltering New York heat was almost unbearable. The sun felt like it was giving the city a bear hug and wasn't trying to let go anytime soon. The pavement felt like it was melting underneath people's feet, and even the buildings were sweating. The residents were trying to keep cool by any means, which meant children playing and keeping cool in open fire hydrants, or running through the sprinklers in the park.

The ladies were sitting on the front steps of walk-up apartments, or lingering on the benches outside the towering projects and fanning themselves continually, trying to overcome the heat, and the men walked around shirtless and scowling, angry at the summer's heat bearing down on them.

Harlem was coming under fire from two deadly forces: the blazing sun above, and the hoodlums at war with each other, shooting up the block and creating casualties. Either way, the residents were getting scorched. With Chico and Apple at war, there was no safe place to hide as even the cops got caught up in the fighting, finding themselves under a blanket of violence.

Several days earlier, a marked car on patrol near the Lincoln Projects was shot up by machine gun fire from an unknown triggerman. Both uniformed officers were hit and barely survived. The mayor was livid, and during his media coverage about the bold attack on the city's finest, he vowed that whoever was responsible for the murder attempt on the officers' lives would be caught and prosecuted to the full extent of the law.

After that latest incident, the city flooded Harlem with dozens more cops in the area. In addition to the young rookies walking the beat through the housing projects, cop cars were cruising the Harlem blocks more slowly now, eyeing and harassing any passing black man as a potential suspect. "Stop and frisk" was the order of the day.

Getting any kind of illegal income in Harlem came down to a crawl. Many dealers were becoming frustrated and angry. A war that had nothing to do with them was interrupting their cash flow, because cops were everywhere in Harlem. Tactical police teams were kicking in doors and making raids in every direction. Snitching was on the rise, and undercover officers were always around, kicking over the nests hustlers had built in the hood. The authorities wanted arrests and indictments for the vicious attack on two of their comrades, and everything was pointing toward Apple and her band of thugs.

Apple's killing crew was paving the streets red with blood. She had come to New York like an unpredictable force of nature, so no one was ready for her. And to make matters worse, while many residents and drug dealers were scared of getting caught up in the crossfire, she didn't give a fuck.

She continued to flaunt her wealth in front of the have-nots, riding around in her Bentley, or some other luxury vehicle, catching envy from others. She went on shopping sprees and sported jewelry that cost more than an average worker's yearly salary. She looked at the people in Harlem like they were something vile and dirty that she would wipe off her five-thousand-dollar boots. She was shitting on everyone and not giving it a second thought.

Apple walked around her penthouse suite in her panties and bra. She took much delight in the air conditioning that flushed the place, keeping her and her goons cool in the heat wave.

She went to the window and gazed at the city overcome with humidity and the glare of the sun. So many things were going through her head. The suite was quiet, since she was alone for the moment, enjoying some much-needed solitude.

Guy Tony had jumped on an early-morning flight back to Houston to handle his business. New York was no longer his home. Apple felt it was for the best. He took a few goons with him back to Houston, leaving Apple with a handful of thugs to continue her vendetta. She didn't have time to fly back to Houston. In fact, it'd been a few months since her arrival, and there was still hell to pay.

Terri entered the bedroom and saw Apple clad in sexy underwear. Her curves were enticing and able to hypnotize any man, but a few scars on her body showed the evidence of the suffering and torture in the Mexican brothel.

Terri stood tall in front of her, ready to carry out any orders coming from the boss lady. He was the ideal soldier in her crew—strong and vicious, but also loyal and subtle. Terri knew his place in the criminal organization and was content with being paid handsomely for his deadly deeds as a contract killer. He allowed Apple to be the brain, while he was the brawn. And he liked being the brawn. He used to feel weak at one time, but the pistol put in his hand when he was a teenager gave him strength. And, before long, bloodshed, murder, and violence became his calling card.

"Any word from Jet yet?"

"Nah. No word," Terri responded coolly.

"How fuckin' long is this shit gonna take?"

"For what you're asking for, it might take a little longer than expected."

Apple sighed. She wanted Sean's head in her lap and his body rotting in the dirt. "I want that muthafucka so bad, Terri. I want him dead."

"I know you do, and Jet is good at what he do. From his pedigree, he ain't gonna fail you."

"I hope not. We're paying him a lot of money."

"The wolves are gettin' a little restless, especially Crunch."

Apple didn't like Crunch. She thought he was just too ignorant—too fuckin' country. He had a provincial way of thinking that bothered her.

"Fuck him!" Apple hissed.

"They need work. They've been cooped up in the same place for almost a week now. Why have muscle around, if they ain't gonna be muscle?"

Apple wasn't so quick to respond.

She had Terri and Chicano, two of the most skilled killers she'd ever come across, and with those two men flanking her, she had all the muscle she needed in New York. Crunch and his Southern boys stood out like a stripper with no nipples. They were just hard to look at and be around. But Guy Tony suggested that Crunch stay, for Apple's protection, so she was left to deal with his nasty odor and tasteless ways. Crunch was a nasty muthafucka with no prudence at all.

Apple continued to move around the bedroom in her scanty underwear. "Fine. I'll have somethin' for them soon."

Terri nodded. His eyes shifted to her legs. Then he walked his eyes up to her chest and face. It was hard for him not to notice her attire, but she was the boss's lady, and he had respect for his boss. It was manifested to him that Apple wasn't in love with Guy, but for some reason, Guy Tony was in love with her. Their relationship wasn't his business. He was paid to kill, not to be a relationship therapist.

Apple felt comfortable enough around Terri to walk around in her underwear. But she was raw like that. She had drastically changed from that young, frightened teenage girl who was hiding from Supreme because she'd owed him money. If only Supreme could see her now. But she'd had him killed. Too bad. He had created a monster.

Over the months Apple grew to trust Terri, and his judgment. Not only was he was smart, but he was the silent and strong type too, only speaking when he needed to. In some ironic way, he reminded her of Chico, before their deadly feud. He was so handsome and vicious, a mix she was attracted to.

Terri lingered by the door while Apple stood around and gazed out the floor-to-ceiling windows.

"Are we done here, Apple?"

She turned and locked eyes with her enforcer. She walked her eyes across his attire. He was wearing a wifebeater that hugged his muscular frame like artwork. The dark blue denim jeans he wore looked good on him. His long dreads were like a thick lion's mane around his face, and his dark eyes were transfixed on Apple.

"Yeah, we're done."

Terri nodded and exited the bedroom, leaving Apple with some unexpected naughty thoughts about him. It had been weeks since she'd had sex, and with Guy Tony back in Houston, it gave her some breathing room to do whatever she pleased.

*

Apple took a pull from the Newport she was smoking as she relaxed in the cultured marble jetted tub, trying to soothe her stressful lifestyle in the warm water. She was yearning for a trip to a top-notch Manhattan spa. Even though she was a gangsta bitch, she was still a woman, and she wanted to escape to pedicures and manicures, sensual massages, steam treatments, and mud baths.

Apple was submerged in the lukewarm water from the neck down. She had her eyes closed and savored the stillness and temporary tranquility around her. Her mind began to drift, and her body to feel appeased.

Just then, her cell phone started to ring near her reach. It irritated her that she brought the damn contraption in the bathroom with her. She saw it was her mother calling. She wasn't in the mood to put up with her nonsense.

She ignored the first call, and the second from her mother. But Denise was a persistent bitch and would keep calling until someone answered.

Apple snatched up the phone after the third call. "What?" she screamed into the phone.

"Something happened to Kola."

"What you mean?"

"Your sister is in the prison infirmary down in Miami. She got stabbed by an inmate."

"She dead?"

"No."

"Too bad!"

"Apple, this is your gotdamn twin sister."

"I don't have a fuckin' sister, Denise. I don't care nothin' for that bitch anymore. If she lives or dies, she ain't my fuckin' problem."

Denise sighed. "Did you have somethin' to do wit' it?"

"You blaming me now for this shit?" Apple barked.

"Kola is awake, and your name came up as the culprit. Apple, did you try to have your own sister killed?"

"You're fuckin' impossible, Denise. Always taking her side, right. I didn't have shit to do wit' it. I ain't the only enemy she got. Fuck that bitch! She deserves everything that's happening to her."

"Apple, you can't be that evil."

"Watch me. I ain't that little girl anymore. And if that bitch wanna blame me for her gettin' stabbed, then so fuckin' be it. But she better keep her ass down in Miami, 'cause I ain't that bitch to fuck wit'. I got an army for that bitch now."

Denise shouted, "What is wrong wit' you?"

"Everything."

"You know what, Apple—You're making the same fuckin' mistakes twice. Look at you, riding around the hood in fancy cars, shitting on the people you came up with, and you're creating a shit list of enemies in Harlem. You're becoming overwhelmed by madness. You're becoming a lunatic. I fear you ain't gonna ever learn. I feel so sorry for you."

"Don't feel sorry for me, Denise. I'm good, and gonna always be good. I don't need you or any fuckin' backstabbin' family around me."

"You gonna always need family."

"You think so, huh? Where you at right now? In the fuckin' projects. And you wanna know where I rest my head at every night—a penthouse suite in midtown, Denise. You think I need Harlem? I don't need a gotdamn thing from that asshole of a place. Fuck Harlem! And fuck you, if you think I'm gonna kiss ya ass and feel sorry for Kola. I'm lookin' out for myself right now."

Denise sighed heavily once again. "I'm gonna tell you somethin', little girl. No matter where you set your throne at, you gonna always need allies if you want to stay alive in this game."

Apple let out a mocking chuckle.

"You think it's funny?"

"Yeah, I do."

"Apple, I pray—"

"What, you prayin' now? How can you pray wit' a dick in ya mouth? Get the fuck outta here, Denise!"

"I just hope you didn't have anything to do with the attempt on your sister's life."

Apple shouted, "And if I did, what that bitch gonna do to me? Huh, Denise? That bitch is lightweight right now, probably a fuckin' cripple too, and she ain't fuckin' wit' me. You can go and personally tell that fuckin' bitch-ass twin sister of mine to kiss my black ass and go fuck herself. 'Cause I ain't the one to come at. So fuck her, you, Chico, Harlem, and your fuckin' prayers! You ain't fooling me wit' that nonsense, Denise!"

"You're impossible, Apple."

"Yes, I am. Ain't nobody gonna touch me. I'm the baddest fuckin' bitch on the block. I'm running things now."

Denise grew a little salty. It was bad enough that her girls weren't looking out for her any longer, but now they were ready to kill each other like they were complete strangers. It left a bad taste in Denise's mouth, and their feud was leaving an ugly stain on the family's name. It was embarrassing to her.

Apple clutched the cell phone tightly to her ear. Her soothing bath suddenly felt like rocks scraping against her. Her mother had soured her evening.

"Do me a fuckin' favor, Denise—Don't ever call me about that fuckin' bitch again. I'm done wit' the both of y'all."

Apple hung up and quickly removed herself from the tub. Her face in a scowl, she didn't bother to dry off. She hurried into the bedroom wet from head to toe and snatched a kimono from off the back of a chair and threw it around her. She plopped down in the chair, lit a cigarette, crossed her legs, and stayed there for an hour, thinking. She knew one thing for sure—there was going to be a family reunion soon. And when that time came for her and Kola to face off, the question would be answered—Who would be the first sister to pull the trigger and take the other's life?

FOURTEEN

Kola woke up in the prison infirmary to a slight pain in her side and back. The light shining over her was bright, and the smell of the infirmary was overwhelmingly stale. She was wearing a hospital gown instead of the ugly, orange prison officials. When she tried to move, the pain from the stabbing shot through her body like electricity. Having survived the brutal attack in the shower, she knew whoever was behind the attempted murder on her would be very displeased that she had opened her eyes to see another day.

Kola's eyes shifted everywhere in the room, trying to become familiar with her surroundings. She didn't know what day it was, or the time.

It was her first time in a hospital. She had to heal, and heal fast. She was sure her foes would come for her again. But there wasn't going to be a second time. She had made bail and was ready to make her exit from the harsh and depressing environment. She raised herself slightly from the bed she was in. The feel of the place was far from comfortable. The staff in the room didn't seem to care about the patients. It wasn't a five-star health care system at all. It was like an infection. The sick and crippled inmates around Kola were starting to make her feel sick herself. She hated to be around the weak. All her life, she was strong and smart, or so she thought, but one slipup had her reevaluating the people around her.

"Nurse!" Kola cried out.

She tried to remove herself from the bed, but the pain in her side was excruciating—like a jolt of lightning had shot through her—and the slightest movement triggered it.

"Ouch!" she uttered faintly, holding her side, where the bandages wrapped around her petite frame were stained with dry blood.

Kola felt in bad shape. She wanted to cry, but being the woman she was, she sucked it up. She moved against her bed like an elderly woman with arthritis.

When she coughed, pain shot through her. "Nurse!" she cried out again.

A short moment later, a slim white nurse clad in blue scrubs walked over to her. "You need to lay back and get your rest, and stop fidgeting around so much," she said in a crabby tone. "You're only going to make things worse for yourself."

"Fuck that! I need to get out of here."

"I'm afraid that's not going to happen. You were hurt really bad. In fact, you're lucky to be alive, and what you need to do is relax, stop fighting, and wait until the doctor is able to come and check on you."

Kola glared at her. *Who is this fuckin' bitch?* She was ready to punch the round-faced nurse in the face.

"I don't have time for any fuckin' doctors. I made bail and need to get the fuck outta here!"

"Your bail will have to wait. Your health is more important right now. You suffered severe stab wounds to your back and side. You were touch and go for a while, but you were lucky no major arteries were hit."

Kola shouted, "Fuck lucky! You think me being in this crippled position is fuckin' lucky, bitch? Go fuck yourself! Get me the fuck outta here! I wanna go home!"

The nurse twisted her face then craned her neck. "You're not going home."

Kola tried to depart from the bed. It was a slow, painful attempt for her, but the nurse placed her hand against Kola's chest and grabbed her arm. It felt like she had the strength of a hundred men when Kola tried to elevate herself and swing her legs over to try and touch the floor.

"I said relax. You're only going to make it worse for yourself."

But Kola couldn't relax. She was angry. She wanted the bull dyke that attacked her in the shower while her guard was down dead. And the people responsible for hiring her, she wanted to hunt them down and destroy everything they loved.

"If you don't calm down, then I'm gonna have to call security over and have you restrained," the nurse said through clenched teeth.

Kola looked past the nurse and noticed the beefy C.O. standing by the door, his chest protruding. The bars on the windows were a harsh reminder that she was still locked in a prison and not in a public hospital. There was absolutely no leaving the place on her own free will.

"I fuckin' need to go," Kola said despondently. "Don't you fuckin' understand, bitch? I'm dead in here."

The nurse looked unmoved by the statement and continued to fight with Kola to keep her positioned in the bed. Even with the pain from her injuries shooting through her body like a thousand volts of electricity, Kola was still determined to get up and make her exit.

The nurse had had enough. "Guard," she called out.

The beefy C.O. rushed over and quickly restrained Kola. He placed the iron bracelets around her wrists and handcuffed her to the bed railing.

"I tried to be nice," the nurse exclaimed.

"Fuck you!"

Kola then sighed heavily. She was a free bitch, but now it felt like the light was slowly fading from her eyes, feeling like she was stuck in a prison within a prison. There wasn't anything worse than being handcuffed to a bed inside the infirmary and surrounded by the ill.

Miami was becoming a nightmare. And Harlem looked more like a blessing every day she suffered down in Miami.

*

The days went by gradually for Kola, and finally the doctor cleared her for release from the infirmary. She was healing well. Now her next step was getting out and getting back to business.

Kola linked up with Danielle soon after her release from the infirmary. Danielle noticed the displeased look on her face and instantly read her thoughts.

"Don't take it there, Kola," Danielle said. "She's in lockdown in the hole, and there's no way to get at her."

"I wanna take it there," Kola replied through clenched teeth. "That dyke bitch tried to kill me. I want her so fuckin' dead!

"I know you're upset, but let it go. You made bail, right?"

"Fuck bail! She stabbed me, and that shit hurt. The bitch almost crippled me."

Danielle let out a heavy sigh. "Go home, Kola. Get out. Don't think on this place anymore, and I'll handle the problem in here."

"How? You gonna kill her? I can't let that dyke bitch walk away free from what she fuckin' did to me, Danielle. I can't forgive that bitch. I want her dead. You do me that favor, and I'll pay you twenty-five thousand. And you know, with my rep, I'm good for it."

"Twenty-five thousand?" Danielle questioned with puzzlement. "You just won't let it go, will you, Kola?"

"She fuckin' made me look weak. And I can't look weak . . . not now, not never."

"If I were you, I would sneak back home to New York, Kola. You made bail, you're getting out, and most of us in here will never see that again."

Kola barked, "You know what, Danielle—If you won't do me this favor, then fuck you! I'll find someone that will. I was tryin' to look out for you, get you paid, 'cause I like you and had some fuckin' respect for you. But you're actin' like a scared bitch. This bitch put a blade through me a few times, and she's still breathin'. Nah, fuck that! Where I come from, we handle bitches like that, and that dyke would be dead in no time. Fuck you! You can rot in this bitch for all I care." She stormed away, leaving Danielle standing there dumbfounded.

The anger in Kola was bubbling. She wouldn't be appeased until she got what she wanted—hood justice—with that justice starting in Miami and then leading back to New York to her sister Apple, if she was truly the one behind the attempt on her life.

Kola's hate for her sister was like a cancer eating away at her from the inside. She wanted to rip out the disease in her life and crush everything from her past that did her dirty. It was time for some housecleaning, and once she was released, she was ready to go ham on everyone and everything.

She had made a new connection with Sassy and her peoples, and once she was outside the prison gates, it would be back to business as usual. One obstacle—one short stint in the Women's Detention Center wasn't going to stop her.

There were a lot of unanswered questions about her sudden incarceration. Nikki was MIA, and OMG had forgotten that she even existed. She made a lot of money for him over the months, and even committed murder, so where was the loyalty? Where was the help when she really needed it?

Kola was ready to make some serious noise again, and she was determined to be heard. She was eager to send out a loud and direct statement to everyone listening—from Miami to New York. People's ears were going to bleed with her violent statements. It was time for both cities to see that she wasn't fucking around.

*

Kola walked out the Women's Detention Center a free woman, but she wasn't happy. She'd spent too much time in hell and had a lot of catching up to do. She knew someone had snitched on her, and then someone had tried to kill her while on the inside. The sun was shining, and the sky was a vast blue. The feel of the bright sun in her face was invigorating, and everything on the other side of the prison wall felt a lot fresher.

The first thing she wanted to do was take a decent shower and go shopping, and maybe get some good dick. She looked ahead and saw the gleaming black Escalade sitting on 24-inch chrome wheels parked and idling outside the gates. She was thankful that Sassy had her back and looked out for her. It felt good to be picked up in style. She once again felt like that bad bitch.

She strutted toward the vehicle and got inside. The feel of the cream leather seats against her was soothing. The stereo was playing Kanye West, and Copper was seated in the backseat waiting for her.

"Good ta be finally out, right?" he asked with a smile. "An' in good health."

Kola nodded. "Fuck that place!"

Copper replied, "Oh, and that problem ya had on the inside, it ain't a problem anymore. It was taken care of. Let's just say, the dyke met karma, and karma won in a vicious way."

Kola beamed. "Finally . . . somebody wit' some fuckin' balls in this city."

"We look out for our own," Copper told her.

"Good to hear."

Kola coolly sat back in the plush SUV, the jail in the rearview mirror. She heaved a sigh of relief. She was ready to see what Copper and Sassy had in store for her. Nothing came for free, and everything was always about business, especially murder. But it was hard to believe that Sassy had clout and connections like that. Kola thought she was just the average hood rat bitch that didn't take shit from anyone. Who knew she could be the brain to a large-scale operation down in South Beach? It was clear to see that there was more to these two than what met the eye.

"Where you takin' me?" Kola asked.

"Sassy's been dyin' ta see you again," Copper said.

"She has, huh?"

Copper nodded.

"I need to make one quick stop first," Kola said, "if that's cool."

"Where to?"

"My old home. I just need to check on somethin'."

Copper told the driver about their new destination, and the Escalade made a sudden U-turn and headed that way.

The truck turned slowly onto Kola's old block in the urban area of Miami, where she and Nikki shared a home, which was their stash house. Nikki had told her that the feds had raided it and took out everything, but Kola felt like something was off, so she decided to do her own investigation.

It was early afternoon, and the block was quiet. The Escalade came to a stop in front of the vacant home. The place looked like it hadn't been lived in since Kola was arrested. The grass was growing wild, and there was some debris in the front yard, but the home didn't look like it was raided by the feds. There was no indication of it—no papers put up, no documentation of seizure placed on the home, and the door was still attached.

Copper looked at Kola. "You gonna check it out?"

"That's why I came here."

Kola stepped out of the truck and approached the house. She went up the steps and checked the door, which was unlocked. *That's odd,* she thought. She slowly entered her old home and looked around. She noticed everything important was gone—the safe, the money, the guns, and the books. The place didn't even look ransacked. There was no overturned furniture, the cabinets weren't rummaged, and there was nothing out of place, except a few key things missing.

"What the fuck!" Kola muttered.

She stepped back out onto the steps and noticed her neighbor watering his lawn in his faded jeans and button-up shirt. She rarely had any words with the man, who appeared to be in his early sixties, and she didn't even know his first or last name. Kola would always catch him sitting on his porch, soaking in the day. The man minded his business. Whenever she did her thing, he would always look the other way. Kola liked neighbors liked him. She decided to have a talk with the man.

She walked over. "Excuse me," she called out.

The tall, black man with grey facial hair and receding hairline turned to look at her. He greeted her with a toothless smile. "Yeah."

Kola smiled. "You remember me, right? I was your neighbor for a few months."

"Of course," he said, nodding. "Pretty girl like you . . . an old man like me can never forget you. Seeing you come and go always brightened up my day."

Kola beamed. "Can I ask you a question?"

The man nodded.

"You remember my cousin, the other girl I was staying with?"

"I remember her too."

"What happened to her? Have you seen her around lately?"

"No. Been a few weeks since I saw that one come and go. I think she moved like a thief in the night some weeks back."

"She did, huh?"

He nodded.

Kola was ready to curse. "And what about the FBI raiding this place?"

The man looked at Kola like she had two heads. "What raid?"

"Didn't the feds raid this home a few months back?"

"If they did, I didn't see a thing, and you know I'm always on my porch, sitting and watching. There was no police raid done here. I figured you two pretty ladies just up and left, got tired of seeing my ugly mug every day."

Kola wasn't amused. In fact, she was furious. She had all the information she needed. Nikki had backstabbed her and run with the goods, so there was no telling what else she had lied about.

She pivoted and marched away without even thanking the old man for his time and information. She went back to the truck and jumped in.

Copper noticed the change in her mood. "Trouble in paradise?" he asked.

"I'm gonna kill my fuckin' cousin."

"When you need help wit' that, let us know."

Copper passed her a cigarette, and she took it and lit up. She needed a smoke. She was stressed. It had been an awfully troublesome time for her lately.

Copper had his driver pull off, and they merged onto the expressway. The drive through Miami was stimulating, with the sun shining from above. Kola sat back and peered out the window, captured by her own thoughts. Nikki was her number one concern.

Copper was quiet. He was wearing a Miami Heat jersey, cargo shorts, and sporting heavy jewelry. He took a pull from his cigarette and looked through the truck window at his city. Miami had always been home. His paradise.

"Thanks," Kola uttered.

"For what?" he asked.

"For this . . . for gettin' me out."

"Ain't no thang. Like I said, Sassy vouches for you, then we vouch for you. Understand?"

"But why? She don't know me like that to vouch for me."

"Business."

"And what type of business y'all want from me?"

"When we get there, she'll explain."

"Didn't know Sassy had it like that." Kola took one last pull from the Newport and flicked it out the truck window.

"There are a lot of things many people don't know, and we like to keep it like that."

They arrived at the Pork & Beans Projects in Liberty City as the sun was fading from the sky. One of the most densely populated areas in South Florida, the area was inundated with drugs, violence, and crime, with its dilapidated shotgun-looking houses and single- and split-level project buildings.

Whatever Sassy and Copper needed her to do, it had to pay well, even though she owed them a favor for bailing her out of jail.

The truck came to a stop in front of a run-down project home with grass that was an ugly brown and full of litter. Copper stepped out, followed by the driver.

Kola was the last one to exit the vehicle. "What is this?" she asked, looking around.

"Opportunity." Copper smiled.

He led the way, and Kola followed.

Copper's demeanor manifested to Kola that he was the king in the streets, the ultimate and fierce ruler of this urban playground. The residents and young dealers lingering in the projects made it their business to acknowledge and say hello to Copper as he walked by, and no one gave him any sly looks or bad attitude. It could've been fear, love, or respect, or maybe all three. His six-two bodyguard was also testimony to his power and wealth.

Kola entered behind Copper into the project home, which was a stash house. There was loud rap music playing, and young dealers scattered about, some loafing around, smoking and drinking, and then there were the workers seated at a table cutting and packaging dope and coke. And the 50-inch flat-screen TV and the high-end sound system seemed out of place with the raggedy décor and tattered furniture.

Everyone instantly began to show Copper respect, and he acknowledged them with a slight head nod.

When Copper had visited Kola in prison, she was under the impression that he was a soldier or pawn, but it was clear to her now that he was the one running the show.

All eyes were soon focused on Kola.

"Damn!" one young hoodlum shouted out. "She bad!"

"Yo, Copper, that's ya new bitch?" another hoodlum asked.

"Yo, listen. Y'all li'l niggas best need ta respect her right here. Understand?"

The goons nodded.

Once the statement spilled from his mouth, the young hoodlums in the room straightened up, shut their mouths, and no longer gazed at her like she was some whore to run a train on, or a jump-off. But she was still confused about why she was there.

Sassy, clad in a pair of coochie-cutting shorts and a skimpy T-shirt that stopped at the belly button, emerged from one of the back bedrooms, pulling on a cigarette.

When she noticed Kola standing in the living room, she immediately smiled. "Is dat my fuckin' bitch right there?"

Sassy rushed over and greeted Kola warmly. The two exchanged kind words and quickly reminisced about how they'd met. But Kola was keeping her guard up. She didn't know these people and didn't know what they wanted from her.

Copper soon cleared the room, telling his young goons to step out for a minute, that he had important business to take care of. He went over to a round wooden table, where there were countless liquor bottles stockpiled, and began pouring himself a shot of Hennessy. He threw it back, and then he looked at Kola.

"I know ya wonderin' why you're here," he said.

"You damn right."

Sassy smiled.

"I'm gon' be frank wit' ya, Kola," Copper explained coolly. "I been hearin' 'bout your reputation, and real talk, I respect you. You a bitch 'bout ya business, and we want you ta come work for us."

"Work for you?"

"Yeah. We need a bitch like you on da team," Sassy said.

Kola felt like she was her own boss, but she continued to listen.

"Ay, we feel you can be a good asset to our team," Sassy added. "We think alike—we 'bout that life and business."

"But we also need that reach."

"'Reach'?" Kola raised an eyebrow.

"Into New York," Copper continued. "Look, we got da fuckin' product straight off da boat from our Colombian connect, purest coke Miami's ever seen, but we're limited down here. And I ain't into havin' limits. I don't have the reach in New York to unload what I have. I need a bitch like you to walk our shit into ya city. We know you have da connects out dat way."

"And what's in it for me?"

"Sixty-forty split," Copper answered.

It was a sweet deal, but Kola was still hesitant. "But you know I got caught up. I got a pending fed case lingering over my head. How you know you can trust me?"

Copper replied, "We know you—Business and money is ya motivation."

"And OMG?"

Copper waved him off like he was a bad odor. "Fuck OMG! Where was he when you got caught up? Muthafucka is a snake. His time is passing. I'm da prince of this city now."

So far, Kola liked what she was hearing. Her funds were crippled tremendously and her clout in Miami somewhat diminished since OMG and Nikki turned their backs on her. And being incarcerated made her business stagnant in the streets. She needed to rebuild and surround herself with better people. But were these better people? It was a risk, but she needed a come-up again.

Copper and Sassy were in her ear about structuring an empire and expanding their sales of narcotics across state lines. Copper was the man in Liberty City, Miami, but he wanted to be the man across the nation. He had a touch of megalomania. He wanted to become the Nino Brown of his time, the *New Jack City* prince.

Copper had always had an obsession with New York—the lights, the structure, the people, the hustlers, and the way it moved. The city alone was a hustler's paradise. The cluster of boroughs that comprised New York had him in awe. So when Sassy had told him about Kola, he knew she would be the key in making that obsession to become king in territories outside of Miami—especially in New York—a reality. So he had to befriend her and bail her out. She was smart, ruthless, and very resourceful, making her the perfect weapon to have on his team.

Kola thought it over briefly. "Let's make it happen," she stated boldly. "But under one condition."

"What condition?"

"You want New York, I want revenge. You give me a crew of killers to come back to Harlem with me, and I'll guarantee, within two weeks time, I'll have Harlem wide open for you to move your ki's. Once we execute the bitches I hate, then we'll be around to pick up the crumbs from the fallout. You wanna be Nino Brown, and I just wanna be the black mamba for the moment."

Copper thought about the request and felt like Kola was asking for more than she deserved. He had already put up a quarter of a million dollars for her bail—money that he would probably never see again, and now she also wanted them to supply her with goons to settle a past beef? Copper and Sassy were about their business. They wanted to expand and make paper. Copper hesitated, and reluctantly stated, "I'll give you what ya need to get what I need. But you got two weeks tops to handle ya business. Fuck me on this and ya dead. No second chances, ya heard?"

Kola heard him loud and clear. "Two weeks."

FIFTEEN

King of Diamonds in Miami was the world's largest gentlemen's club, boasting 50,000 square feet of full nudity and full friction. The venue was armed with fourteen super skyboxes, thirty private VIP suites, full body massages, a fine dining menu, and a roster of over 300 provocative dancers of every nationality.

The place was packed with people. Scantily clad women were everywhere for the men, and even women to enjoy—pure eye candy from wall to wall. The ladies were dark skinned, redbone, high yellow, thick, slim, petite, and voluptuous. Some were tatted up, others not, but they were all beautiful and unique. Some of the girls were working a few stages strategically situated throughout the club. The dancers twirled themselves around the long poles, booty-clapping and pussy-popping to "Sex Room" by Ludacris and Trey Songz, and some got really acrobatic on the pole, showing off their flexibility and skills while completely nude.

Kola sat in the VIP section with Copper and Sassy. Copper stood up, laughing with his crew of goons from Liberty City. He was popping bottles like a playboy, and spending large amounts of dollars on bottle service and making it rain ones, fives, and tens on the strippers. The money was tossed up in a knot and started sprinkling down like green snow.

*

Not too long ago, this was Kola's world, what she was about, and where she made her money—pussy. It had opened doors for her in New York. Her parties attracted some of the best group of people in New York—the elite, the socialites, the bosses, the athletes. She ran with the best of them. But then she made that transition into drug dealing and never looked back. She and Cross had a very strong relationship and were becoming the power couple in New York City. They were unstoppable, but jealousy and a few bad apples in their organization destroyed all of that.

Kola hadn't heard from Cross since his incarceration. The last she knew about him, he took a plea to the gun charge, and the judge handed him a seven-year sentence. It was the best his lawyer could do for him. Cross and his organization had become incapacitated, but she didn't miss him. He'd put her life in jeopardy with Eduardo and cheated on her with a Brooklyn bum bitch. But Kola had other sights and motives to worry about. To reflect on the past was a death sentence.

*

Kola downed her champagne and smiled. After spending months in hell, this was paradise to her. Sassy sat opposite Kola, and the wild, young girl was beautiful. Kola found herself staring at her. Sassy, in her tight clothing, chest protruding, her long hair in braids, and her curvy hips, could easily be confused for one of the strippers in King of Diamonds. Like Kola, her body was crazy.

Sassy always carried a pistol, and she was always cursing someone out and ready to fight if she had to. Every nigga tried to get into her pants, but she was very selective about who she fucked. Copper was her cousin, and the two shared a sister/brother type of love between them.

Kola crossed her legs. Her white floral minidress was really short and was riding up her thigh. She had the goons' attention, but having respect for Copper, they put their hands and attention on the strippers and left her alone.

Kola gave a few fleeting looks toward Sassy. There was something about her that excited Kola. It had been a while since she'd been with a woman. Sassy noticed Kola's minor glances at her, and the two locked eyes. They both talked with their looks for a moment, and both of them had smiling eyes. The attraction between them was magnetic. The activity going on around them—the music blaring, the men laughing, the strippers flirting, and people drinking—all became irrelevant at the moment.

Kola wanted something from Sassy, and she spoke what her needs were through her dynamic gaze and body action, and Sassy picked up on it.

"You good?" Copper asked.

Kola nodded.

The place became really packed, and there was a slew of athletes and A-list celebrities in the building.

Kola was feeling drained and decided to leave. It was two a.m., and there was no indication that their group was leaving anytime soon. It didn't surprise her that Sassy agreed to leave with her.

The two ladies left alone, sneaking out while everyone else was getting pissy drunk. They got into one of the trucks that was part of their high-end motorcade, and Sassy drove away. While en route to Liberty City, the two both admitted the attraction they had for each other, and they wanted it to lead to something more. Sassy was an open bisexual, and she'd made it clear in her hood that she loved dick and pussy.

The two quickly locked lips once inside the home. It was dark and still, but their hungry moans for each other boomed into the dimness. Then they went into the bedroom and locked the door.

Sassy embraced Kola fervently. Her slim arms were locked around Kola's curves, and she little by little raised Kola's white floral minidress, exposing the pink panties she wore.

"Nice." She ran her hands across Kola's shapely hips.

Kola smiled. She wanted to dive in and devour her pussy, make it an experience the two of them would never forget, but first, there was the foreplay. The gentle kisses against brown skin and pleasant lips. The firm touching. The fondling and cupping of breasts.

Kola continued to place her mouth on Sassy's lips. Their lips parted, their tongues found each other's, and the wrestling was on. Immediately, Kola's pussy began to throb and pulse. It was getting wetter every time Sassy kissed her and touched her in places that stimulated her. It felt like intense heat shooting through her body.

Slowly, their clothes were being peeled away, and the appealing feminine flesh they carried was revealed to each other. Sassy found herself lying naked on her back in the tender grasp of Kola.

Kola kissed her way down Sassy's neck, tasting her skin and pressing her lips to all of her erotic hot spots. Kola had her writhing, twisting, panting, and so turned on. She reached her collarbone and sucked on it like she was a vampire.

"Ooooh, it feels nice," Sassy cooed.

Kola licked everywhere. Methodically, she sucked on Sassy's nipples. While Kola kissed and tasted Sassy, she took her fingers and gently spread Sassy's pink lips and started to finger her pussy. Sassy continued to squirm. Kola continued on with her gentle, wet kisses, making her way down her lover's body, until her face was between Sassy's spread-eagle legs, and her mouth, lips, and tongue were gently licking on her exposed clit.

Sassy shoved her pussy in Kola's face, wanting her to suck harder. Every nerve in her body was alive with pleasure. Sassy gripped the sheets tightly, while Kola's tongue wiggled across her clit and she thrust her fingers into her honey pot.

Sassy moaned, "Mmmm! Ooooh shit! That feels so nice. Don't stop. Ooooh! Squeeze my tits. Eat that pussy. Ooooh, yes!"

Kola went from sucking pussy to sucking on tits and nipples, and their bodies became entwined, flesh against flesh. The weight and the fullness of Sassy's hard, dark nipples in her hands were sensory overload. Kola was going into her primal beast mode in the bedroom, sucking on Sassy's nipples like they were tasty treats. She then lowered her forte between Sassy's legs again and devoured her pussy, while reaching down between her legs to stimulate her own needy clit and pussy.

Sassy rolled over and positioned herself over Kola, pussy rubbing against pussy. It was Kola's turn for her pussy to be ravaged and devoured. She arched her back and let out a hiss as Sassy shoved her face between the depths of her thick thighs. Sassy took to Kola's pink folds like a well-paid porn star, sucking and licking, licking and sucking.

The piercing moan escaped Kola's lips. "Ooooh!" Her breathing was short and raspy. She snatched Sassy's head and held it close to her honey pot. The tongue inside her was pure bliss. Her eyes fluttering, she wrapped her legs around Sassy and felt her legs go numb. She sputtered profanities, screaming out loud how good the shit felt.

Sassy slid her body around and placed her pussy against Kola's once again. Their pussies soft and wet, the girls massaged their clits against each another. The sensation Kola felt, the hot breath against her thighs and pussy, the rubbing and fucking, the fingering, and the kissing led to one intense orgasm. The ladies cuddled against each other, spooning, and looking spent.

Kola fell asleep briefly, and when she woke up, she departed from the bedroom, leaving Sassy, the gangster bitch of Liberty City, asleep and looking harmless.

*

OMG's arrest at his Miami home in the early-morning hours was all over the news, and his face, an outdated mug shot, was plastered across the television. The media portrayed him as a ruthless kingpin who ran a multimillion-dollar drug empire that fueled violence, murder, and extortion. At the raid on his home, the police seized hundreds of thousands of dollars in cash, kilos of cocaine, and several guns. Over twenty individuals and associates of the Miami drug crew had been arrested within a forty-eight-hour period.

OMG and his crew had been under federal investigation for several months and were finally brought down via snitches and an undercover agent who had infiltrated his organization.

Kola sat and watched the news coverage in awe. It was getting ugly in Miami. The heat had been turned up, and there was no escaping the kitchen. The blaze was everywhere. With OMG locked up, there was going to be a void in the underworld. Kola knew there was going to be a power struggle for Miami.

Kola was indecisive about remaining in Miami, but she also had some unfinished business there, like hunting down her cousin Nikki and maybe putting a bullet in her head. And with her pending fed case, and OMG's arrest, it was more than likely that she would be considered a snitch.

The one thing Kola knew for sure—she wasn't dying in Miami, or getting locked up for the rest of her life so far from home. Jumping bail and returning back to Harlem seemed like the better option for her, where she also had unfinished business. And it was home.

SIXTEEN

Denise stood still in her bathroom, gazing at her reflection in the mirror. Her two daughters were at war, and her life was almost in shambles. The community was holding her responsible for her daughters' ruthless behavior, especially Apple's. The bitch was unforgiving and rotten to the core. Harlem was ready to lynch Apple, and was belittling Denise. But Denise was also wrestling with her own demons. They say karma is a bitch, and she was finding that out.

*

When Apple had kicked her out of her home after their fight, Denise vowed to get back at her in the worst way. She was upset that Apple had shot at her and then evicted her, sending her crawling back to the ghetto. The best way Denise knew how to strike back was to attack her looks. It was what the twins cherished the most. So she hired a crackhead to throw a cup of acid in Apple's face.

Denise fought with herself every day since the incident. She had turned her daughter into a savage beast. It was only to teach her a lesson, but now her daughter was coming back with a vengeance. And she was afraid that the truth would be heard soon.

Apple had tortured men and women to find out who was responsible for the attack on her. The crackhead Denise had hired was brutally murdered; shot to death on the project roof. His mind was too far-gone from drugs to remember who'd paid him. Denise thought her dirty little secret was safe, but there was one problem—Her friend, or ex-friend, Nina knew about the dirty deed too.

After her eviction from Apple's place, Denise went on ranting nasty things about her daughter to Nina. The two were chain-smoking at Nina's apartment, where Denise was staying temporarily. Denise then went on to say how she wished her own daughter was dead, or how she could hurt her. Nina sat and listened quietly, sipping on alcohol and just being a good listener to an upset friend.

Denise then went on to say how she should pay someone to have her own daughter disfigured. The heinous idea slipped out loosely, but Nina laughed and somewhat agreed. The talk was taboo, but several weeks later, the sudden attack on Apple with the acid occurred.

Now Nina, with her own financial troubles and an eviction looming, came to Denise for help, but Denise denied her. Nina was an alcoholic, and when she got to drinking, her lips got to talking. Now, Nina, in her sober mind came back at Denise with blackmail. The projects figured Denise was still paid—still had some kind of illicit income coming in from her daughters, and Nina wanted a piece of the pie. If Denise didn't pay her what she asked for, then she would start yapping.

∗

It was Friday night, and Denise had her regular card game going. Jay-Z's voice could be heard faintly from the living room, which was packed with friends seated at a square folding table. The music was blaring, and everybody had a cup with liquor in hand, as cigarette smoke lingered in the air.

Denise needed a timeout from everything. She thought playing cards and gambling with friends would help her escape her worries, but her guests weren't any help either. All they did was yap their mouths, talking shit about things in the hood that didn't concern them. They were like the damn media. They were becoming a bunch of gossiping bitches, and that bothered her. Did they forget that she had mothered both girls? She had to excuse herself and retreat into the bathroom.

Denise exhaled loudly. With one daughter in Miami, and in the hospital, and the next one acting like a savage, it was putting a grave strain on her. And Nina and her blackmail efforts were making her lose her hair. She had already lost weight from lack of sleep.

As Denise gazed at her tired reflection in the bathroom mirror, her cell phone, which was lying on the sink, rang. She looked at the caller ID and noticed it was Raymond calling. It had been a week since she'd last heard from him, and two weeks since she gotten some dick. Seeing his name pop up made her think of pleasurable things again, like a good, stiff dick pushed inside of her.

Denise answered his call. She tried to smile when she heard her young lover's voice, but the stress was overwhelming her.

"Hey, Raymond."

"Where you at right now?" Raymond asked urgently.

"Home. I'm having my regular card game. You comin' through to see me tonight, baby? I could definitely use some tonight."

"Get the fuck out ya place now!"

Denise was confused. "What?"

"I said, drop what the fuck you doin' and leave, 'cause some niggas are on their way over there right now to kill you."

Denise was horrified and panic-stricken. The thought of being murdered in her own home made her knees shake and her legs wobble. All of a sudden she wanted to throw up.

"What the fuck are you talkin' about, Raymond?"

"There's a hit out on your head," Raymond shouted. "And Chico has some heavy hitters comin' ya way. Denise, just drop what the fuck ya doin' and leave!"

Denise knew Raymond was serious. "I'm leaving now."

She hung up and rushed out the bathroom. The living room was still crammed with her guests playing cards, smoking, and drinking. Denise was wide-eyed with panic. *Are they at my apartment door already?*

The atmosphere in her home was still loud and jolly.

"Denise, what's wrong wit' you, girl? You okay?" Damien asked, smiling and laughing.

Denise ignored him. She rushed by everyone and made her exit out the apartment, hoping when she opened her door, her life wouldn't be snatched away. As it turned out, the hallway was clear.

"Denise, girl, where the hell you rushing off to?" Penny asked. "You okay?"

Denise slammed the door as she left, not giving her guests any warning of the imminent danger approaching. She was in panic mode and too scared to think to utter anything to them. Her heart beat so hard it felt like it was about to tear from her chest.

She rushed down the hallway and banged on Ms. Simpson's door. "Ms. Simpson, it's me, Denise. Open up, please," she cried out. Her eyes darted up and down the hallway, especially focusing on the elevator, praying her killers didn't step out.

She continued to bang on Ms. Simpson's door. Finally, Ms. Simpson swung her door open, and Denise rushed inside and collapsed.

"My God! Denise, what is wrong?" Ms. Simpson asked. "You look like hell is chasing you."

Denise couldn't say a word. She was in shock. When she tried to explain, her voice went mute. The guilt of leaving her friends inside the apartment started to trouble her, and she began to cry.

Ms. Simpson walked over and began to console her. "Denise, what is wrong? Talk to me."

"I gotta warn them."

"Warn who?"

*

Stone and Easton were two hardcore killers hired by Chico's people. Stone stood six two, was very muscular, black like space, sported a bald head, and had cold, chilling eyes. Easton was six foot, slim, and pure evil. He styled his long dreads into a ponytail, had a thick goatee, and was deadly. They had been a tag team for years and had a resume for killing that stretched an arm's length.

The two killers casually strutted into the project lobby, which was clear of any residents. Both men wore dark shades, and they were dressed in jeans and jackets over T-shirts. Under their jackets they had concealed pistols. Stone had a .45, and Easton had a Glock 19.

They moved coolly and in sync, like one unit. Easton pushed for their floor, as they stood erect and silent. The elevator came to a stop at the floor they pushed, the metal door slid open, and the men stepped out. The second they entered the hallway, they heard an apartment door slam shut. Easton and Stone stared in the direction of the door slamming but saw nothing. They craned their necks toward Denise's apartment and made their way in that direction. The men heard loud music coming from the apartment. They knew there was a party or something going on, but that wasn't going to deter them from their mission.

When they got to the apartment door, both men screwed silencers onto the barrels of their pistols. Then they looked at each other and nodded. Easton raised his fist and knocked hard on the door.

No response.

Easton knocked again, louder this time, and a moment later, the door swung open. A man said, "Damn! Denise, you forgot your keys to your—"

Before the man could finish his sentence, Easton forced his way inside, pushing the man off balance and shoving the gun in his face. Stone quickly followed him.

The people in the apartment were suddenly plagued with fear. The card game, the laughter, and the good times came to an abrupt stop.

A few ladies screamed, but Easton waved his gun at them and shouted, "Shut the fuck up!"

Within the blink of an eye, the two men had the room under control. The music was still playing, but the joy in the room had been squelched. In total, six people were held hostage.

"Where is she?" Stone asked.

"Who?" a male replied.

"Denise."

"She stepped out. I swear to you, we don't know," the male returned, his voice quivering with fear.

Easton nodded toward Stone, and he disappeared down the hallway, checking each room methodically. He came back and shook his head.

"Where is she?" Easton pushed the end of his pistol against the man's temple.

"I don't know! I swear to you, I don't know!" he cried out.

"Someone in this room must know," Easton replied.

Easton and Stone eyed their hostages. They came to send a message to Apple. It was their instruction—Send a harsh statement to that bitch. Make it clear that Chico wasn't fucking around any longer.

"Fuck it!" Stone raised his pistol to the man's head and fired.

Poot!

The body dropped to Stone's feet. There was more screaming and panicking. The door was shut, and the killers had the only exit blocked.

Easton followed suit, firing his pistol too.

Poot! Poot! Poot!

The bodies began to drop. The screaming was fading quickly, and the smell of death occupied the room.

The remaining survivors tried to scramble for cover, but safety inside the small apartment was limited. They were too high up to jump from the window.

A young lady in her late thirties was cowering behind a sofa, crying, shaking like a leaf. Easton walked toward her and raised his pistol to her forehead.

She stared up at Easton with her tear-stained face and cried out, "Please, don't do this! I don't wanna die! I'll suck your dick . . . right now."

Easton smirked and squeezed the trigger.

Poot!

The woman fell dead to his feet, blood pooling around her head.

Stone killed a man running into the bathroom. He tried to lock the door behind him, but Stone kicked in the door violently and shot him multiple times, and blood splattered everywhere.

The two killers left the apartment nonchalantly, like they'd just stopped by to see an old friend. No one was left alive.

The war between Apple and Chico had reached a whole new level.

SEVENTEEN

Chico heard the news about the carnage in Harlem. Six were dead. It was on every news channel, headline news for all the newspapers, and even caught national attention to some extent.

He stood alone at Chelsea Piers on the docks of the Hudson, waiting to meet with Ion. It was a beautiful day, with a vast blue sky and calm winds, and the pier was filled with people and activity. He glanced at the time. It was late in the evening. Ion had selected the meeting location. Chico didn't understand why he wanted to meet in a public place. There were too many people, mostly white folks with their kids, enjoying the day, indulging in the fun-filled amenities the pier had to offer, as well as police and security. The atmosphere was making him somewhat nervous. He didn't like people in his business, or being so close to police.

Chico kept his cool and stood near the sports and entertainment complex that offered a variety of athletic activities like golfing, skating, batting cages, a gym, and a spa. He took a pull from his cigarette and kept his eyes open, moving gingerly, trying not to make himself look suspicious among the crowd.

Chico noticed a yellow cab pulling up. It made its way toward the curb and stopped just short in front of him. The driver was paid, and a man got out. The man wore beige cargo shorts, a basketball jersey, and a white fitted. He had brown skin, cropped hair, and stood about five nine with an average build. And he wore black specs and carried a book bag.

He stared at the stranger, watching carefully. *Nah, this can't be Ion,* he thought. The man looked like a cross between Steve Urkel and a black Bill Gates.

The man walked up to him, shook his hand like a gentleman, and quickly said, "Buy a ticket to the batting cage and meet me there." Then he walked away, looking cool and harmless.

Chico was taken aback, but he did as he was told. He bought a ticket to the batting cage and walked inside. The cages were made of a chain-link fence and were rectangular in shape, and there was a pitching machine at the opposite end of the cage. The interior floor of the batting cage was sloped. The place wasn't crowded; only a handful of white boys occupied the place, practicing hard on their swings. You constantly heard the cracking noise of a bat as it connected with the baseball that was traveling at ninety miles per hour.

Ion was positioned in one of the cages in a baseball hitter's stance. He gripped the metal bat in his gloved hands and focused on the pitching machine. Chico took the cage next to Ion's and emulated his position. Except for occasionally watching his younger brother's games, he wasn't a fan of baseball and had never played the sport.

The ball flew out from the pitching machine, and Ion swung and connected with a powerful hit. Only the cages surrounding the area prevented the ball from soaring in the air. He repeated the feat again and again, making a direct hit with the ball every pitch and sending it flying.

Chico tried but came up empty on a few tries with continuous strikes.

During a break between pitches, Ion uttered, "I heard you need help."

"I do," Chico said.

"My services are expensive," Ion said coolly. "I can tell you are already judging a man of my stature."

Chico was confused. "Judging?"

Ion chuckled. "You thought I would look like a monster."

Ion swung and made the hit again, while Chico swung his umpteenth strike.

"Fuck!"

"Well, I am a monster," Ion said. "I may not look like the one you pictured, but I am."

"A monster is what I'm payin' for," Chico replied.

After a few more pitches, Chico started to get the hang of things, making a few consecutive hits of his own, but Ion was killing it. It seemed like he couldn't miss.

"My fee is sixty *K*."

"But—"

"Do not say his name," Ion interjected quickly. "No names."

Chico nodded. "You right."

"And it is only because of him, that I'm having this meeting with you," Ion said. "But sixty *K* is my price. There's no negotiation."

The hitting continued. The cracking of baseball bats echoed throughout the batting cage. The two had enough privacy to talk business, because no one gave the men a second look. It seemed like two people just shooting the breeze and chitchatting.

"It's thirty up front, and another thirty after the job is done."

Chico nodded.

"And I do things my way."

"I just want the problem gone."

"And it will be gone."

"And how do you want payment?" Chico asked.

"I'll reach you later with the details, but for now, our meeting is done."

Chico nodded. He left the batting cage, leaving Ion swinging at baseballs, the cracking of his baseball bat ringing out repeatedly. He made his way toward the exit thinking about how eccentric his hit man was. He was impressed. And if Ion did the job he was being paid to do and killed Apple, then Chico was ready to triple his fee.

EIGHTEEN

The black S-Class Benz with the Miami plates came to a stop in front of the Lincoln Projects late in the evening, and the streets were quiet for once. The fading sun was still burning down to some extent, and the humidity was still soaring high, making it sticky and uncomfortable. A few faces peered down at the S-Class Benz out of their apartment windows, trying to keep cool. Rap music played from another project window, and a mother yelled at her kids from a distance.

Kola stepped out from the passenger seat of the Benz and looked around with a slight smile. It felt so good to be back home. It was a long trip on the I-95 highway, and she was somewhat exhausted. But touching down in the concrete jungle was bringing back old memories for her.

She stood erect in her chic heels and gazed at everything. Home was so much different from Miami. The towering project buildings looked like giant cocoons in her eyes.

She hadn't told anyone she was coming back to Harlem. She wanted to keep a low profile for now. But she came with company—two shooters from Copper's crew, Mondo and Sags. They had been tasked to protect her like she was the president of the United States.

"So dis Harlem, huh?" Sags said, looking around from his seat in the car.

Kola didn't respond. She continued to take in everything. First, she had to find Denise, and hoped she was still living in the projects. Kola had been gone for months. But already, she saw that things weren't the same. Her home didn't look natural. She could smell the trouble around her. She could sense the tension. She had been hearing the news about Apple and her bandits tearing uptown apart.

Sags and Mondo exited the Benz, standing out in Harlem like black people at a KKK rally. They had "dirty south" written all over them, with their box braids, the gold and diamond grills in their mouths, the strong Southern accents, and their style of dress.

Kola was ready to make her play, take out the trash and start new. "I need to make a phone call," she said.

Mondo passed her his cell phone.

"Not here," she uttered. "My sister done pissed a lot of people off, and I look just like her. I'm not safe here."

Mondo nodded, and the trio got back into the Benz and drove away.

*

Kola stepped out of the Benz and stared at Saint Raymond's Cemetery for a moment. She felt hesitant in proceeding forward. She felt her heart drop into her stomach and her knees get weak. It was a heartrending moment for her, but she needed to be strong and walk in. It had been too long now.

Sags and Mondo were about to exit the car and follow her into the cemetery.

"Stay in the car," she told them. "I'm gonna be okay."

"You sure? We were told to stay by your side, no matter what," Sags said.

"I'm fine. Just stay in the car. I need to do this alone."

Sags nodded.

Kola let out a heavy sigh and walked forward. Every step closer to Nichols' grave was a challenge for her. She didn't do cemeteries. And she hadn't been to the gravesite since they'd buried her little sister. It was just too painful to endure. Every time she thought back to the moment Nichols was murdered, she cringed. The unspeakable way her sister was raped and slaughtered fueled her hatred and angered her, and that feeling had made her a raging bitch. Many people had already paid for their sins against her family, but there was still a handful of guilty people out there who had to be dealt with.

Kola strutted across the manicured grass. It was an awkward feeling, knowing the dead were underneath her feet, many probably burning in hell, and that she was responsible for sending a few of these people to their graves. She had a haunting thought about her final moment on this earth, whenever it came. *But how will I die? Will it be quick?* It was a scary and paralyzing thought, but she refused to dwell on it.

She snapped out of the daze and continued walking in the cemetery, which seemed to stretch on endlessly with grave after grave, the Throgs Neck Bridge in the distance.

Kola barely remembered where they'd buried Nichols, but it suddenly came to her as she continued walking. She started to remember where her sister's plot was. It was near some thick shrubbery, shaded from the burning sun. A few tears began to trickle down her face.

Kola heaved a hard sigh and peered down at Nichols' grave. The pretty flowers that once covered her grave were dead and scattered, and the area around it was littered with debris. The granite headstone displayed Nichols' name, along with her birth and death year, and engraved into it was "We love you, Nichols. You'll be forever missed."

Kola stood near the plot for a moment, her fists clenched, and a deep scowl on her face. Her tears continued to fall. She missed Nichols so much. Nichols was the sweetheart and the smart one in the family.

She knew Nichols was going to graduate from high school and go off to college. She was about to become a scholar; she had the brains for it. She was going to escape the ghetto and make something of her life.

Nichols' death left a void in Kola's life. Her little sister was so young, so loving and caring. The monsters who took her life needed to burn in hell. Kola had vowed revenge for her sister's death, and so far, she had executed it. But the one truly responsible for Nichols' death, Apple, was a thorn in her side. Kola couldn't forgive Apple for her stupidity.

"I miss you so much, Nichols," Kola proclaimed with her watery eyes. "You were the one so easy to talk to. You was always special, Nichols, and you still are. A lot done happened since your death, and I know you gotta be lookin' down at us and shakin' your head. You gotta hate what you seeing right now—Apple and me at war wit' each other." She released a slight chuckle.

"But I can't stand the bitch. She's so fuckin' stupid! Her stupidity got you killed. But I know you, Nichols. You would hate to see your two sisters like this, and you would be the peacemaker, like you always were, and would try to be the one to piece us back together again. But I don't think there's no puttin' us back together again. She did this to you. You had so much potential to do somethin' wit' ya life, and this fuckin' place, this ghetto took all that away. How can I forgive her, Nichols? Huh? Look at you, rotting in the fuckin' ground like shit, when you were supposed to be blossoming every year of your life."

Nichols was the glue that held the family together, and now that the glue was gone, everything had fallen apart. Standing over Nichols' grave, Kola started to feel a calm settle around her. She started to talk freely, release her emotions and feelings, like she was in therapy. The tears continued to fall, and the calm around her continued to grow.

"I have been goin' through a lot. I was stabbed in Miami. I almost joined you in the afterlife, Nichols, but I survived it. I'm on top now, little sister, and I've been tryin' to avenge ya death, even if I gotta get at Apple."

Kola suddenly felt a feeling of uncertainty. For some reason, it didn't seem right to be vilifying Apple and Denise's names while standing over Nichols' grave. Nichols wouldn't have liked it. So Kola stopped her rant and sighed, wiping away the tears sliding down her cheeks.

"I want to forget about it, but I just can't, Nichols. How can I forgive the people that did this to you . . . that put you in that ground?"

Kola bent down and removed the dead flowers and rubbish from Nichols' grave, trying to make her sister's final resting place a little more decent. She planted her knees into the grass, wanting to get comfortable and continue her talk with Nichols, not caring if she stained her expensive Seven jeans.

She leaned forward and kissed the headstone and then wrapped her arms around it, hugging the inanimate object like it was Nichols herself. "What should I do, little sister?" she asked meekly. "I know you wouldn't want me to keep on hating our family, but I have so much rage and resentment in my heart. Someone needs to pay for your death. But I know you wouldn't want me to go against Apple. You loved us both so much, as we loved you."

Kola, hugging the granite headstone with love, felt a calm and tranquil feeling sweep over her. It felt like there wasn't anything wrong in her world. It almost felt like all her problems had been erased. She didn't know if it was Nichols hugging her right back spiritually or what, but it was a warm feeling.

Kola embraced the headstone tightly, and she started sobbing like a baby. "I miss you so much, baby sister," she cried out.

Kola remained at the grave for over an hour. It gave her some comfort and insight. She regretted waiting so long to pay her respects and vowed to visit her sister at least once a month. She rose up from off her knees and stood tall, drying her tears. "I'll be back, Nichols. I promise."

She pivoted on her heels and walked toward the exit. As she made her way toward the Benz parked outside the cemetery gates, with Sags and Mondo posted on the hood of the car, smoking a cigarette, she knew this war with her sister had to come to an end soon. It'd dragged on too long. But how it would end was the million-dollar question.

"Ya good?" Mondo asked.

Kola nodded. She climbed into the S-Class and remained quiet. She couldn't show her weakness.

Mondo and Sags shrugged and got into the car. Sags got behind the wheel and waited for Kola's instructions. "Where to?" Sags asked.

"Back to Harlem. I got some unfinished business to take care of."

Sags nodded, started the car, and pulled away from the curb, leaving the cemetery behind them in the rearview mirror.

Kola closed her eyes and tried to preserve the memory of her baby sister. Visiting her grave had stirred something else inside of her. She couldn't pinpoint the emotion, but she felt she had to snap out of the weird trance. But she just couldn't stop thinking about Nichols.

NINETEEN

People had been seeing Kola around, and the word was out.

"That fuckin' bitch is back in town, huh," Apple said to no one in particular. "She shoulda kept her ass down in Miami. I'll kill that bitch if she gets in my way."

"Talk about sisterly love," one of the goons joked.

Apple shot him a sharp glare.

"My bad," he said, apologizing quickly.

She took a heavy pull from the Newport and gazed out the passenger window of the Range Rover filled with goons and guns as it sped north on FDR Drive. Terri kept quiet while he drove and Apple ranted about Kola's return to Harlem.

*

Denise had been constantly blowing up Apple's phone. Her mother was scared to death after the murders in her apartment. She had no support or muscle in the streets, and she refused to tell anyone where she was hiding out. The cops had questioned her for hours immediately after the massacre, but she'd remained stubborn and silent, refusing to name anyone who might want to end her life. Denise thought that her only hope was via Apple or Kola. She'd heard that Kola was back in New York, and she'd reached out to her daughter immediately.

*

The black Range Rover with the tinted windows and chrome rims moved through the Harlem streets and turned slowly onto 135th Street.

Apple carried a scowl as she smoked her cigarette. She eyed everyone moving in the streets like they were prey. Under her seat was a loaded Glock 19, which she was ready to use without hesitation. She'd heard rumors of the feds running a joint task force with the NYPD to put an end to the violence and lock up the major players, but she was still hell-bent on causing chaos and destruction. Shaun, Kola, Chico, and Blythe; they all had to die.

She wanted Shaun the most. She wanted to tear him apart piece by piece and make him suffer slowly and painfully. Next on her list was Blythe. Unbeknownst to Blythe, she became a mark the minute she started fucking Chico. Apple couldn't stand the pretty, sassy bitch. Chico, she wanted him dead yesterday for his betrayal. And Kola, Apple was going to save the best for last. It took a special kind of evil to kill your own kin. The neighborhood used to say that Apple was the good twin and Kola was the rotten one. Now, both twins were rotten to the core, but Harlem really despised Apple.

Apple's phone rang. It was Denise calling. She let out a frustrated sigh. "I'm fuckin' sick of this bitch."

"Why don't you just answer it?" Terri suggested.

"She just don't fuckin' get it! I heard about the shootin' at her place, and now this bitch is lookin' for me to help." Apple chuckled at the thought. "Fuckin' scared lil' bitch she is. She wanna disrespect me and now come crawling back to me so I can save her ass. Fuck her!"

"I don't even see why we gotta come out here tonight," Terri said.

Apple cut her eyes at him. "What? You havin' a change of heart all of a sudden?"

"No, not at all. I'm fuckin' cold-blooded wit' this shit. I just need you to be smart about things, and not impulsive."

Apple hissed, "I *am* smart about this—come at family, I go after ya fuckin' nuts and cut 'em off."

"But you don't give a fuck about ya moms."

"It ain't the point, Terri, and you know this. I can't look weak!"

"You ain't weak, Apple. I think Harlem understands that clearly by the work and bodies that we been dropping," Terri replied. "And they say niggas got egos."

"Fuck that! I'ma clip Chico's nuts and stuff them in his fuckin' mouth!"

"You the boss," he said dryly.

They made it to the west side of Harlem, continued driving toward the GW Bridge, and crossed into New Jersey.

It was a lengthy drive into Lyndhurst, New Jersey. The roads were shaded and quiet. In a nearby park adults and teenagers were enjoying a ballgame on a warm summer night.

Apple stared at the soccer moms and coaches. "Fuckin' gimps."

"The American dream," Terri joked.

"It ain't *my* American dream," she replied.

"Then what is?"

Apple remained quiet. From the front seat of the truck, her eyes stayed on the crowd in the park. She scanned the area looking for a particular face. The baseball field was packed with people cheering, the bright lights in the park flooding the area, making it look like daytime. Apple's ruthless Mexican thug, Chicano, and Kori, her silent killer, sat in the backseat, both itching for some action.

Apple's eyes never left the park. She took a few drags from her cigarette and waited patiently. In her world, everyone was a target. Young, old, it didn't fuckin' matter. She was looking diligently for Chico's little brother, Terrance. He was eighteen, and a baseball fanatic.

Terrance and Chico were complete opposites. Chico was the gangster in the family, while Terrance was the square, a straight-A student who never got into any trouble. She'd met Terrance once, when he came to a birthday party in Harlem for Chico. He was very handsome and smart. Chico adored his little brother and always looked out for him.

Now Apple was hunting for the little nigga. She was ready to send a violent message back to Chico. He thought his little brother was safe in the suburbs in New Jersey, but Apple was about to prove him wrong.

She'd found young Terrance via the Internet, through his Facebook account, and befriended him under an alias. She looked into his page, studied the activity on his wall, and soon found out about his hobbies, his likes and dislikes, and that he was in a relationship. It didn't take rocket science to track him down. Terrance was very vocal open on his Facebook page, letting the world know about all his activity, even his baseball games.

"What this li'l nigga look like?" Kori asked.

"When I see him, I'll point," Apple replied coldly.

"A'ight." Kori pushed the loaded clip into his 9 mm.

The park was loud and vibrant, so no one noticed the dark Range Rover with New York plates parked in the distance. Everyone around the baseball field was focused on the game. It was the last inning and a tied ballgame. The warm summer night became boisterous whenever there was a hit or home run, or a difficult catch by one of the outfielders.

"Bingo!" she uttered, smiling.

"Got him?" Terri asked.

Apple nodded. She gestured to the player stepping up to bat next. "Number twenty-four."

Apple grinned. It was too easy.

"Fuck it." Chicano opened the door with the Mack-10 in his hands.

"Chicano, chill," Apple told him. "Not now."

"Why not now?"

"'Cause I wanna watch him play for a moment . . . see if he's any good."

Chicano shut the door, growling.

Apple watched Terrance step up to the plate, the crowd cheering. The teen got positioned into his hitting stance and clutched the bat, looking like Derek Jeter at the home plate. With the game tied and already two outs for his team in the final inning, this was it—clutch time. Win or lose.

The pitcher threw his pitch, and it was an automatic strike. The crowd booed. Terrance kept his calm and remained focused. The pitch was thrown again, and it was a ball. Count one and one. The third pitch was a ball, and the fourth a strike that Terrance swung at and missed. The game was becoming tense, and everyone was on their feet.

Terrance raised the bat, held it tightly, and stared at the pitch like he had the eye of a tiger. The baseball came at him at ninety miles per hour. Terrance swung and connected, sending the ball flying out the park. It was a home run. The crowd cheered, and Terrance's teammates came running out the dugout screaming and yelling. Terrance slowly made his way around the bases, all smiles. He had won the game for his team.

"Little nigga got talent," Apple said.

"Too bad," Kori said.

Terrance was enjoying the attention. His team was going to the finals. He hugged and kissed his girlfriend. She was young and beautiful, and clearly proud of her boyfriend. He was on his way to bigger things, like attending college in the fall with a full athletic scholarship, and possibly playing in the major leagues.

Fifteen minutes later, everybody started leaving. Terrance walked to his car with his girlfriend on his arm. They were nestled together with love. He was talking and laughing with his teammates, receiving pats on the back and praises. He escorted his girlfriend into a burgundy Camry, a birthday gift from Chico a few months back.

Apple turned to her shooters and gave them the nod.

"It's 'bout damn time," Kori uttered.

He and Chicano stepped out the truck and moved toward their victims. The crowd in the park became sparse, with everyone either in their cars or walking home. The two shooters hastily made their way toward the Camry that sat idling in the parking spot. Terrance was kissing his girlfriend passionately. The windows to the Camry were down, and the occupants' attention was focused on each other.

Chicano walked up toward the driver's side window, while Kori crept toward the passenger side, their guns out and ready to be put to use. Terrance's girlfriend noticed the men first and screamed, but it was a short, piercing scream right before both men opened fire.

Tat! Tat! Tat! Tat! Tat! Tat! Tat! Tat!

Bak! Bak! Bak! Bak! Bak! Bak! Bak!

The MAC-10 tore into Terrance's flesh, jerking him violently in his seat, while the 9 mm slugs ate into his girlfriend from the chest downward. Blood splattered everywhere, spraying the windshield and coating the seats with a crimson hue.

Terrance slumped over the steering wheel with his brains leaking onto the dashboard, stomach spilling all over the seat, while his girlfriend drooped against the passenger door, their bodies contorted with death.

The sudden shots stirred the attention of the remaining spectators at the park, but Chicano and Kori quickly left the scene, walking quickly but not worriedly toward the Range Rover. They climbed into the truck, and no one said a word.

Apple released an impish smile. She stared at the gruesome masterpiece created by her two killers as the truck drove by the dead. She would pay handsomely to see Chico's reaction once the news hit him about his little brother. It would be a priceless moment to witness.

"Checkmate, muthafucka," she said, tossing her cigarette out the window.

*

The new location was more discreet and not so cozy for Apple. It wasn't the Trump Plaza, but she felt safe there. She had to relocate. Things were getting hazardous for her, and she didn't feel secure staying at one location too long. And besides, the Plaza was too busy and congested; too many upscale residents and too many unfamiliar faces were always coming and going. The Plaza was posh, but it wasn't made for her and her crew. Her goons were always catching attention from security, and with the automatic weapons they wanted to house, the Plaza wasn't going to work.

So she and her crew moved into Brooklyn, renting out a spacious loft near the Brooklyn Bridge. The area was secluded—no neighbors, not too much traffic, and there were only two exits, which Apple had covered with security cameras. Inside the loft was a small arsenal of machine guns, automatic weapons, grenades, bulletproof vests, and gas masks.

Apple heard the news of Terrance's murder had hit Chico hard. She heard he went mad and was in pure rage mode. He viciously attacked the messenger that gave him the news of his brother's murder. The murders made headlines, and it didn't take long for the media and investigators to link the gruesome murders to a drug war and a drug kingpin in Harlem. The papers were all over it, with one newspaper's headline being, "Harlem Kingpin's A-student Brother Gunned Down in Park."

Apple felt rejuvenated as she stood out on the rooftop with its picturesque view of the Brooklyn Bridge and the city's skyline. She had just gotten off the phone with Guy Tony. He wanted her to come back to Houston.

"Come home, Apple," he'd said.

Apple declined. New York and Harlem was her home, Houston wasn't.

Guy Tony became upset. He told her he was missing her, but Apple wasn't missing him at all. She thought he was stupid to accept her back into his life after everything that'd happened. Letting bygones be bygones was a far-fetched theory for her. Apple was a leopard that wasn't changing its spots, despite his kindness toward her. Guy Tony was a ruthless thug/ kingpin in Houston, but Apple was confident she still had him wrapped around her finger. She was the one pulling the strings. Once she was done taking care of unfinished business in Harlem, she planned on going back to Houston and cleaning house.

The rooftop gave Apple some solitude from her crew and the world. She peered at the Brooklyn Bridge as she smoked her cigarette on this calm night. She marveled at the city's infrastructure. The city was alive with noise and bustle as it was every day and night. It appeared so strong and enduring, weathering many storms and the times.

She wanted to become the same as the city—massive with a lasting infrastructure. She missed home so much. However, her personality shifted greatly.

The only way Apple was able to cope with what happened to her was through violence. She hated the weakness she felt while being a whore for Shaun, and the thought of the abuse and rape she'd suffered made her clench her fists and narrow her eyes. The nightmares wouldn't stop. Every morning, or during the middle of the night, she woke up bitter and furious, her mind infested with horrid memories of being held captive. Apple couldn't cope with emotions anymore. She couldn't sleep. The only thing that gave her satisfaction was murder and death. She had transformed into a snarling, bloodthirsty creature everyone feared.

She felt everyone was responsible for her pain and heartache—Nichols' murder, the betrayal of Cross with Kola, the acid being thrown in her face, the embarrassment, the kidnapping, the abuse, rape and torture, and the cruel snatching of the daughter she gave birth to, which would drive any woman over the edge.

Peaches, her baby, came to mind out of the blue. "Peaches," she uttered faintly. She closed her eyes for a moment and shed a few tears for her missing baby. The feeling for Peaches came unexpected. The father was an unknown trick who paid for pussy, but Apple didn't care. Motherhood was the one emotion she couldn't turn off.

No one knew about the birth, which had been kept a secret. But thinking about her daughter in Mexico ate away at her. For a brief moment, while she held her newborn child in her arms, she'd felt some peace in her life. While she was living in hell, Peaches felt like an angel in her arms.

Now, that moment seemed so far away. It had been almost a year since she had given birth and had last seen her daughter. And if she was to even look for her, she wouldn't know where to start. But Shaun knew where to start. Apple had a sudden realization that Shaun couldn't die right away. He needed to talk. He needed to tell her who he sold his daughter to. She knew Peaches was sold in the black market; affluent couples were willing to pay handsomely for healthy babies. She needed to find her baby, another problem on her agenda.

She called Terri up to the rooftop, and he came immediately.

"What is it?" Terri asked.

"Contact Jet, and tell him that there's been a change of plans."

"Change in plans? Like what?"

"I want that muthafucka alive."

Terri raised his eyebrow, looking bewildered, "Alive?"

"He has something valuable of mine that I need back"

"A'ight. I'm on it right now."

Terri faded from the rooftop, leaving Apple alone again. She was consumed by her thoughts. She lingered there for an hour, contemplating her next move. Chico would come heavy; it was inevitable. But Apple was ready for him.

She took one last look at the city skyline and was ready to depart from the roof. As she made her way toward the exit, her cell phone rang. It was Denise calling again. Apple was hesitant in answering the call, but she did take it.

"What?" she barked.

"We need to talk," Denise said.

"You and me have nothing to talk about," Apple replied sharply.

"I think we do, Apple."

"You been a fuckin' pain in my side for too long, Denise."

"I'm your damn mother, Apple," Denise shouted. "And you gonna give me my fuckin' respect!"

Apple laughed. "Really? And why?"

"'Cause"—Denise paused, hesitant to say what was on her mind at first, but spat it out anyway—"'cause, I know who was the one responsible for tossing that acid in your face."

"What?"

"I know who it was."

"Who the fuck was it?" Apple exclaimed through clenched teeth. "Don't fuckin' play wit' me, Denise. Who the fuck was it?"

Thinking back to the acid incident infuriated Apple. She touched the side of her face where the scars once were. It made her blood boil to find out that all this time, Denise knew who was responsible for disfiguring her.

"Denise . . . "

"Meet me somewhere and we'll talk," Denise said.

"Where?"

"Tonight, in New Jersey. I'm in East Orange."

"You better not be fuckin' around, Denise."

"I'm not."

Apple got the information from her mother and hung up. She stormed down into the loft where Terri and her crew were lounging around, and shouted, "Get y'all fuckin' guns. We're leaving!"

"What's up?" Terri asked.

"I'm about to have a family reunion," Apple returned.

*

Chicano, Kori, Crunch, Terri, and Apple piled into two trucks and sped toward Jersey, fully loaded and anticipating anything.

Apple didn't know what her mother had up her sleeve, but she wasn't taking any chances. Kola was also back in town, so they both were probably trying to plot against her and cause her demise. But Apple knew one thing for sure—she was going to get the truth from someone, even if she had to kill for it.

She tried to fight the emotion, but as the Range Rover forged ahead, she turned her head from Terri to gaze at the city, to hide her sentiment. The tears started to trickle down her cheek as she thought about her daughter and the pain of being disfigured.

She gripped the pistol tightly and took a deep breath. She'd had her moment of sentiment, and now it was back to vengeance. She dried her tears and exhaled.

"Kill 'em all," she muttered.

TWENTY

The dense and dark backwoods of upstate New York seemed to travel for miles, with mountains as far as the eye could see. An hour's drive from the city, the rural area with the tall trees and tall grassy field was a different world for the urban gangsters traveling in the gaudy Durango. It was late in the evening, and the green Durango traveled hastily on the dirt road that led up to the mountains. Turn after turn, and ascending further into the hills, the truck was swallowed deeper into the woods, with the main road being miles back.

The Durango came to a stop at a log cabin perched on an elevated hilltop that seemed to look out at the heavens. The view of the mountains was phenomenal. The cabin was nestled in the woods like a dirty little secret. The nearest town was eleven miles away. This cabin belonged to Chico and was unfurnished and had no amenities or decorations. He had only one use for it—torturing muthafuckas for information. With them nestled so deep into the woods, the victims' screams wouldn't be heard for miles.

The rap music shut off when the engine was cut off. The four doors to the Durango flew open all at once, and the occupants stepped out onto the grassy field. Chico stuffed the pistol into his waistband, his face awash with anguish. The news of his little brother's violent murder hit him really hard. It was painful to hear how Terrance was killed. It had him on the brink of insanity.

He stared at Rome and shouted, "Yo, get those muthafuckas out the back."

Rome nodded, and he and Bad walked around to the hatch of the truck and lifted it open. Inside the back were two men, their limbs and faces swollen and bloody, their wrists bound tightly behind them with duct tape and their mouths gagged with it also. They squirmed and became wide-eyed when they saw Rome smirking at them.

Rome quickly grabbed one captive by the shirt and yanked him out of the truck and pushed him onto his stomach in the dirt with a loud thud. He then kicked the man in the stomach. "Bitch-ass muthafucka!"

He then grabbed the second man and yanked him out of the truck by his dreads and threw him to the ground on his face, bruising his face more than it already was. Both captives were in serious pain, but their attempted screams were muffled by the duct tape over their mouths.

Bad and Torrez grabbed up both men and dragged them into the private cabin. A scowling Chico clenched his fists, ready to tear into them like he was Jaws and they were fresh swimmers. There was going to be revenge for his little brother, and people were going to die in extremely gruesome and painful ways.

Once inside, the men were stripped naked and forced into rickety wooden chairs and bonded with wire and duct tape. They continued to squirm, but their effort was fruitless. Torrez hit them multiple times with his fist, blood leaked from their mouths, and more bruises formed on their faces.

Chico walked up to Raymond, one of his soldiers, and ripped the duct tape from his mouth. He was furious with him for tipping Denise off about the hit on her. He knew Raymond was fucking her, but now he let his dick interfere with his business, so now he had to pay for his betrayal.

He stood over the badly beaten Raymond and scowled. He pushed his .44 Magnum against Raymond's frontal lobe. "You dumb muthafucka!"

"Chico . . . listen, man, it ain't gotta be this—"

Chico started to pistol-whip him, and the butt of the .44 went crashing against his skull, splitting open flesh and tissue, nearly knocking him unconscious. Blood oozed from his face, and his body went limp.

"Where is she?" Chico demanded to know through clenched teeth.

"I don't know," Raymond replied weakly.

"You pissin' me the fuck off, Raymond. I'm gonna ask you once—Where is she?"

"I'm tellin' you, I don't know."

"You fuckin' ignorant, but you gonna fuckin' learn, muthafucka!" Chico turned to Bad and nodded.

Bad went into the next room and came back out carrying a can of gasoline and a fire extinguisher. Raymond's eyes showed absolute fear as Bad began to douse him with gasoline. The other man tied in the second chair began to squirm in panic, the duct tape still over his mouth.

"What the fuck is this, Chico? C'mon, nigga, what the fuck!" Raymond screamed out. Gasoline started to drip from his naked body while he fidgeted in his chair, but he was tied too tight.

Bad lit a match and held it close to Raymond.

"Where is she?" Chico asked again.

"I don't know," Raymond cried out, his voice dripping with fear.

"Wrong answer."

Chico gave the signal, and Bad tossed the burning match at Raymond, who instantly went up in flames, his screams loud, piercing, and agonizing. Chico and his goons stood nonchalantly and watched him burn.

Chico then nodded.

Bad picked up the fire extinguisher and began putting him out. The foam covered Raymond. He was breathing hard. He was screaming. He was a mess.

"Talk," Chico said.

"Chico . . . please, I'm sorry."

Chico nodded to Bad, who set Raymond on fire once more. And the piercing screams started again. He burned longer this time. Chico then gave the signal to put him out with the extinguisher again.

Raymond was barely clinging to life. The wire and duct tape were hardly holding him up from collapsing. Several times, they set him on fire, watched him burn, and then put him out.

Chico found humor in the malicious act. "Nigga, you startin' to smell like barbecue. Talk, muthafucka!"

His goons laughed.

"He ain't talkin', Chico," Bad said.

Chico glared at Raymond. His eyes were bursting from the sockets, and half his face had started to melt. The duct tape and wire had liquefied into his flesh.

Torrez said, "He done, Chico. This nigga a dead man tryin' to live."

Chico shook his head. "Cancel this nigga then."

Bad set Raymond on fire one last time, and his loud screams faded as he burned to a total crisp, his flesh and skin dissolving rapidly under the intense heat. When they were satisfied he was dead, Bad put him out with the extinguisher one last time, and then he kicked over the chair. Raymond's charred body hit the wood flooring with a thud. He was burned beyond recognition.

Chico stood over the body and put two bullets in Raymond's skull. He then turned to scowl at his next victim and uttered a chilling, "Next!"

The man fidgeted harder, and his eyes began to tear up. He was trying to say something underneath the duct tape, but it was incoherent. Darren was an associate of Apple from back in the days, a once close friend and, some might say, an ex-boyfriend.

Chico tore away the duct tape from Darren's mouth and placed the pistol against his frontal lobe, just as he did with Raymond. "You see that muthafucka on the floor?"

Darren nodded. "Please don't kill me," he cried out. Darren had peed on himself and was trembling uncontrollably.

"Nigga, be a fuckin' man," Chico barked. "You wanna make this easy on you, right?"

Darren nodded.

"Then just tell me what I fuckin' need to know about that bitch."

Darren nodded fast again, looking like a bobble-head doll in the chair.

Bad stood behind him, and Torrez and Rome were ready to watch the fun start.

Chico removed the gun from his forehead. "What you know about that bitch?"

"I haven't seen or spoken to her in three years," Darren replied, tears trickling down his face.

"Wrong answer." Chico gestured to Bad.

Darren began fidgeting in his chair when Bad started pouring gasoline on his body. He screamed out, "No! No! No! Please, I'll tell you anything! Anything! Don't do this to me!"

"Talk, muthafucka!" Chico said. "I need something current."

"Nasty muthafucka," Torrez said, when he realized Darren had shit on himself.

Chico was becoming impatient with Darren taking too long to answer. "Fuck it! Light his ass up!"

Bad lit the match, and Darren screamed out, "No, I know somethin' about her moms, though!"

"Like what?"

"She's stayin' wit' a friend somewhere in New Jersey," he said quickly. "She's scared to come back to Harlem, from what I heard."

"You got a name, a fuckin' address?"

"I just know the friend's name is Yandy. That's all I know about anything. You gotta believe me," Darren hollered.

Chico stared him down and spat, "You useless muthafucka!"

"What? I gave you what you needed."

"Fuck you, and her, and anything associated wit' that fuckin' bitch. I'm killin' anything connected to her. Anything she loves is gettin' destroyed," Chico proclaimed through clenched teeth.

"I told you somethin'. She don't love me; she never did. Please don't do this to me! I have kids! I have a life. I don't wanna die! I don't wanna die!" he begged and screamed out.

"Light his ass up, Bad."

Bad stood near Darren with the burning match in his hand. Darren, his eyes flooded with tears, fought and fidgeted harder in his seat, but his restraints held him in place. The horror manifested on his face looked like he was staring at the devil himself. He continued to scream out, "Oh God, help me! I don't wanna die! I don't wanna die!"

Bad tossed the match, and Darren lit up like a barbecue grill, his body at once engulfed in flames. He screamed out loud. It was a bone-chilling sound. Darren, while burning, actually broke free from his restraints and tried to run, but he only got to the door before collapsing from the intense heat. And he was dead right away. Everyone stood around smiling as they watched him burn to death.

Bad stepped up to put him out, but Chico stopped him, saying, "Nah, let that muthafucka burn some more."

Darren's body was no longer visible under the intense flames. What was once flesh and skin had turned black and contorted and looked like charcoal on the floor.

Chico stood and continued to watch Darren burn. He didn't know this man at all, but he wanted him to die in such an inhuman way because word had gotten back to him that he and Apple once had a thing going on a few years ago. Anything Apple loved or used to love, he was going to hunt down and kill in a gruesome way.

"Now put that muthafucka out," Chico instructed.

Bad stepped in with the extinguisher and put out the flames surrounding Darren's burning body.

"Now, let's get back to business and on this hunt," Chico said. "We don't fuckin' rest until that bitch and her family is dead."

TWENTY-ONE

Everybody was on edge, and Chico was no different. Killing those two fools up in the cabin did nothing for him. He was still hurting from the loss of his little brother. He missed Terrance greatly.

He took a swig of Hennessy Black. He had been drinking all night. He sat back in his La-Z-Boy chair and stared at the television in the dimmed living room of his home. He had the channel on the nightly news, but his mind was heavy on war, with the .38, .357, and .45 handguns all within his reach. He wasn't taking any chances. If anyone dared to come through his front door unannounced, they were going to be in for one hell of an awakening.

Shirtless and in a pair of jeans, he sat slouched in his seat. He'd long ago dried his tears for his brother. He switched the channels, but his attention wasn't on any TV show.

He glanced out the window when he heard a noise. It was dusk out. His thugs were on the hunt in the streets. He'd given the word—a hundred thousand for Apple's head. And he had Ion on the hunt too. He was becoming angrier every day that bitch was allowed to breathe.

When he heard the same noise coming from outside again, he reached for his .357 and raised up from the chair slightly, staring out the window, poised with the gun in his hand, and ready to open fire.

When the noise from outside the home moved closer, Chico stood up, his cold, black eyes transfixed on the door. Then the door handle moved a little.

"Muthafucka!" Chico aimed the gun at the door.

The front door opened slowly. Then he heard voices. Chico gripped the gun tighter and was ready to react. Since the room was dim, he would see them before they saw him.

In walked a shadowy figure. It was hulking and dark.

Chico fired. *Boom!*

A woman screamed.

"Chico, what the fuck! Oh my God!"

The lights came on, and the reality of Chico's harsh actions came to light. He had just shot Blythe's bodyguard in the head.

"What is wrong with you, Chico?" she screamed. "Oh my God! Are you crazy?"

Chico stared at Frank's dead body. He had hired him to be Blythe's personal bodyguard, not wanting to take any chances with his woman's safety.

"Baby, just put the gun down," Blythe said to him, approaching him slowly.

"This fuckin' bitch got me trippin', baby."

"Chico, just calm down and relax. I know it was an accident. But what if it was me walking through that door? Baby, you gotta think. You're too fuckin' paranoid right now."

Chico wasn't releasing the gun. He locked his eyes on Blythe and continued scowling. His anger was rising more and more every day his war with Apple raged on.

Blythe, matching his scowl, shouted, "I can't do this anymore! I can't take this shit with you, Chico. Look at what that bitch is doing to you. You fighting that war out there and in here with us! I'm tired, Chico. I'm so fuckin' tired! Look at this. Look at Frank!" She pointed down to her dead bodyguard. "Is this what you want . . . to be surrounded by death constantly?"

Chico remained silent.

Blythe's tears trickled down her face. She stared at Chico and tried to hold back her sudden contempt for him.

Chico finally spoke, "What you want from me?"

"I want this to end."

"It ain't gonna end until either me or that bitch is dead."

"I can't live like this."

"Then fuckin' leave, bitch!" he screamed madly. "Ain't anyone asking you to stay. This is my fuckin' fight, not yours!"

"I can't believe you. I love you, baby, and I want us to be happy."

"Fuck *happy*. You see this?" Chico raised the pistol and showed it off. "This is gonna keep us alive, keep us happy. Frank was just a casualty of war, that's all. I just gotta get you a new bodyguard."

"I don't need anything else from you, Chico. I don't need shit from you, if you're gonna continue on with this insanity. You're too fuckin' blind to see what is happening with you. Look at you! That fuckin' bitch got you sadistic and twisted. She got you chasin' behind her like some damn fool! Who's the fuckin' bitch, you or her?"

Chico snapped. He rushed toward Blythe, wrapped his hand around her throat, and pushed her against the wall with tremendous force. A few pictures on the wall were abruptly rattled and fell against the floor, shattering.

Blythe's eyes opened wide in fear. This wasn't the man she'd fallen in love with. He was choking her, draining life from her body. "I can't breathe," she managed to say, gasping for air.

"I'm no one's bitch. You fuckin' understand me? You dumb bitch! I'ma have that bitch's head in my fuckin' lap real soon. I'm gonna kill her, so stay the fuck out my way," he growled. He released his strong grip from around her throat and took a few steps back, gun in hand.

Blythe was dumbfounded and upset. She was done. She couldn't believe Chico had attacked her. She wanted to throw up. She ran off into the bedroom and began packing her things. Enough was enough. If Chico wanted to throw himself over the edge, fine then, but he wasn't going to pull her over with him.

Chico took another swig of his Hennessy Black and gazed out the window, the .357 in his hand, down by his side. He heard Blythe in the bedroom crying as she packed but made no attempt to soothe her pain. He no longer cared about her needs or happiness. The only thing on his mind was bloodshed.

Twenty minutes later, Blythe came storming out the bedroom wheeling her suitcase.

Chico turned to glare at her. He remained silent.

Blythe took a deep breath and locked eyes with her man. "Goodbye, Chico," she said matter-of-factly.

Chico didn't reply. He only stared at her with contempt. She was weak. And he refused to be around anyone that was weak. There were bigger issues to deal with than to worry about some bitch.

Blythe lingered at the door for a moment. "You're not going to say anything?" she asked.

"Fuck you!"

Blythe began to cry again. They'd been together for over a year, and now, everything came to an abrupt end. Frank's body by the front door was proof enough that things were too dangerous for her to stay. And she no longer felt safe in her own home. She could have easily been the one he'd shot.

Blythe collected herself and made her exit. She had no more words for Chico. She loved him dearly, but she couldn't tolerate it anymore. He'd become a monster, and she would rather leave and start over somewhere else than to feel unsafe and unloved in her own home. She stepped over Frank's body and left the front door open.

She cried as she walked toward the cab. She looked back at her old home one last time and got into the idling cab. "Fuck you too, Chico," she muttered under her breath.

She knew Chico wasn't going to chase after her. He was too stubborn. He was fighting for everything else other than their love. Their relationship was a done deal. The cab pulled away from the curb with Blythe in the backseat shedding tears, and she refused to look back again.

Chico stood by the window. He saw the cab pulling off, and he didn't give it a second thought. What was done was done. Now it was back to business. Blythe was a good woman, and he felt in order for her to stay alive, he had to let her go.

His heart ached for her, but there was no room for love and emotions. With his enemies on his heels, he had to become withdrawn.

The ringing cell phone snapped him from his thoughts. He went to answer the phone. "Who the fuck is this?"

"Listen carefully," the unknown caller stated. "We both have a common enemy at the moment."

"What?"

"I want a meeting wit' you," the caller said.

Chico didn't recognize the voice. He barked through the phone, "Why the fuck would I want to meet wit' you, nigga? Who the fuck is you?"

"Once again, listen carefully. A friend of yours has something to say to you."

"Yo, Chico, I'm sorry, man. I fucked up," Bad said.

Chico was outraged. Someone had kidnapped one of his prime lieutenants. Bad was a beast in the game and was always careful with his movements in the streets. Who had caught him slipping?

The unknown caller got back on the phone and said to Chico, "Do I have your attention now?"

"I'm listening, muthafucka! Speak ya damn business."

"Come to this warehouse in an hour. It's in the Bronx," the caller said. He gave Chico the location and some instructions.

Chico hung up, furious. He was ready to add more bodies to his growing body count. But he knew the unknown caller was smart and savvy in the streets. How this unknown caller had captured Bad had Chico in bewilderment. Would his lieutenant still be alive once he showed up? It was a sticky situation, and Chico was ready to make it even stickier.

He got on the phone with Rome and Torrez, and they quickly headed out to the Bronx, heavily armed and ready for the unthinkable . . . if it came.

*

Chico stopped his ride in front of the industrial warehouse on Chesbrough Avenue in the Bronx. It was a three-story corner commercial building consisting of two loading docks, one garage door, and a freight elevator. The block was dark and quiet, and there weren't any residential neighbors around for blocks, since it was an industrial area.

Chico was hesitant to proceed as he sat behind the wheel of the Durango. It probably was a setup. Apple was a sneaky, conniving little bitch who he had truly underestimated in the past three months. She always seemed to be one step ahead of him. He had to find a way to become one step ahead of her.

"You trust this shit, Chico?" Torrez asked.

"Not one bit."

But Chico didn't have a choice. Good soldiers like Bad came rare in today's game. And losing Bad in a time of war would be crucial to his crew.

Rome suggested heatedly, "I say fuck it. We go in shootin'. Let muthafuckas know not to fuck wit' us."

"Nah, we go in and talk, but just us two," Chico said, referring to him and Torrez. "And, Rome, if we ain't out that bitch within fifteen minutes, you know what to do."

Rome nodded.

Chico stuffed his pistol into his waistband and stepped out the truck. Torrez did the same, and the two walked toward the rolling gates out front. The area was lifeless. It felt like he was in a bad low-budget horror movie. Anything was possible. This caller maybe wanted to talk, or maybe he wanted Chico dead. It was a risk coming into unknown territory with little muscle. Chico knew one thing for sure though—if it was a setup, then he wasn't going out without a fight.

Torrez knocked on the side door. The two men took a step back and braced themselves for the worst. Anything could be behind this door—business or war.

The steel side door opened, and a slim soldier wearing a red bandanna, red beads, and sagging jeans emerged. He scowled at the two men. He was a Blood member.

Chico locked eyes with him. "You know what the fuck we here for. Don't act stupid."

"Yo, fam, don't come up in here wit' that. I ain't the one," the young soldier said.

But Chico was far from intimidated.

The young soldier stepped aside and allowed them entry into the warehouse. Chico and Torrez walked into the 8,750-square-feet space with the 20-foot ceiling. The place was filled with boxes and junk and hadn't been used in months.

The Blood soldier showed that he was carrying a pistol. He continued to glare at Chico and Torrez.

"Who we here to see, yo? 'Cause I ain't got no fuckin' time to waste," Chico said.

"Just follow me." He led the way, and Chico and Torrez followed behind him.

They walked into an empty office, and there was Bad, tied to a chair, surrounded by a half dozen other Blood members, flaunting their red bandannas, beads, and tattoos. One soldier held a gun to Bad's head, and he looked like he could easily kill a man in a heartbeat.

Chico looked around. He took in the atmosphere and situation instantly. "The man in charge, where the fuck is he?"

No one said anything. They kept mute and acted like he didn't speak English.

"Y'all niggas deaf? Who the nigga I spoke to on the phone?" Chico demanded to know.

"That would be me," a voice boomed from the shadows.

Chico and Torrez turned to see a figure approaching. Chico couldn't make out who it was immediately, but as the man and the voice loomed closer, Chico flared up.

"What the fuck do you want, nigga? Is this a fuckin' joke?"

"No joke, Chico. You and I now share a common enemy, and we both want her dead," Shaun said coolly.

The air in the room became a lot tenser. Chico was taken aback. *Is the enemy of my enemy now my friend?* It was an age-old question.

Shaun, clad in a wifebeater and jeans, approached Chico. He looked really fit. His head was shaved, and he had some serious muscle behind him.

"I'm a hunted man, Chico. I know Apple wants me dead like yesterday, and she's come close on a few occasions. I got a heavy bounty on my head. And I'm being hunted by this man who calls himself Jet. His team cornered me in Brazil, there was a shootout, and Jet took a couple slugs. I barely got out alive. I know you and I once had our differences. I know you loved that bitch once, but she's a threat to both of us now."

"Nigga, what you did to her in Mexico is what caused this shit wit' her," Chico said. "You fucked her head up."

"And that's the past, and we both won't live to see the future if we let that bitch continue to rage on."

Chico continued to frown upon Shaun. He didn't trust him, but he was desperate to end this war. "And I'm supposed to trust you after this shit with Bad, and wit' one of your men holdin' a gun to my lieutenant's head?"

"I had to get your attention. So do I have it?"

"And how are you supposed to get at this bitch? I've been tryin' for months. She's hard to fuckin' kill. And what's your fuckin' way of handling this bitch?"

"Simple—I have somethin' she craves and might want back."

"And that would be what?"

"She's has a daughter."

"A daughter?"

"Yes. And I know where she is."

Chico's mind was spinning. Was the child his?

TWENTY-TWO

Denise stared out the living room window from her friend's apartment on South Munn Avenue, an elegant pre-WWII apartment in East Orange, New Jersey. She had a perfect view of the street from the fifth-floor window.

Denise had known Yandy for years now, and she was one of the few friends she could trust. Yandy was from Harlem, and the two of them had grown up together, and were once thick as thieves. Yandy had moved from Harlem years ago. When Denise needed a place to escape to or hide out, Yandy welcomed her friend with open arms into her home.

It was dark, and after midnight, but Denise was up and nervous. Denise was chain-smoking by the window and waiting for Apple to show up. She knew Apple was coming. Her daughter had been craving to find out who was behind the acid attack. Yandy thought Denise was insane for snitching on herself, but she did have a conscience. And it was hard to look at Apple's disfigurement, knowing she'd paid someone to make her daughter ugly.

She couldn't relax because Apple was unpredictable. *What would she do once the truth came out?* she thought.

"Shit!" Denise muttered when she saw Apple's over-the-top trucks pull up in front of the building. She took one last pull from the Newport and flicked it out the window. She watched Apple and her goons trickle out of the two vehicles, a Range Rover and a Tahoe. *What have I gotten myself into?*

*

Apple instructed Crunch and Chicano to wait by the truck, while she went into the building with Terri and Kori. She turned to Terri and said, "This bitch better not be wasting my fuckin' time."

Terri only shrugged. On his hip was a holstered and concealed Desert Eagle. He was Apple's shadow. He was observant and adept at protecting her from any dangers, and Apple trusted him with her life. Terri immediately didn't like the idea of driving out to East Orange so hastily. They didn't know the area or what they were walking into. In his mind, everything was a potential setup.

Apple peered up at the building, and then she, along with Terri and Kori attempted to cross the street. But they were unaware they were being watched and targeted from afar.

*

As Apple strutted across the quiet four-lane street, she was in perfect sight of a high-powered rifle. The scope of the rifle followed her vigilantly as she crossed the blacktop. Ion was perched on a nearby rooftop and waiting for the right moment to fire.

Dressed in black and nestled in the cover of night, he was suspended on the edge of a five-story building. He gripped the high-powered rifle with his finger on the trigger, poised like a trained sniper. His military pedigree had taught him how to become invisible and use high-end technology.

Tracking Apple down was easy, since he had the best toys. He had been on Apple for one week. He'd tapped into her phone lines and had access to all her conversations. He had pictures of her doing various things.

Within a week, he'd learned about her family, Guy Tony, her twin sister, Denise, and a few other details. He'd listened in on her conversation with Denise, which had led him here, ready to strike. It was only a matter of time before he devoured her with his umpteenth kill and introduced her brains to the moonlight.

*

Apple walked with a scowl, gliding in her high heels toward the front entrance, but before she had the chance to step into the building, she lost her footing and stumbled on the curb. One of her high heels had gotten caught in the jagged concrete, and she nearly tumbled over.

"Shit," she muttered, trying to break her fall, her arms outstretched.

Then it happened. A split-second shot, and Kori's head exploded, spraying Apple with his blood. He dropped to the concrete.

"What the fuck!" Apple shouted. The shot had been quiet and seemed to come out of nowhere.

Terri quickly went into action. He snatched out his .50 and moved toward Apple. "It's a hit!" he shouted. "Get down! Get down!"

Crunch and Chicano started to run over with their guns drawn. Another shot was fired at Apple, who came out her heels and tried to run for cover. A third shot was fired, and the bullet ripped through her back and dropped her near the building entrance hall. Then she was shot again, and a slug tore through her side.

Apple managed to escape into the building to find cover. She was howling from her injuries. She felt like she was burning up, like her insides had been set on fire. She stumbled against the lobby walls, smearing her blood all over. She felt herself becoming dizzy, and when she tried to walk, she stumbled and collapsed on her side, her body numb and weak.

Apple was disoriented. She buckled near the elevators, all her strength suddenly drained from her. Where was Terri? Was he hit too? Who had attacked them? She lay against the tiled floor bleeding profusely. She knew she was dying.

She remained wilted against the lobby walls, her blood pooling around her. She could barely keep her eyes open. She grunted from the pain that throbbed all through her, and her breathing was becoming erratic.

She looked around crazily, and she couldn't help but to feel fear. Then, suddenly, she noticed a familiar face approaching, a face with features that matched her own.

"Fuck you, Kola!" Apple hissed weakly.

Kola, clutching a .45 in her hand and fueled with resentment, stood over her sister's bullet-riddled body. She ached for this day. She blamed Apple for everything, and this was karma coming back on her. She aimed the .45 at Apple's head and asked, "Did you do it?"

"Do what?" Apple managed to say, coughing afterwards.

"Did you try to have me killed in Miami?"

With blood discharging from her mouth, Apple released another nasty cough. She faintly replied through hard breaths, "I don't know what the fuck you talkin' 'bout."

Kola cocked the gun back.

"Just fuckin' kill me, bitch!"

Kola started to tear up. *Just do it.*

"Do it, you fuckin' bitch!" Apple coughed again.

Terri abruptly charged into the building, and Kola spun around and pointed her pistol at him. He emulated the action, and now the two were in a tense standoff.

"I'll drop you, bitch!" Terri shouted, his gun trained at her head.

"Don't do this," Kola replied. "This ain't your beef."

"Like hell it ain't!"

"I don't have a problem with you, but we can mix it up if you don't back the fuck down."

"Bitch, I will kill you where you stand."

They soon heard police sirens blaring in the distance, as they continued to eye each other intensely.

"It don't make any sense all of us gettin' locked up or killed at this moment. Till next time then." Kola lowered her gun and took a few steps back from the threat aimed at her.

Terri still kept his weapon trained at her, but he wasn't going to fire.

Kola turned to look at her sister and said, "You better not die on me like this. I still got unfinished business wit' you."

Apple was too weak to respond. Simply breathing had become difficult for her.

Kola eyed her sister and then went the opposite way, leaving Terri alone with Apple. He immediately rushed to her aid.

Apple was against him staying. "Leave, nigga!" she managed to say weakly.

Terri looked confused, but then he suddenly understood. He would be no good to her if he were incarcerated. The police were coming, and he was a known felon carrying a large gun. Kori and Crunch were dead, and Chicano drove away in the Range Rover, after Terri advised him to. The vehicles were dirty, and the last thing everyone needed was the police snooping all into their shit.

"I'll be back." Terri darted into the darkness, leaving Apple alone.

*

Police came rushing into the lobby with their guns drawn. They flooded the area like ants and found Apple lying unconscious in a pool of blood. They didn't know if she was dead or alive.

Ten minutes later, EMS workers came storming inside pulling a gurney behind them. They saw the chaos and rushed toward Apple and began trying to save her life. The paramedics quickly assessed the situation and began placing an endotracheal tube into her lungs to help her with her breathing. And then they started an IV to give her fluids.

*

The trauma unit hurriedly wheeled Apple into the ER of East Orange General Hospital. Apple was in critical condition. One bullet nearly pierced her heart, and the second bullet left her with a collapsed lung. The hot bullet was still inside of her, moving around freely, causing extra damage to her bodily functions. After she was wheeled into the ER, every available doctor and nurse in the trauma center was aiding to keep her alive. They had to stabilize her blood pressure and repair her damaged lung, and they had to remove the bullet, if possible. She'd also suffered swelling in some crucial areas.

The doctors had to perform surgery fast. They cut the bloody clothes from her skin and began prepping her for surgery. Her blood pressure had dropped dramatically, and she was touch and go, barely clinging to life. The medical staff was clueless about her history. The only thing these doctors saw was a young girl shot by a high-powered rifle, and by some miracle, she wasn't dead.

After three hours of surgery, the doctors had stabilized Apple's condition, but the danger was far from over. They were able to remove the bullet, but she was still in a risky stage and had to be monitored twenty-four/seven.

*

Terri sat outside the hospital in a parked truck seething with rage, his pistol on his lap and specks of blood on his face and clothing. He refused to leave Apple. He had to make sure she was okay, confirm that she was still alive. He knew she was vulnerable to her enemies. It was easy access to her, and he needed to prevent it. The shooting came suddenly out of nowhere, and if Apple hadn't missed her footing, she would have been dead.

Terri gripped the pistol with a frown. He was watching the hospital entrance like a hawk. He needed to go inside and check on her, but he didn't want to draw attention to himself. He needed to clean himself up, but he couldn't be in two places at once.

"Shit!"

He noticed two federal agents walking into the hospital. He knew they were FBI by their dark, sharp attire. In fact they walked like the feds. And Terri knew exactly who they were going to see. With the FBI visiting Apple, he definitely couldn't go see her now.

He got on his cell phone and dialed Houston. Guy Tony picked up.

"We got a problem," he said.

"What is it?" Guy Tony asked indifferently.

"Apple's in the hospital. She's been shot."

"What the fuck, Terri! How did this shit happen?"

"We walked into an ambush. A sniper hit us."

"How bad?"

"It's bad. I think she's been shot twice. And the feds just walked into the hospital."

"Fuck me, Terri. You're supposed to be keeping her alive. And the feds . . . what the fuck is goin' on up there?"

"I know. I fucked up."

"Yeah, you fucked up. You my best man, Terri. How'd you allow this shit to happen? You do whatever possible, but you clean this shit up ASAP!"

"I understand. And I will."

*

Guy Tony hung up, leaving Terri pondering his next move.

Guy Tony wasn't as forgiving and loving as he appeared to be. He needed Apple alive because she was his key in escaping the RICO charge developing against him. He had a few government officials in his pocket. He'd paid off cops and agents generously, and they were feeding him inside information on upcoming raids, indictments, and other drugs crews in the city on a regular. He'd found out that prosecutors were ready to open a RICO case against him for his dealings in the Southern underworld and his ties with the Mexican cartels. Jail wasn't an option for him. An inside official advised him to find someone to take the fall. He needed a scapegoat, a much bigger target for the feds and special prosecutors to chase, and Apple was it.

He'd rescued her from that Mexican brothel for his own selfish reasons. He took her in, gave her love, and allowed Apple into his world, familiarizing her with his organization. He knew she would take the bait. She'd once played and manipulated him to kill Supreme, but he would now turn the tables against her. She'd take the fall when the feds came knocking with a slew of indictments.

Guy Tony knew Apple would be hell-bent on revenge against Shaun, and that meant a war, and war meant bodies and bloodshed. And the multiple and brutal murders going on in Harlem because of that bitch was becoming national news. The nation couldn't ignore it.

He'd sent Apple to Harlem to do what was expected of her, and she didn't fail him. She was doing a fine job as a terrorist in her community. He had Terri, one of his best killers and soldiers, to protect her, because he didn't want anything to happen to her. So when the feds came knocking, he would point the finger at her as the HBIC—head bitch in charge. It was a genius plan, and so far, it had been going fine . . . until this shit.

TWENTY-THREE

Denise rushed into the hospital with tears in her eyes, her heart feeling like concrete. She had Yandy by her side.

"I need to see my fuckin' daughter!" she screamed out. "Where is she?"

The overnight receptionist was taken aback by Denise's loud outburst. The screaming mother was catching everyone's attention.

The feeling of guilt and apprehension became overwhelming for her. Yandy was there for comfort, but it seemed like everything was going from sugar to shit. It was unbelievable. Denise was so traumatized after the hearing the news, she threw up for hours in the bathroom.

Denise pounded her fist on the receptionist's desk and shrieked, "Where is my fuckin' daughter? I need to see her, right now! Oh my God, this can't be happening. Not now. Not now."

"It's gonna be okay, Denise. We gonna find her," Yandy said.

"Don't tell me it's going to be okay, Yandy! What the fuck is goin' on?"

"What is your daughter's name?" the reception asked.

"Apple. She was brought in a few hours ago. Y'all need to hurry the fuck up! My daughter better be okay!"

"Ma'am, there's no need to get so hostile."

"Don't fuckin' *ma'am* me. I need to see my fuckin' daughter!"

Two security guards walked over and tried to defuse the situation.

They towered over Denise.

One of them said, "Miss, just calm down."

"I don't need to fuckin' calm down."

"Denise, relax!" Yandy chimed. "I'm here. We're going to get through this. Just let them do their jobs, okay?"

Denise glared at Yandy. She was in fear for her own life but came out of hiding to tend to her daughter's well-being. The tears trickled down her face. And the truth of what her life had become over the years suddenly came to light in her eyes. She had been a no-good mother for so many years, teaching her girls the wrong values. She made them dishonest, and taught her babies to manipulate and take advantage of niggas, especially weak-minded niggas, the way she'd done with their father, who'd killed himself, leaving the twins without a father in their life.

As Denise stood in the bustling hospital area, the realization suddenly swooped down on her like a heavy downpour—she was alone, bitter, scared, and a marked woman. Too many years, she'd whored herself to the drug dealers, pimps, and ballers in the hood, straddling the fence with her kids' well-being, causing Nichols' demise. Too many years, she'd lived on Section 8, making a living through tricking and stealing. Too many years, she'd scolded and abused her daughters. Too many years, she had been that unemployed, lazy, ghetto-trash, alcohol-drinking, cursing, cigarette-smoking, partying black woman living in the projects.

Denise suddenly felt lightheaded. She stumbled against the counter, nearly collapsing in front of everyone.

One of the security guards grabbed her. "Miss, you okay?" he asked.

When she didn't respond, Yandy said, "Get her some water."

The security guard helped her over to the row of chairs lining the wall and made her take a seat.

Denise's tears continued to trickle. "I've been a terrible mother to them, Yandy."

"Don't beat yourself up about this, Denise. You and her are going to get through this."

"I don't know. I just need to see her."

A cup of water was brought for Denise to drink. She refused, but Yandy insisted she take a few sips. The stress was making her dizzy and sick. Denise gulped the water down and rested a little. Her temper had calmed down, and she was at ease for the moment.

A half hour later, Denise walked into the ICU room to see Apple. The sight of her daughter made Denise's knees almost buckle. She felt like she was ready to fall over in grief again. Her baby looked like a character out of *The Matrix*, with the tubes and wires protruding from her. She was connected to several machines to help her breathe, and to keep her alive. Her vitals were steady, but she was comatose.

The room was cluttered with ventilators, a patient warming system, a feeding pump, infusion pumps, and other critical care machines, all humming and buzzing in the still room.

Denise's eyes were transfixed on her daughter. Yandy stood behind her. Her own eyes became cloudy with tears. She'd watched Apple grow up, and now her life had taken another sad turn, and the pretty little wide-eyed girl with so many dreams and hopes was looking like a monster once again.

"Look what they did to her." Denise sighed heavily. She moved closer to her daughter and took her hand into hers gently. "I'm guilty of this, Yandy. She was comin' to see me. You know I was ready to tell her the truth, despite the consequences, and look at this shit. Can it get any uglier than this?"

"Just pray for her, Denise. We both can pray." Yandy walked over and stood next to them both.

Soon, a few doctors entered the room to inform Denise of her daughter's condition. She was lucky to be alive. The team of doctors told her the surgery was successful, but it was going to be a long recovery.

Denise took comfort near her daughter, gently holding and massaging her wilted hand. Her own near-death experience had changed her greatly. The two hit men that rushed into her apartment with their guns blazing gave Denise a whole new outlook on her life. She vowed to change for the better, and it had to start with family. For all the grief she'd caused in her daughters' lives, she knew it was time to become the devoted and loving mother she never was.

*

Ion sat parked outside the hospital, determined to finish what he'd started. He was truly disappointed with himself. He'd never missed a target. The bitch stumbled, and her life was spared. It infuriated him that Apple was still alive. Now he had to finish the job, or his reputation for killing would be questioned.

When Chico had heard about the failed hit, he'd shouted, "Muthafucka, how the fuck did you fuck this up? I'm payin' good money for that bitch to be dead, and you miss? What the fuck is wrong wit' you?"

"I will finish it," Ion told him. "No need to worry."

"You better . . . because you came highly recommended. And if you don't finish her off, I'll get someone to finish you off."

Ion didn't take kindly to the threat on his life. He understood Chico was upset, and at the moment, he was his employer, but Chico would be the one in danger if he threatened his life again.

Ion watched everything from the black gypsy cab outside the hospital. He calculated what needed to be done, and how it would be done. He wanted to be in and out as smoothly as possible, but the problem was, Apple always had company. If it wasn't her mother caring for her, then it was the goons standing outside the hospital and her room. And then there were the federal agents lingering in the building inconspicuously, or so they thought. But Ion noticed it all; he had a trained eye.

Ion cracked his knuckles. His high-powered rifle was in the trunk of the car, and a few automatic weapons also. The two shots Apple took should have killed her, but the bitch had survived by a miracle. Ion had killed many men, and it took a young girl to disrupt his track record. Now, it was personal.

It was time to make his move—now or never. He had waited around for a few days to learn the inner workings of the hospital and its staff. He'd infiltrated the computer systems, learned the names of certain doctors, patients, and staff members. He'd also taken a mental note of all the exits and stairways.

Without anyone knowing or becoming suspicious of him, Ion had walked the halls of the hospital numerous times, checking every floor and even passing by Apple's room a couple of times and taking a glance inside. He'd observe Denise seated by Apple's bed, holding and stroking her hand. No one knew what he looked like. He kept his identity a secret. In everyone's eyes, he was either a visitor or a staff member moving about. But Ion was watching and scheming. He knew the exact time to strike.

Ion stepped out the gypsy cab in a white lab coat, blue scrubs, and his fraudulent hospital ID—Jonathan Meyers, M.D.—attached to his lab coat. He had altered his physical features somewhat, with a different hair color, a fake goatee, different color contacts, and nerdy frames. He also carried a small leather briefcase. He looked harmless, like another doctor getting ready to work the midnight shift, but underneath his long lab coat was a holstered 9 mm with a silencer.

It was late in the hour, and the staff was sparse. Most of them had gone home for the night, and the hospital floor was quiet, with security walking the floors. Ion needed to change that. He needed a distraction.

His first move was into the men's bathroom. He checked his image in the mirror and was pleased with his appearance. He was official, as always. He looked around, taking in everything. The bathroom was empty.

Ion saw only one possible way to cause distraction, and he was ready to implement it. He removed a pipe bomb from the leather briefcase and walked into one of the bathroom stalls. The bomb was set on a timer, and was to go off in fifteen minutes.

Next, he took one of the yellow signs that said, "Closed for Cleaning," and placed it near the bathroom entrance. Then he went on the stairway and pulled out a disposable cell phone and made the call. He dialed the hospital, and a female worker answered.

Ion was blunt with the information. He told her, "There's a bomb in the hospital that's set to go off in thirty minutes. You need to evacuate everyone immediately." He hung up, leaving the young female petrified.

Next, Ion pulled the fire switch in the stairway, and a loud, unsettling alarm went screaming throughout the hospital. People started to panic. The movement in the hallways became heavy.

The worker Ion had called instantly notified the police and other staff members about the bomb scare. Ion just lingered in the hallway for a few short moments and waited for the right time.

Ten minutes later, the serene atmosphere in the hospital was suddenly transformed into chaos and panic. The nurses and orderlies were running from room to room, and the patients were crippled with fear.

Ion made his way down the hallway in a calm manner. With the confusion and disorder going on around him, no one noticed how cool this doctor was. He approached Apple's room, which was a few doors down, his pistol concealed underneath his lab coat.

Denise was in the doorway. She shouted, "What's happening?"

"Miss, we're going to have to evacuate her soon," a staff member told her.

"Why?" she screamed out. "What's goin' on here?"

"We notified the police. We just need for everyone to stay calm." The staff member hurried off to tend to the other rooms.

"Police? What the fuck!"

Ion approached Denise with his calm smile and said to her, "Miss, I'll help you with everything. Just trust me, we're going to get your daughter to safety very soon."

Denise saw his outwardly appearance and nodded. She felt he would help out with everything.

Ion stepped into the room. He gazed at Apple. He peered at his work with admiration. Even though she wasn't dead, his two shots had fucked her up really bad. Now it was time to end this.

He turned to Denise and said, "I'm going to need your help."

Denise nodded frantically, willing to do whatever it took to get her daughter to safety.

KABOOOOM!

The explosion rocked the floor beneath them and sent a wave of panic throughout the hospital, with screaming, yelling, and crying. People were running and taking cover. The alarms screamed louder and the sprinkler systems were automatically activated, showering each floor with a monsoon from the ceilings.

"Oh my God! Oh my God!" Denise screamed.

"Miss, I need you to be calm." Ion subtly reached into his lab coat and gripped the butt of his pistol.

"Do somethin'!" Denise screamed frantically. "Please do somethin'!"

"I plan to." Ion removed the 9 mm from the inside of his lab coat and pointed it at Denise's head.

"No! Please!"

Ion's warm and caring eyes all of a sudden altered into cold, black slits at his victim. He lurched closer, his arm outstretched with the pistol.

Denise stood frozen in front of the barrel, like a deer caught in headlights.

Within the blink of an eye, her savior loomed by the doorway amongst the chaos, his .45 aimed at Ion.

Ion felt this sudden threat behind him and pivoted on his heels, fast like lightning, to counterattack, but he was a second too late.

Bak!

The shot struck Ion in the chest, and he stumbled backwards, the gun still gripped in his hand. He was able to let off a shot, but he missed his target by meters.

Terri rushed into the room and fired again, and the bullet slammed into Ion's skull, dropping him dead by Apple's bed.

Terri had seen him coming. He knew the killers wouldn't rest until Apple was dead, and he was determined to prevent that. It was only a matter of time before they sent someone to finish the job. And if he hadn't been paying attention, Ion would have succeeded.

First, the man in the white lab coat getting out of the gypsy cab caught his attention. And then instead of going through the front entrance like every other doctor and staff member, he went around through the service entrance. Terri watched him closely, and when the alarm had been set and panic ensued, Terri knew the deal.

Denise was grateful to Terri, but they weren't out of hot water yet. The dead man in the room wasn't a good look, even though he was a killer.

Terri couldn't be around for any questioning. He advised Denise on what to do next, and she nodded steadily. He moved briskly before he was seen by anyone, leaving Denise in complete bewilderment while standing near her comatose daughter.

Police sirens were blaring, and cops and the SWAT team were storming into the hospital. It was a scene straight out of the movies, and Denise could barely believe what she had witnessed.

TWENTY-FOUR

Kola smashed the crystal glass against the bedroom wall, upset with herself and the events of the past weeks. She'd had the opportunity to kill her sister right then and there but didn't pull the trigger. So what went wrong? She continued to pace the floor in the spacious Bronx apartment she was renting, trying to collect herself.

Sags peeked his head into the bedroom and asked, "Everything okay in here?"

"Just leave me the fuck alone for a moment," Kola barked.

Sags quickly closed the door and gave Kola her alone-time.

The men hired by Copper to protect Kola wouldn't leave her side, no matter what, and she started to feel like a prisoner in her own hood. She had made Copper a promise and owed him a great deal. She had promised him Harlem, vowing that they would distribute kilos coming from Miami, but lately, things hadn't been going as planned.

Kola had made enemies with a few dangerous men and major players in the underworld. The list went on for her—OMG, Cross, Chico, Apple, and Eduardo.

She missed her team of shooters, her girls that she trusted, Candice and Patrice, who had been wiped out by Eduardo's hit men. The muscle she once had was washed out like a surfer going against a crippling wave.

And over the past months, she had to rely on her street smarts and wits to survive.

She was once the queen of Harlem and the princess of Miami when she was down with OMG's crew and Nikki had her back, but now all that was gone. The noose around her neck was tightening, and her breathing was becoming restricted.

The TV in the bedroom blared out, *"Breaking News in East Orange, New Jersey,"* and images of a hospital in complete turmoil started to flash across the screen.

Kola stared at the television and realized it was the same hospital Apple was in.

The anchorwoman announced, *"An explosion happened at East Orange General Hospital this evening, leaving three dead in the chaos. It's understood that a bomb scare was called in by an anonymous caller right before the explosion."*

Kola turned up the volume to hear more details on the story. *Is Apple one of the dead?* Her eyes were transfixed on the images the news were displaying—firefighters and police everywhere. The entire hospital had been evacuated, and a few bomb-sniffing dogs were brought out.

"Fuck this!" Kola muted the television. It was getting too depressing.

If her sister was dead, then so be it, but for some odd reason, she didn't think Apple was among the dead.

She walked to the window and peered outside from her two-story walk-up. The summer heat was making things very uncomfortable. She looked down at the Bronx Street below her. Her view was that of a dark alley littered with trash. She hated the Bronx, but the apartment she was keeping low in was cheap and in the cut. With a few bounties on her head, she had to keep a low profile. And supposedly no one knew about this location. She turned her attention away from the window, sighing heavily. The night seemed to drag on like a four-hour church service. The fighting, survival, and having an open fed case was taking its toll.

Kola had taken a few extra security measures to maintain her survival. Lying on her bed were two pistols, a .380 and a Ruger LCP, both fully loaded. While Sags and Mondo were killers, they weren't the best. They were almost like two stooges with guns. They knew how to shoot, and were wild thugs, but they were far from cream-of-the-crop assassins.

Clad in a pair of jean shorts and T-shirt that accentuated her breasts, she peeked out into the hallway and heard the two men shouting and yelling. They were in the living room playing Xbox. She closed the bedroom door and took a seat on the bed. She raised the volume on the TV and changed the channel to see if there was more news coverage about the hospital bombing, but there was nothing new.

All of a sudden, she heard, *Chk-Chk-Boom!*

The sound startled her. She leaped from the bed with her .380 in her hand and rushed toward the bedroom door. The shotgun blast was followed by deafening automatic gunfire in the living room.

Kola knew Sags and Mondo were already dead. Then she heard a man yell out, "Yo, find that fuckin' bitch!"

Her heart began to beat fast. "Shit!" She slammed the bedroom door, locking it.

But it wasn't going to do any good. She was trapped in the bedroom, and the killers were approaching fast. She didn't know who'd sent them, but it didn't matter. There wasn't going to be any negotiation about her life. These men were a few feet behind her door, and they'd come for only one reason—to spread death.

"Think, think!" she said to herself.

She looked at the window. The fire escape was her only way out. She rushed toward the fire escape with only one gun in her hand. She opened the window and started to climb out of it as she heard the killers approaching.

The killers smashed open the bedroom door and right away shot up the room with their automatic weapons. By that time she was already on the first floor and could hear the bloodcurdling gunfire above her.

"Where is that fuckin' bitch?" a man shouted.

A man looked out the window and yelled, "There!"

"Fuck me!" Kola cursed. She had never been so scared.

The killers propelled their weapons out the window and started firing down at her. Bullets ricocheted off the fire escape, barely missing her.

She jumped from where she was and landed on her side, scraping her elbow, but she'd made it to the ground alive.

"Fuck! Get that bitch! Get that fuckin' bitch!"

Kola was in the dark, littered alley, the .380 by her side. She snatched the gun up, picked herself up from the dirty ground, and made a run for it.

She ran into the street, ready to shoot at the first thing coming her way. She glanced at her building and noticed a dark green Durango with chrome rims parked outside, a man seated behind the wheel.

How did they find me?

Kola hid between two parked cars in the shadows and watched as the three men who'd tried to kill her ran out the lobby. She recognized Chico. "Muthafucka!" she muttered under her breath. She saw him looking up and down the block.

Sirens stared to blare in the distance, breaching the stillness on the Bronx Street. The block was about to be swarming with police.

Chico screamed out, "Fuck! We out."

The men climbed into the Durango, and the truck went screeching off and faded down the block.

Kola removed herself from between the two cars, not wanting to stick around either. Sags and Mondo were dead, and she was left alone with nowhere to go. The only company she had for protection was the .380 in her hand.

*

Kola smiled as she looked up at the apparition. The woman was even more beautiful than Kola had remembered her. Her eyes lit up like two huge quarters, and the warmth around her was comforting. Kola finally felt peace in her life.

She reached out to this angel approaching and wanted to take her hand, to escape the madness she had been engulfed in. Kola knew once she took her hand, everything was going to be okay, that all her pain, suffering, and misery was going to be wiped away clean.

Kola stood up from the ground and felt whole once more. She took this angel's hand and smiled, tears of happiness trickling down her face. And the darkness that surrounded her was suddenly transformed into a bright, flowing light.

"I missed you so much, Nichols," Kola said with a smile.

Nichols smiled at her. Clad in a long, white gown, and her hair flowing like the wind on a nice spring day, the look on her face was welcoming. Her baby sister looked marvelous. She was pure perfection.

Kola wanted to hug Nichols and never let her baby sister go. Everything was angelic about her, just the way it was before her death almost three years ago. Nichols hadn't changed at all.

Kola was ready to just let go, and go with her sister, but that was impossible. Her sister was dead, so why was she all of a sudden seeing her?

Nichols comforted Kola with a heartening hug and then whispered into her ear, *"It's going to be okay, sister. Just let it go. Be with family. Be with family."*

Nichols then pulled herself away from Kola's arms and started to shed tears of her own.

"What's wrong?" Kola asked.

"Be with family. Be with family," she repeated, her tears continuing to fall.

Out of the blue, Nichols' pure and transparent form was becoming distorted, becoming darker. Kola knew her sister was leaving. *Be with family? What was that about?*

Nichols didn't speak again, and then, just like that, she was gone, leaving Kola behind in full-blown tears.

The feelings from the violent loss of her baby sister resurfaced again, and she remembered that anger she had for Apple. It was all her fault. All this was her fault.

All of a sudden, Kola felt herself sinking into the ground. The muck and dirt was swiftly consuming her, trying to swallow her whole and then digest her like a tasty snack. Feeling paralyzed, she screamed for help, but her cries were muted. She fought to pull herself from the danger, but the more she fought, the faster she started to sink.

*

Kola was jolted awake, the sun beaming in her face. It was early morning, and there was a light breeze. She had slept in the cemetery near her sister's grave. The realization that it was only a dream made her sigh with relief. But it felt so real to her. She was actually talking to her sister. She'd missed her very much, and recently had been having many dreams about her.

Kola took comfort in the cemetery, trying to evade her enemies. It was a temporary feat. Nichols' grave was the only safe haven she had for the moment, until she could come up with a safer place to stay. She had run out of options and friends.

She gripped the .380 in her hand and looked up at the sky. *Where to go from here?* she asked herself. How had things fallen apart so fast in her life? Only a few months ago she'd had power, wealth, and soldiers who would kill for her at the drop of a dime. Now, she was homeless, hungry, and tired, and had the threat of death and jail time looming over her head. Kola only had one option, so she dialed Copper. He picked up immediately.

"Yo."

"I fucked up," she began. "Things got a little funky out here. I need you to send me reinforcements and some paper until I get back on my feet."

"Come again?" Copper seemed distracted.

"Is Sassy around?"

Suddenly, Copper heard something in Kola's voice. "Nah, she ain't here but whaddup?"

"We ran in to some beef, and let's just say Sags and Mondo are casualties of war." Kola sighed. "I need you to send me some more goons so I can get at those punk muthafuckers!"

"Ya ass lost my men? My men are fuckin' dead! Up North . . . what da fuck am I 'posed to tell their family?" His voice was menacing and gruff with outrage over Kola's lack of progress. "I gave you a short leash to handle ya business so you could then handle my fuckin' business 'cuz my cousin vouched for you. Your dumb ass couldn't get that on and poppin'? I'm starting to think ya whole rep is manufactured!"

Kola listened to his rant, unfazed. She knew she was a thoroughbred. "I get mines and I hold my own."

Copper let out a hearty laugh. "Bitch what you get? You get locked the fuck up, that's what you get. You get shitted on by your own family—yeah, you get that too. You also get my men murked. But right now what ya *ain't* getting is that paper and those connects! And ya silly ass sure ain't holding ya own if ya calling me and digging in my pockets!"

"Calm the fuck down 'cuz right now you actin' like a li'l bitch!" Kola was tired of being belittled. Her name rang out up and down I-95. Who the fuck ever heard of a Copper or a fuckin' Sassy? "Everybody knew the risk. What fucking line of business you think we in? We move weight, and people get rocked to sleep!"

Copper's voice took on a creepy tone. "I don't know what you do for a livin', ma, but I own a barber shop"—there was a pregnant pause, and then, "Listen, why don't you come back here and we could get all this shit mapped out? Ya feel me? I apologize for losing my cool, but it's all good, right?"

"Leave New York and come back to Miami?"

"Yeah, take a few weeks off. Maybe you and Sassy could go shoppin' and do that shit you girls do ta get ya mind right."

Kola knew at that point she had fucked up by talking reckless over the phone, especially when she hadn't lived up to her end of the deal. For someone who had just caught a federal charge to be yelling about moving weight and committing murders was a red flag. Copper was most likely thinking she turned snitch and was trying to pull him in to her case. She knew that if she went back to Miami that she would return back to Harlem in a casket.

"A'ight . . . I'm on my way," Kola lied. "And you better not front on the shoppin' when I get there 'cuz a bitch is fucked up right now."

"One thing about me, ma, is that I always keep my word."

Kola hung up knowing two things: She wasn't ever going back to Miami and she now had to add Copper to her list because she'd failed to deliver what she had promised and had gotten his men killed. Copper had made it clear to her that she was a dead bitch walking.

She rested against Nichols' tombstone and continued to talk to her sister. She didn't want to leave the cemetery.

Hours had passed, and Kola stood stationary by her sister's grave. She could feel Nichols' sweet voice in her ear, talking to her, trying to advise her. The dream was trying to tell her something.

Kola got on her knees and leaned toward the tombstone, tears falling. She kissed Nichols' tombstone lovingly, and said in a whisper, "I'm only doin' this for you, baby sister, 'cause I love you and I miss you."

"Be with family" was perpetually replaying in her head.

But how would this reunion turn out? Her mother was a raging bitch, her sister was a fuckin' lunatic, and she wasn't a rose garden herself.

TWENTY-FIVE

Night and day, Denise remained by Apple's side, sometimes getting little sleep and having nothing to eat. She hardly left the hospital. With the attempted attack on Apple's life two weeks earlier, Denise and Terri weren't taking any more chances. They'd moved her under an alias to a more secure hospital in Long Island, and Terri had his goons watch her room and the hospital day and night.

Denise talked to her daughter daily, repeatedly confessing to her that she was the one responsible for the acid attack. Denise would brush her daughter's hair and stroke her hand. And even though Apple was unconscious, Denise figured that talking to her was a good start.

"I'm sorry, Apple. I'm sorry for being the type of mother I was to you for so many years. I was jealous of you and your success. Y'all were so pretty. I was jealous of you and your sister. I hated y'all once. My own daughters I hated. And look at what our family has become—fucked up! You being in this coma, and hating your sister, Kola's out there somewhere, and Nichols being dead . . . it shouldn't be like this." Denise shook her head. "It shouldn't be like this."

Tears trickled down Denise's grief-stricken face as she confessed her sins to her daughter. She wanted to become a changed woman. The world she lived in had become so ugly and disastrous. She felt her life was spared for a reason, and now she intended on taking advantage of her second chance at life.

Terri silently watched Denise's confessions from the doorway. It was a touching moment. But he was only there for protection. If anything happened to Apple, his life would be on the line. He also had received a second chance. Guy Tony had made it clear to protect her at all costs.

Terri was smitten by Apple, but he wouldn't say it. He had gained a lot of respect for her. She was willing to go where no man would go. And the lengths and measures she used were extreme. She was going head to head with one of New York's most notorious kingpins and winning. He couldn't help but respect a woman like her.

Terri didn't involve himself with Denise and her time with Apple. His time at the hospital was limited. He showed up, stayed briefly, and left. The feds were steadily sniffing around, and state detectives were snooping too. That violent incident at the New Jersey hospital had opened up a can of worms, and many branches of law enforcement were investigating the bombing and the murders.

Ion had been identified as an ex-Navy SEAL gone rogue, causing the death of a prominent doctor and a staff member. The bombing and murders had made the national news. And the murders at the hospital had been linked to the ongoing drug war in Harlem. Apple now had the attention of the press, who paraded the story as a hit gone wrong. The mayor of New York held a press conference and vowed to stop the gun violence in New York. Something had to be done.

Terri knew the kitchen was getting hot. Too hot. And Guy Tony was loving every minute of it. News about Apple's deadly episodes took the heat off him, and now the nation was watching her.

Terri, on the other hand, was ambivalent.

He came to New York to perform a job. It was to keep Apple safe, and have her back, even if it meant risking his own life. But he started liking her more than he should. He kept his feelings about Apple a secret. He had to keep his actions about business.

Terri gazed at Apple and then shifted his eyes over to Denise. "I'm about to take off," he said.

Denise glanced at him and nodded.

"You have my number. If you need anything, or if anything changes, do not hesitate to give me a call."

Denise nodded.

"I got two men watching this place, but I doubt anyone knows she's here."

Denise only listened. She didn't reply.

Earlier, Terri had slipped her a .38 for protection. She had the revolver in her purse. She wasn't a stranger to guns. And she wouldn't hesitate to use it if her daughter's life was put in danger again.

TWENTY-SIX

Kola stepped into the seedy motel room in Jamaica, Queens. The cozy room with the provincial décor was comfortable enough to get business done. It was inexpensive, clean, and far away from the threat, if only temporary.

The man she walked behind, the one who'd rented the motel room for the evening, was desperate for some action. He had a predatory smile as he sat on the bed and gazed at her. He had just picked up the young girl from the track on Rockaway Boulevard and couldn't wait to get a piece of that candy.

"You thirsty?" he asked.

"No. Let's just get this done," she replied dryly.

"Okay. A hundred, right?"

Kola nodded.

"You look so nice and sexy. I just want to touch you all over," the chubby man with boyish features said.

Kola rolled her eyes. She had no cash and hardly a place to stay. Too many men were after her, and keeping a low profile in Queens was her only option.

"Come close," he said, smiling.

"You got condoms?"

"No."

"Well, I do," she said, reaching into her purse.

The man started to unzip his jeans. He couldn't wait to sink his manhood into such a pretty young girl. Her shapely body had him drooling, making his dick hard. He pulled down his jeans, revealing the tighty whities he had on. He sat back, ready for her.

Kola wanted to throw up. *What kind of man wears underwear like that? Pathetic.* She stepped closer to the trick.

"Ooooh, I want you to suck my dick first," he said, his eyes wide, ready to be pleased by the young, dark-haired beauty. "You're so beautiful."

"I know I am."

And in the blink of an eye, she pulled the .380 from her purse and shoved it into the man's face. She scowled at him. "I'll blow ya fuckin' head off, muthafucka!"

The trick became wide-eyed with terror. "What the fuck! You're robbing me?"

"Shut the fuck up!"

Kola struck him with the butt of the pistol, and he tumbled over and started to bleed. He knew she wasn't fucking around.

Kola, needing some quick cash, made herself the perfect decoy. Being young, sexy, and beautiful, what dumb trick wouldn't pick her up from the track and take her to a room?

"Take off your fuckin' clothes," she instructed.

The man hesitated.

Kola raised the .380 to his head and cocked back the hammer. "Either way, dead or alive, I'ma take what I need from you."

He grimaced and did what he was told. He took off the remainder of his clothes slowly and tossed them to the floor.

Kola snatched his pants from the floor and removed his lumpy wallet. She quickly went through it. He had nothing but twenties and fifties on him—five hundred eighty-five total in cash. She removed the cash and his car keys.

"A'ight, you fat fuck, get ya fat ass in the bathroom," she said, waving the gun at him.

He slowly stood up and moved toward the bathroom. He didn't take his eyes off Kola, fearing she was going to shoot him in the back. "Why are you doing this to me?" he asked.

"'Cause you deserve it." She pushed him into the bathroom and shut the door. "And don't come out for a half-hour. If you do, I'll kill you."

Kola hurriedly snatched up the man's clothes, along with his cash and car keys and left with them out the motel door. She climbed into the front seat of his Chevy Cavalier and sped away. The money wasn't much, but it would be very useful to her.

Now she had to make a second stop.

*

Kola ran up behind the young soldier and placed the pistol to his head, catching him off guard. He was coming out the liquor store and walking to his car. She slammed him against his car and shouted, "You lie to me, and I'll blow ya fuckin' head off!"

The young soldier was ready to cooperate.

"I'm gonna ask you some questions. You tell me what I need to know."

"What the fuck do you want from me?"

"My sister, what hospital do they have her in?"

"I don't know."

Kola hit him with the butt of the pistol, and he went down stumbling. She stood over him with the gun trained at his head. "You think I'm the bitch you really need to fuck wit'?"

The young soldier looked up at her, holding the side of his head. She glared down at him, ready to snatch away his life.

Tommy was one of Terri's goons. He was a loyal soldier, hard-core and careful, but he wasn't careful enough. He didn't look like much physically, but he had the heart of a lion.

Kola had done some investigation of her own, and had started to follow the crew closely. It took time, but she finally got hold of a reliable source, and he disclosed the information she needed to know, which led her to Tommy.

She stepped closer to Tommy and aimed the gun at his dick, threatening to blow off his family jewels. "Where is she?" she asked through clenched teeth.

"Terri's gonna kill me if I tell you anything."

She cocked back the hammer. "What you think I'm gonna do?"

"Okay, okay. Shit. They took her to Long Island Jewish, but she's protected. If you think you gonna take her out, it ain't gonna be so fuckin' easy."

"Who said I was goin' to kill her?"

The soldier looked confused.

Kola wanted to kill him, but the gunfire would draw too much attention to her. So she removed the 9 mm he was carrying in his waistband and left in a hurry.

*

Kola sat parked across the street from the hospital with a small arsenal under the driver's seat. She sat low and watched the foot traffic come and go from the hospital lobby. The stolen Chevy she was in looked inconspicuous amongst the other cars on the block. The area was populated by white people, families, and medical staff parking their high-end cars in the parking lot across the street.

Long Island Jewish Hospital was nestled in an affluent community in New Hyde Park. The suburban street with the two-story homes and manicured lawns was a contrast to her world, which these residents would never understand. It seemed like paradise out there with the tree-lined streets, pricy homes and cars, and two-car garages.

"Fuckin' Brady Bunch," she said to herself.

In Kola's eyes, these people would be food in the hood. The wolves would devour everything they had in minutes.

She sat for over an hour, trying to come up with a way to execute her plan. It was going to be difficult. Or maybe not. After all, she was family. But once she stepped into the hospital to visit Apple, what would the reaction be? She knew there had to be undercover agents all over the place, watching and observing visitors.

And Apple's goons were lurking about, but they would be easy to spot. In a place like Long Island Jewish, where white folks were predominant, a scowling black goon trying to fit in would be easy to pick out.

Kola stuffed the .380 into the purse she carried and stepped out of the Cavalier. Clad in tight-fitting blue jeans, a trendy black shirt, and a pair of white Jordan's, she gave herself an innocent college student look, styling her hair into a long ponytail. The Kola that strutted toward the hospital was cool and smiling. No one would guess she was a stone-cold killer, drug dealer, madam, and once led a violent drug crew from Harlem to Miami responsible for a half-dozen unsolved homicides.

Kola stepped into the pristine lobby of the hospital, which was busy with staff and patients moving about. No one looked at her strangely. In their eyes, she was a pretty, young girl visiting a family member, maybe a grandma or a parent.

She quickly took in her surroundings, and nothing seemed odd. There were more white faces than black, which was to be expected. She walked toward the reception desk and looked at the lady in the blue scrubs. The fair-skinned employee had her head down, reading something on her desk, and behind her were other female staff members engaged in their daily duties.

"Excuse me," she said with a smile.

The woman picked her head up and looked at Kola. "Yes."

"I need some help. I'm lookin' for my sister. I think she was brought into here a few days ago."

"Her name?"

"Apple Martinez."

The lady started to type into her computer, logging into the main database and searching for the name. It only took a few seconds to look up, but the woman began to shake her head, indicating there was no record of an Apple Martinez being admitted into the facilities.

"I'm sorry, but there's no one by that name here," she told Kola. "Are you sure this is the right name of the person?"

Kola was sure. But then it came to her. Apple had enemies itching to see her demise, so she had to check in under an alias. Now it became difficult. Apple could have been admitted under any name, which would be like trying to find a needle in a haystack.

Fuck! She thought. She didn't come this far out to Long Island to be turned away. The lady gazed at Kola.

"Thank you. I might be at the wrong hospital."

Kola walked away, but she didn't plan on leaving. There had to be a way to find out what name her twin sister was admitted under, and what room she was staying in. She walked toward the modern-style cafeteria and looked around and waited. The place wasn't too busy. People were spread about eating and talking.

She had to be extra careful as she moved about. Anybody could be watching, and her enemies came in all forms. Her eyes darted everywhere, from the hallway to the individuals dining in the cafeteria. She was looking for that one particular person who would stand out, that goon she could catch slipping in a haven like Long Island Jewish.

To fit in, Kola went to one of the several vending machines lining the entrance wall and got herself a few snacks to munch on. Then she took a seat at a table that had a panoramic view of the whole cafeteria, where she could see people coming and going.

A half hour later, Kola zeroed in on one particular individual walking into the cafeteria. He stood out by his street attire—dark jeans, long T-shirt, Timberland boots, a skewed Yankees fitted on his head, and tattoos on his forearms. His whole demeanor screamed out trouble—he was a soldier.

Kola watched him like a hawk. He went to the lunch counter and ordered a cheeseburger, French fries, and a large Coke. He then went over to the nearest table and began chomping down on his meal. Kola could tell that he wasn't the sharpest knife in the drawer. She figured he had to have an ankle piece on him, probably trying to be discreet with his weapon in such a public place.

Bingo! Kola thought.

It took him less than five minutes to devour his food and burp it out like he was trying to win a contest. The rude burp attracted some attention from the other customers in the cafeteria, but everyone minded their business and continued eating and talking, mumbling under their breaths. The man got up and left his trash on the table.

When he made his way out the exit, Kola stood up and started to follow him. She watched him go into the men's bathroom. Now was her chance. She glanced around to make sure everything was clear before rushing into the bathroom. She found him taking a piss in one of the urinals.

He noticed Kola coming into the bathroom and commented, "Damn, ma! You know you in the wrong bathroom."

He took a second look and suddenly realized she was Apple's twin. He tried to react, but Kola had already pulled out her pistol and aimed it at him.

"You fuckin' move, and I'll shoot ya dick off!"

He stood frozen by the urinal. "What the fuck you want?"

Kola moved closer. She crouched down a little to check underneath the stalls to make sure they were alone. "My sister's room number and her alias, give it to me."

"Fuck you!"

Kola screwed her face, becoming angry at his resistance. She had no time to waste. She was in a difficult situation, where anything could go wrong in the matter of seconds.

"That's a nice gun. What . . . a three eighty? A gun like that can make a loud noise in this small space."

"So you're not as stupid as you look."

"I'm no genius, but I have my ways."

"Well, you know me, right?"

"Your name rings out."

"All I'm asking for is my sister's information. Let's not make this difficult. I know ya muscle, but I need to see her."

"What? To talk it out? You know she's in a coma, right? And, last I heard, you two hate each other."

"Things change."

"Fuck that! What's in it for me?"

"Everybody's out for self," Kola replied, shaking her head.

Kola reached into her purse and pulled out a few hundred-dollar bills, money from different men she'd robbed. She tossed him three hundred dollars. "Is that incentive enough?"

He picked it up. "Yeah. She's in room five twenty as Jenny Sampson."

"A'ight. And your gun."

He smirked. "What gun?"

"The one you carry on your ankle."

He chuckled. "You peeped that, huh?"

"A bitch can never be too careful. I don't want any incidents with a bullet in my back."

"If I'm gonna kill you, believe me, I want you to see it coming."

"Very well. Now, gun please."

He slowly reached down and pulled up his pants leg to reveal the holstered Glock 27 on his right leg. He removed it and slid it over to Kola. "Enjoy," he said matter-of-factly.

Kola picked it up and placed it in her purse. It was better safe than sorry. She then slowly made her way out the bathroom, leaving him dumbfounded. She got what she needed; now it was time to see her sister.

The trip to Apple's room seemed like the longest walk for Kola. The hallway was cluttered with doctors and staff, along with patients, and no one noticed the young, pretty girl in their domain. Kola moved naturally, wanting to give the impression that she belonged. She continued to keep an eye out for anyone or anything that stood out, meaning Apple's soldiers. But on this floor, if you weren't in a lab coat, scrubs, or had a nametag, then you were considered an outcast, a visitor.

Kola spotted room 520. She took a deep breath and proceeded forward. So far, everything looked cool. There were no threats looming, and no one gave her any odd looks. She moved toward the doorway and there she was, Apple, dormant and looking like part machine and part female, with several wires and tubes protruding from her listless frame. And, surprisingly, there was Denise by her side looking like the loving mother. Kola was shocked to see her mother in the room.

Kola just gazed at her twin sister from the doorway. Every time she saw her sister, it reminded her of Nichols' murder. But she had to control that rage and anger toward her sister. Now wasn't the place or time to be violent or hold any grudges. Apple was already suffering.

Denise suddenly turned around. When she saw Kola standing in the doorway, her eyes got really wide with shock and worry. "Kola."

Kola remained silent. She stepped further into the room.

"How did you find us?" Denise asked.

Before Kola could answer, the sound of a hammer being clicked back alerted her to the threat behind the door. She stood still. It was a gunman watching over Apple. "Don't move," Terri said in a whispery growl.

"I didn't come as a threat," Kola returned, keeping her cool.

Terri kept the gun to her head. He wasn't taking any chances. He asked for her to give up the purse, and Kola let him know she was carrying multiple weapons. He snatched the purse from around her arm and tossed it into the chair, keeping the gun close to her head while remaining in the shadows, out of the public's view.

"If I wanted my sister dead, then she would already be dead."

"Why are you here?" Denise asked.

Kola gazed at her mother. "You two made up now?" she asked sarcastically.

Denise stood up from her seat. It was an awkward moment to have her twin daughters in the same room. She eyed Kola with suspicion, waiting for an answer.

"Can you please tell him to take the gun away from my head? I'm no longer a threat."

Denise nodded, and Terri lowered the gun and took a few steps back, his eyes on Kola.

"Thank you." Kola focused on her mother and continued with, "I went to Nichols' grave earlier. I had to. It's been too long now."

"Why?" Denise asked.

"Why? Are you serious? Have you been to her grave since it happened?"

Denise remained quiet.

Kola sighed. "With a fuckin' mother like you, it's no wonder why we all turned out the way we fuckin' did. We never had a chance. Look at her. Look at us."

"So all this is on me now?"

"It might as well be. You were always a selfish bitch, Ma. Always! I remember growing up, we were just a fuckin' burden for you in the projects. And then you started showing off your twins off like we were toys, like we were little fuckin' trinkets. Yeah, we dressed nice, but that's all you ever gave us, nice things from the men you used to fuck, and who would sometimes try to fuck us."

"I always defended my daughters."

"Only when you felt embarrassed by it. The only time you would care about us is when it benefited you. You treated a nigga wit' a big dick and some cash better than you did us. And now look at her." Kola pointed to Apple. "And look at where Nichols' is at, Ma. We all fucked up, and now you have the audacity to sit by Apple's bed like you really fuckin' care. What? You plan to benefit from us now, huh?"

Denise locked eyes with Kola, and her tears started to fall. She knew Kola was a hundred percent right. Even though she was a changed woman, there was no hiding from her past. But was it too late?

Kola continued to chastise her mother. For so many years, she had been holding the anger and pain inside, and now it had been unleashed in the streets and at her mother like the perfect storm. She was tired of fighting. She had accumulated so many enemies and contributed to so many deaths, she just wanted to disappear for a moment, start fresh somewhere. But where? Her foes were everywhere, and they had connections far and wide. One slipup, and it was lights out.

Denise took the tongue-lashing from Kola. She knew it was the hard truth. "I'm sorry," she said, tears trickling down her face. "I know I wasn't the perfect mother, but I'm tryin' to do right by y'all right now."

Kola rolled her eyes. "You almost lost your life to some killers, so now you wanna have a change of heart? You just scared. Ain't nothin' changed wit' you."

"Is it too late for us, Kola? Huh? Do you hate me and your sister that much?" Denise asked in a trembling voice.

Kola glared at her mother. "I don't know anymore." She wanted to go off and punch the bitch in the face, but she kept her cool.

Kola looked at Apple and realized she could have been the one lying in that bed. She'd escaped death so many times, she was like Houdini in the streets.

Kola and Denise were silent for the moment.

"I can't do this shit," Kola said.

She turned and started to leave, but Denise called out to her, "Kola, no. You stay. I'll leave. If you can't accept my apologies for the sins from my past, then fine. But, as a mother, I don't want to see my daughters fighting wit' each other anymore. It stops here, Kola. No more of this shit between y'all."

Kola was somewhat taken aback by her mother's straightforwardness. "Oh really?" she snapped back.

"Yes. Someone tried to murder y'all both. Now think about it. The both of y'all are more powerful together than apart. I know you're alone, Kola, but you don't have to be. And I know you hate me for many things . . . for Nichols' death, the way you was brought up, and that's your choice, but I don't hate you. I love you, and I will always love you. But I made amends with myself for the things I've did."

"Amends?"

"Yes. As I confessed to Apple in her coma, I was responsible for havin' someone throw acid in her face. I was jealous of y'all, and it pains me that I had that done to my own daughter. Whatever punishment haunts me for my sins against my own flesh and blood, then I'm okay wit' it. But you don't hate her anymore. If you want to hate someone, then hate me. But y'all two need to fix this. If the two of y'all are dead, then there is nothin' left, and Nichols' death was in vain. You know Nichols wouldn't want this shit happening between y'all. She loved y'all both, so, for her, you and Apple fix this."

Denise was done talking. She walked by Kola and made her exit. It was the first motherly speech she'd given to her daughter.

Kola looked intently at Apple lying in the coma. She clenched her fist and tried to fight her emotions. But the tears were trickling down her face, her mother's words lingering in her head.

TWENTY-SEVEN

Chico stared at the beautiful baby girl in the crib. Shaun was right. The baby resembled Apple in so many ways. Her light brown skin and big walnut eyes were hypnotizing. Chico reached down and picked up the sleeping infant. As he cradled her in his arms, his goons were rummaging through the affluent home in San Antonio, Texas, treating themselves to the treasures inside.

It was a three-day drive from New York to San Antonio. And once arriving in San Antonio, they met up with Shaun, who gave Chico the information he needed to find the family and the child, and it was as easy as one, two, and three.

Shaun had sold Peaches on the black market for babies, and the family paid a tidy sum for the healthy newborn. But he'd always kept tabs on them, knowing that one day he might need to come back for the infant.

As Chico held Peaches in his arms, Shaun entered the room. Chico looked at him, and asked, "What now?"

Shaun replied, "Now we have some fun."

*

The team of doctors followed Apple's condition closely. For fourteen days, they observed her vitals thoroughly and continuously checked for swelling in her brain. But she was healing fine. On the seventeenth day, she started to show signs of recognizing voices once again—her mother and her sister.

Apple finally awoke from her coma to see Kola standing over her. She gazed at Kola silently. At first she didn't recognize her own twin sister. It was like she was seeing a stranger for the first time.

Denise was smiling, but Kola remained pensive and somewhat uneasy. This was the first time Apple had emerged from a vegetative state.

By the twentieth day, Apple was responding to simple commands, such as, "Show me two fingers."

On the thirtieth day, she was no longer in need of intensive medical care, and was transferred to a rehabilitation center in Long Island, with a team of physical, occupational, and speech therapists, as well as a psychologist to help with her long recovery.

The situation was awkward for Kola. For so long, Apple was the enemy, the raging bitch in Harlem, but seeing her sister weak and vulnerable felt unreal. It almost became a brand-new world for her, learning to walk and talk again one painful step at a time.

Kola was there to assist her sister. At first she was reluctant, but then this transformation came over her, and she wanted to see Apple get better. Despite their horrid relationship, this was still her sister; they shared the same blood and suffered the same loss. She wondered, though, once Apple regained her full strength, would she revert back to her old, deadly ways and turn on Kola once more?

The streets were quiet for now. Chico had been MIA for several weeks, and their foes had been dormant. But Kola knew their enemies were still a threat to them, still looming about somewhere in the shadows. These two sisters caused havoc and death on an unprecedented level in the streets, and they owed a debt to too many major figures in their world who weren't just going to allow them to walk away so easily from the game. Kola knew this was only the calm before the storm.

Terri became a major help with Apple's recovery. He cared for Apple and wanted to see her heal. Whatever the sisters needed, he got for them. He also gave Guy Tony continuous updates about Apple's condition. Guy Tony refused to fly into New York to see Apple. He tried to distance himself from her, convinced the feds were about to come down on her like a shit storm.

Guy Tony was ready to save his own ass and testify to a grand jury. It was his revenge against that bitch. Death would have been too easy for her. He'd rather see her rot and die slowly in a federal prison. He was smiling in her face while slowly pushing the knife in her back. The shooting did put any indictments on hold, but the feds and detectives were sniffing around Apple's criminal affairs and watching her recovery.

Kola knew it would only be a matter of time before word got out about Apple's true condition. The wolves were out there pounding the pavement, and one whiff of the sisters' vulnerability would bring them around. And they would like nothing better but to tear these twins apart. Their safe haven was only temporary, and the doctors would be ready to release Apple soon.

Denise was with her twins almost twenty-four/seven, and she had become a different woman, behaving like a mother, not a ghetto girlfriend. She helped feed Apple, brushed her hair, and gave her daughter sponge baths.

But the miracle came when Apple and Kola started to communicate with each other. Apple was becoming her old self, and her memory was coming back to her. She was haunted by the shooting, though. And Terri informed her that Ion was dead, but Chico was still alive.

As Apple's rehabilitation continued, the twins had a heart-to-heart with each other. Kola made Apple realize that if they didn't stand tall together, then it was inevitable that they would die separately. Kola was the first to apologize.

"That thing wit' you and Cross, I'm sorry. I know what he meant to you, and I shouldn't have taken it there. But if it pleases you to know, he wasn't shit anyway, and he ain't gettin' out of lockup anytime soon. Muthafucka got what he deserved. And I'm sorry about what happened to you in Mexico. No one deserves that type of punishment. No one," Kola said genuinely. "I was really hurt over Nichols' death, and I hated you for it . . . for sleepin' wit' the enemy, for being stupid. But that's a while ago, and things have changed."

Apple remained silent. She never took her eyes off her sister. For too long, the demons controlled her, and revenge was the only way she felt fulfillment. She needed to confess her part too.

"I didn't have anything to do with your stabbing in Miami, and that's the God's honest truth. And I'm sorry about my relationship wit' Supreme. That bastard had me brainwashed somehow, but I dealt wit' him. Had him shot down while he slept," she told Kola. "How did it get so hard for us?"

Apple and Kola talked out their differences, putting everything out into the open. And then they started to make a list of all their enemies—Shaun, Chico, Cross, OMG, Copper, Nikki, and Eduardo. They began plotting against their foes, deciding if they fell, then they would fall together.

TWENTY-EIGHT

Denise sat slumped in the passenger seat of the Ford truck, trying to keep a low profile. Samson, the driver of the truck, was also her muscle. He drove into New Jersey with a screw face and armed with a Glock 17. She felt uncomfortable being back in the hood, even if it was East Orange. But the phone call she'd gotten from Yandy sounded really important, and Yandy insisted that she had to speak with Denise in person. Denise owed Yandy that favor and decided to leave the comfort of Long Island and drive miles away to New Jersey. So Denise was a nervous wreck, because she barely went anywhere unless it was important.

Samson came to a stop in front of the elegant pre-WWII apartment in East Orange. It was early evening, and the block was quiet.

"You ready?" he asked.

Denise nodded.

Samson stepped out first, and Denise followed. He played her closely, his eyes darting back and forth. With his dark shades on and clad in a black T-shirt that highlighted his muscle, he looked like an intimidating figure.

Denise followed him into the building, and they took the elevator up to the fifth floor to Yandy's apartment.

"I wonder what's so important that she gotta see me about," Denise said to Samson.

Samson kept quiet. It wasn't his business to know. He was there for only one purpose—protection. He was one of Terri's trusted soldiers in the game, and he had bodies on him like a small cemetery. "Shoot first, fuck questions" was his motto.

Denise stood outside the apartment door and knocked twice.

"Who?" she heard Yandy shout from the other side.

"It's Denise."

"Okay."

The two could hear the door being unlocked from the other side. Samson kept his hand close to his gun.

Yandy opened the door and smiled. "Hey," she greeted. "I'm glad you came," she said, opening the door wider.

Denise stepped inside first. Samson wasn't too far behind her. Once Denise was in the foyer, she hugged Yandy.

"What's goin' on, Yandy? Talk to me."

"I'm in trouble."

"What kind of trouble?"

Yandy walked into the living room with Denise, and Samson followed behind them. But when he stepped into the clear, a gun was thrust to the side of his temple.

"Oh shit!" he uttered.

Boom!

Samson's brains splattered across Denise, the walls, and the floor, and his body dropped. Denise screamed.

"Shut the fuck up, bitch!" Chico shouted. He pushed his gun into her face and threw her to the floor. "You know what we here for," Chico continued.

Denise was wide-eyed with pure panic, and Yandy stood frozen by the window. Her tears started to trickle down her face. Bad grabbed Yandy by the arm and pushed her into the chair.

"I'm sorry, Denise," Yandy cried out. "They beat me and raped me, and they were going to kill me."

"What y'all niggas want?" Denise shouted.

"Ya fuckin' daughters, bitch," Chico replied through gritted teeth.

"Fuck y'all!"

"No. That's what we gonna do to you, if you don't play ball, bitch! I hated ya ass for a long time, but now it's my turn to have some fun wit' that ass." Chico glared at her. "This is too easy."

"Fuck you!" Denise hissed.

"You know what?" Chico said, "We gonna make things fun. But before the games start, you need to know somethin', you dumb bitch."

Shaun walked out the bedroom holding baby Peaches in his arms. The child was crying. Denise looked at him with bewilderment as she hugged the parquet floors, shivering with fear. She didn't know what was going on. Who was this baby?

"Say hello to your granddaughter Peaches." Shaun squatted down closer to her, so she could get a look at the baby. "Oh yeah, ya slut daughter Apple, she had a baby while in Mexico. Ain't that a bitch? But, yeah, look at her. This ya granddaughter, your one and only."

"Oh my God!" Denise cried out. Tears started to stream down her face. She wanted to hold her.

She reached out for the baby, but Shaun pulled back.

Chico shouted, "Nah, you don't get that fuckin' pleasure."

"What do you want from me?" Denise screamed out.

"Your daughters and your life," he replied.

Chico grabbed Denise by her hair. She kicked and tried to fight him off, but he was too strong. And he had help from his thugs in subduing her. They placed duct tape over her mouth, beat her, and stripped her naked. Then they tied her to a chair and watched her squirm and cry.

Chico said, "Now, your daughters . . . where are they?"

Denise remained quiet.

"You wanna be stubborn, you stupid bitch?" Chico looked at Torrez and nodded.

Methodically Torrez walked toward Yandy, who tried to ward him off. Her small fists were no match for the trained killer. His massive hand grabbed a handful of her hair, yanked her head back, and then slit open her throat. She let out a quiet gasp before succumbing to her injury.

Denise began to tear up again, and her eyes registered complete fear. She mumbled something incoherent underneath the duct tape. She gazed at the baby Shaun was still holding. Her grandchild was in the arms of a killer, and she felt helpless. It was a nightmare she wanted to awake from. With all her strength, she tried to free herself, but her restraints were strong.

Chico, towering over Denise, lit a blowtorch, and the blue flame came to life. Denise's eyes grew wide. She fidgeted in her seat like it was the electric chair.

He told her, "You gonna talk to us one way or the other."

Then he placed the burning flame to her exposed nipple, and the excruciating pain that followed almost made Denise faint. But her screams were muffled by the duct tape over her mouth.

As Chico tortured Denise for information on her daughters, her teary eyes stayed fixed on her granddaughter in Shaun's arms. She wanted to hold and feel the child. It wasn't going to happen, though. It was the worst kind of torture, not being able to hold her granddaughter, and dying right in front of the baby's eyes. Death was coming for her, and there was no escaping it.

She felt her skin dissolving under the intense flames, and her body started to go into convulsions as the hot blue flame from the blowtorch ate into her skin like acid. But Denise wasn't going to give up her daughters. She was willing to die for them. It was her last chance to be the mother they needed.

As the torture continued, she kept her eyes on Peaches, knowing this was the only time she would get to see her granddaughter.

TWENTY-NINE

The messenger came to Terri and whispered the news into his ear.

"Shit!"

Kola and Apple were in the room talking, but when they turned to look at Terri after he received the message, his expression said it all to them.

"What happened?" Kola asked.

Terri walked toward the twins. There was no easy way to deliver the message, so he just came right out and said, "Your mother is dead. They found her body in a city dumpster."

"What they do to her?" Kola asked, gritting her teeth like a madwoman.

"They burned her alive. She was naked, cut up, and barely looked like a woman."

Apple was quiet. The emotions that stirred in her were contradictory and confusing. No matter what she felt about Denise, at the end of it all, she had come through for her and had been a mother to her these past weeks.

The sisters knew it was Chico.

"Chico, that muthafucka gotta go. I swear, I'ma cut his fuckin' heart out," Apple said.

Kola was silent, her mind spinning with a thousand and one things.

No matter what they did or where they went, their enemies were going to hunt them down like animals until their family tree was annihilated. They only had each other now.

"We can't stay here," Terri said. "It's a risk now. There's no telling what your mother told them."

"She didn't talk, I know it," Apple said.

"Yeah , but we can't take that chance."

Kola knew Terri was right. Chico would have the hospital overrun with shooters in a heartbeat.

Terri got on the phone and began making preparations for the twins' departure. They didn't have any time to waste. Every minute, every second counted.

Despite their differences with their mother, the girls vowed retribution on every single last muthafucka that played a hand in her death, Apple getting shot, and Kola getting stabbed.

As Terri and Apple started packing and making arrangements for their safety and retribution, Kola contemplated the next move. It was the only way to survive this bloody war and kill all their foes with one huge blow.

✳

Kola stepped into the stylish café in Washington Heights, located on the corner of Broadway and 181st Street. It was a bustling shopping area with numerous people out and about with family and friends, going in and out of various stores that lined the street.

It was a huge risk for Kola to be anywhere in the city, especially in Washington Heights, which was so close to Harlem, and so close to danger. She had a huge bounty on her head. But with great risk came great reward, so she was willing to take her chances.

She turned heads entering the building in a sexy off-the-shoulder knit top with elastic ruffled detail and bow accent, and a pair of tight black leggings that highlighted her curves. And the red bottoms she wore made her look like she was ready to reach the heavens.

Inside the café, with its brilliant ambiance, clean floors, top ceiling, and bright view to the outside, a few Colombian gangsters were enjoying the good food and great wine. When Kola walked in, the conversations abruptly stopped, and all eyes were on her. She hoped she was making the right moves, because one mistake, and she wouldn't walk out of the place alive.

Kola stood by the doorway and watched these gangsters suddenly stand up from their tables and glare at her like she was a demon. A few started to display their guns, their smiles quickly transforming into scowls. She was behind enemy lines now, so there was no turning back.

"I didn't come for any trouble," she spoke.

"Then you're in the wrong fuckin' place, *puta*," one of the suited gangsters replied through clenched teeth.

"I need to speak wit' Eduardo." Suddenly, Kola found herself surrounded by these men, and leaving the café became impossible.

"You have some nerve, Kola. You think Eduardo wants to see you, after everything that happened? You set him up."

"It wasn't me."

"Like hell it wasn't." The man then smirked at Kola. "Stupid bitch!"

Kola remembered Domino from the penthouse in New Jersey. He was tall and handsome with his well-groomed beard and brawny physique. He was a soldier back then. Now it looked like he had been promoted to lieutenant.

"You got balls, bitch. Stupid, but you got balls," he said.

"I just want to explain myself to Eduardo. That's all I'm asking for. I need to meet wit' him."

Domino stared at Kola like she was a piece of meat. He wanted to tear into her flesh so badly, he felt his dick growing inside his pants. He knew it would be a waste if they had to kill her right away and not have some fun with her first.

One of the men snatched Kola's purse from around her arm and quickly went through it. He removed her .380 and dumped all of the contents from her purse on the floor. But Kola kept her cool. She just wanted to see Eduardo and speak to him. They had history together, and she needed to clear a few things up with him.

Domino continued to glare at Kola. "How did you know to come here?"

"I have a good memory." She locked eyes with Domino. So far, he was the shot-caller in the café. It was up to him to make the call to Eduardo or not. "I know I fucked up, Domino, but just make the call to him and have him decide what he wants to do wit' me. I'm here, so fuck it."

Domino looked to be in deep thought. He stepped away from Kola and removed his cell phone from his hip. He decided to make the call to Eduardo.

Kola watched him closely. She had put herself in this situation. One word from Eduardo, and she could be leaving out the backdoor wrapped up in a plastic tarp and thrown into the trunk of a car. They had the power to make her disappear, and the hood would be none the wiser.

After the call, Domino stepped toward the pack again, his cold onyx eyes fixed on Kola. He was silent for a short moment, and then he said, "It's your lucky day, and you get to breathe easy for a moment. He'll meet with you."

Kola tried not to let them see her sweat. "When?"

"Right now."

Suddenly, the suited Colombian gangsters snatched Kola up and dragged her toward the back of the café and into the kitchen area. The staff and cooks working their shift minded their business and acted like there wasn't anything going on. They carried Kola into a back room, where it was cold and dark, and placed duct tape over her mouth. Then they tossed a black hood over her head and bound her wrists behind her. She was starting to feel like she'd made a huge mistake.

She felt herself being carried over someone's shoulder and tossed into the trunk of a vehicle like a sack of potatoes. Then she heard the engine start. Kola tried to breathe and keep cool, but she was scared. Eduardo was very unpredictable.

She felt the vehicle moving at a fast speed, zigzagging through the city streets. The trunk she was concealed in was spacious and empty.

Relax, Kola, she thought. *Just relax.*

The vehicle came to a stop after a two-hour ride. Kola was in a daze. Her limbs felt sore, and she had the urge to pee.

The trunk came open abruptly, and she felt a blast of sunlight. They pulled her out of the trunk by her arms and made her stand up. She had no idea where she was, since they'd kept the hood over her head.

They pulled Kola up a flight of stairs with support, and then she was forced into a room, where they pushed her into a soft, comfortable leather chair. They cut her restraints, and she was able to move her hands. And then they removed the hood from her head and tore off the duct tape. It hurt like hell.

Kola grimaced at the suited thugs that stood around her. She looked around the room and didn't know the place. The room was huge and well lit with sunlight coming through the floor-to-ceiling windows.

Kola's heart felt like it was in her stomach as she waited for several minutes. When Eduardo stepped into the sunlit room, Kola kept her cool. She refused to show him any emotion.

Eduardo gazed at Kola as he puffed on a huge cigar. The room got silent once he'd showed his mighty presence. His men stood still and waited on his orders.

Kola couldn't take her eyes off Eduardo. A feared figure in the underworld, he was still a gorgeous man with his curly black hair, hazel eyes, and honey-colored skin. And he was well built from head to toe and looked enticing with his precisely trimmed goatee.

Eduardo wore white cargo shorts and was shirtless and barefoot. And around his neck he sported a thin gold chain with a small cross. He approached Kola.

"Kola, you have some nerve showing your face to me again," he said coolly.

"Let me explain."

"Explain what? I should have my men tear you apart for your fuckin' betrayal." He rushed toward Kola, wrapped his hand around her slim neck, and put the burning cigar close to her eye. "I should take out your fuckin' eye right now!"

"It wasn't me, Eduardo," she cried out.

Eduardo squeezed tighter, restricting her airflow.

Kola felt the urge to pass out, but she kept her hard stare on him. "Let me talk, please," she managed to say between gasps.

Eduardo released his hold from around her neck and stood upright, his menacing gaze still aimed at her. Now that she had his ear, she had to convince him if she wanted to remain alive.

"We have dead on both sides, Eduardo, mine and yours. But that attack on you in New Jersey, I had nothin' to do wit' it. I swear to you."

"I lost heavily over that."

"I know, but Cross was responsible for that. I was unaware of his actions until it was too late. He was jealous of you. He always was. He thought we were fuckin'. He had me followed and then decided to move against you."

Eduardo stared at his goons and ordered, "Leave us, now!"

His men didn't ask any questions. They left the room hurriedly, closing the door behind them, leaving him alone in the room with her. Kola didn't know what to expect.

"You know our business was good, and I would never betray our friendship and business, Eduardo. I had a good thing goin' wit' you. I was making so much money wit' you, so why would I fuck that up? Everything was on Cross. He was such a jealous muthafucka!"

"I will handle Cross in due time. I'm aware of his whereabouts. He's not going anywhere anytime soon."

"And what about me? Are we cool?"

Eduardo let out a chilling laugh. "Cool? You forget who the fuck I am?"

"I never did."

"You come to me, tell me this story, and you look for my forgiveness?"

Kola swallowed hard. Eduardo was always a man hard to persuade.

"I'm not lookin' for any forgiveness from you. I came to you to tell you the truth about the situation."

"And you think you gonna leave here alive?"

"You was in love wit' me once, or was that a lie?"

Eduardo chuckled. "You were nothing but an opportunity for me, and one I have yet to take advantage of."

Kola knew what he was hinting at.

"But you are a very impressive woman, Kola, I must admit. And I'm no fool. I know your true reasons for this unexpected visit. The fact that you were able to locate Domino shows your memory and senses were always sharp."

"I'm still the same woman."

"But things have changed between us. And I know and hear everything," Eduardo said in a civil tone. "Everything. I know you are weak and frightened at this moment." He dowsed his burning cigar against the granite countertop and moved closer to Kola, his eyes burning into her.

He touched her gently, admiring her beauty. "You are still a beautiful woman, Kola. Any man would be lucky to have you in his life." He ran his fingers against her smooth skin and then through her dark, long hair.

"Stand up," he said sternly.

Kola stood up, and Eduardo circled her slowly. He admired her luscious backside, plump hips, and curvy waistline.

"Such a young and pretty girl with so much ambition. You know that can get you killed sometimes. I know about your problems with Chico, and your trials and tribulations down in Miami. You thought you could run from me. I always knew you would be back, that you would come to me on your fuckin' hands and knees and begging for my forgiveness."

Kola wasn't going to beg, but she didn't want to infuriate him any more. She needed his help, if he didn't kill her first.

"Look at you . . . looking like a lost bitch."

Kola kept quiet, but she refused to be intimidated by him. She locked eyes with the Colombian kingpin and remained still as his hands continued to roam her body.

"Is this what you always wanted from me, Eduardo . . . pussy?"

"I wanted much more from you, Kola. I wanted your love, and I wanted your heart, but our business came first. I could have taken sex from you a long time ago, but I had respect for you and wanted it to come from you willingly."

"And what's stoppin' you now? I know you have power. I never disputed that. And I'm not foolish to go up against you, Eduardo. You know me. I was never that stupid."

"You sure about that? I've seen smart people do very stupid things." He stood behind her, wrapped his arm around her waist, and pulled her closer into him, so that her backside was pressing up against his pelvis. She could feel his breath against her neck and his genitals rubbing against her.

"You want this, huh? You want me to take something from you that I've yearned for, for so fuckin' long?" he whispered in her ear.

"I need your help."

"Of course, you do. And why would I want to help you?"

"'Cause you still love me," she replied boldly.

Eduardo took a fistful of Kola's hair and all of a sudden yanked it back like he was tugging at the reins of a horse, causing her neck to snap back. And Kola winced from the sharp pain.

"And why would you think I'm in love with you?" he asked through clenched teeth.

"Because I'm still alive."

"You're a dumb, naïve little bitch, Kola."

Eduardo forcefully cupped her breasts, but Kola didn't fight him. She couldn't. She had nowhere to go. She didn't know where she was, or whether she was still in New York. In fact, after the long drive, she could have been in Pennsylvania, New Jersey, Connecticut, or even upstate New York.

Eduardo ripped off Kola's sexy off-the-shoulder top, exposing her breasts, and then he pulled down her tight leggings, revealing that she didn't have on any panties. He curved her over the chair and spread her legs and quickly undid the zipper to his cargo shorts.

"You want my help, you silly little bitch, I'll give you my fuckin' help."

With one powerful thrust, he pierced the one hole Kola wasn't ready for. He pounded his fat, long, rock-hard manhood into her asshole, causing her to yelp. He grunted as he slid in and out of her rectum, while she winced from the pain. He held her steady with one hand and her hip with the other. Her hole was the tightest.

"Ugh! Ugh!" he grunted. "You want my fuckin' help, then you take all this dick, bitch."

Kola had plenty of dicks before, but Eduardo was hung like a horse. The agony she felt from the fierce penetration made her dig her nails into the leather furniture as she bit down on her bottom lip and cried out. Eduardo continued to invade her rectum walls, the head of his thick dick swelling inside of her. She had to take it; she had no other choice. He used his muscles to flex his dick within her, causing her to close her eyes and wish she was somewhere else.

Eduardo fucked her from the back like that for a good moment, moaning and grunting with each thrust, as he continued to hold Kola by the back of her neck, pushing her face into the cushioned chair and ravaging her asshole.

He could feel the come boiling in his nuts and was ready to shoot his load inside of her. He growled savagely as his orgasm reached its height.

He pulled out and shot his hot come all over Kola's gaping asshole. His breathing was heavy, and he was a little sweaty. It was an intense fuck, and he enjoyed every minute of it.

Kola collapsed by Eduardo's feet, and she couldn't stop crying. She felt weak and abused. She couldn't move. She never felt so violated. It hurt. Eduardo had ripped her apart physically and mentally.

Eduardo stood over her as he fastened his shorts, looking proud. "You want my help, then you gonna owe me, and owe me big . . . you and your sister. Nothing comes free in this fuckin' world, not even a nut."

Kola knew what that meant, but without Eduardo's help, the sisters wouldn't last long in the streets. Their time was running out. She had too many enemies, and she wanted them all wiped out. And Eduardo was the only one with the power and resources to kill 'em all.

"From now on, y'all bitches work for me. You understand me?"

Kola hesitated to respond.

"Bitch, do you understand me? If you want my help, then you speak."

Kola slowly gazed up at him with her teary eyes and nodded. "I need your help," she said sadly. Kola had never been broken, but one not-so-pleasurable moment with the Colombian kingpin nearly tore her spirit into pieces.

Eduardo smirked. He believed her story about Cross, but he was about business. And Kola proved that she could become a valuable asset to his drug empire. She was too beautiful and smart of a woman to just kill. She would become his personal concubine, for pleasure and business. It pleased him that he had her where he wanted her, in his pocket, under his control, and indebted to him.

He gazed at Kola with his hard, cold eyes. "Now go and bury your fuckin' mother, collect your sister, and come home to Daddy, because we got a lot of work to take care of. And, Chico—consider him and your other adversaries memories. One snap of my fingers, and these *putas* will be dead by sunset."

Kola stood up on wobbly legs and nodded. She knew she had sold her soul to the devil.

THIRTY

Kola and Apple watched silently as their mother's bronze casket was slowly lowered into the ground. There were no tears or loud outbursts at her burial. They were saddened by the tragic loss, but it was the game—the hand they'd been dealt. Their whole lives, Denise had been a wicked and self-centered woman, and a few weeks of motherly love couldn't take back the hardship they endured while living under her roof. There were good times and bad times, but mostly bad. The twins had simply come to pay their respect to the woman who gave birth to them and leave.

Apple clutched the wooden cane for support. Her recovery was coming along smoothly. She was becoming more agile every day. But her mind was plagued with so many worries, from Shaun to Chico, and her infant daughter was on her mind heavily. She'd kept Peaches a secret, figuring she would never see her daughter again. Shaun had sold her off, and unless she could find him and get him to talk before she tortured and killed him, then seeing her baby again was a lost cause.

Terri stood by their side as he watched the twins bury their mother. He had been to plenty of funerals over the years, having caused many himself, but he wasn't too keen on being in cemeteries.

He eyed Apple from where he stood and admired her bravery. He had never met a woman like her.

Terri knew the feds were watching them closely, even at the cemetery; he'd noticed the dark sedan parked across the street in the distance, with a few agents seated in the car snapping pictures of everything. He knew the routine.

A federal indictment was coming down, and it was inevitable that the twins would be prosecuted. Kola already had an open case in Miami, and Guy Tony wanted Apple to suffer. He was a snitch, but he didn't look at it that way. At this point, Guy was secretly working with the feds to save his own ass, becoming a borderline informant.

*

Kola convinced Apple that they needed to leave the country to escape prosecution and death. If they didn't, then their fate would be sealed. She'd told her sister about Eduardo, telling her he had the money and means to give them new identities and passports and could have them out of the country within twenty-four hours. But they would be indebted to him.

Working with Eduardo would give them an unlimited supply of coke and dope, money and security. Apple was somewhat reluctant. She couldn't leave the country without seeing Chico and Shaun dead. And then there was Peaches.

"We can't stay," Kola said. "If we do, then we're both as good as dead."

Apple understood their situation, but her ego couldn't let it go. What Shaun did to her was unforgivable, and Chico had not only tried to kill her but had mercilessly murdered Denise. She wanted to see him suffer.

Kola finally convinced Apple to go along with the program. She assured her sister that Eduardo had a team of assassins already on the job. But Apple wanted to be there when they caught up with Shaun and Chico. She wanted to see the look in their eyes as they were about to die. She didn't want that moment taken away from her. She wanted to take pleasure in seeing them die slowly and painfully.

Kola looked at her sister and asked, "You ready to make your own moves?"

Apple nodded.

*

Clinton Correctional Facility, the maximum-security prison in Dannemora, New York, was known to house violent inmates and redneck guards. It was late evening when Cross was leaving his work detail in the kitchen. He was doing a seven-year bid on the gun charges he'd caught a while back. It was the best deal his lawyer could work out for him, since he had priors for drug trafficking and murders. He had gotten off easy. He was keeping a low profile on the inside, aware that he was a marked man.

Word had been getting back to him about the murders and violence in Harlem, and Kola's return. His peoples were dead, and he felt like he was the last one left. He just wanted to do his time and get out. He didn't want any problems.

As he moved through the narrow corridor, Jingles said, "Yo, Cross, what's good? You got any smokes on you, man?"

Jingles, a former gang member and ruthless enforcer in his late forties, used to terrorize the Bronx streets in the eighties and early nineties. He had a life sentence and a lot of regrets. Cross had befriended him when he'd first arrived at Clinton. Jingles had never had any problems during his incarceration because everyone knew his fierce reputation.

"Jingles, how's it been?" Cross replied.

"Same ol', same ol', my dun. Time moving slowly, and I'm moving slow wit' it."

"I hear you."

Cross passed Jingles a cigarette. He lit it up and the two started to walk down the corridor, talking and laughing. Cross had a lot of love for

Jingles. When he'd first arrived, Jingles took him under his wing, and they became friends, sharing stories of their wild, hustling ways.

As they walked, the hallway dimmed, and within the blink of an eye, Cross felt a pair of strong arms wrapping around him and pulling him into a darkened corner.

Jingles' smile rapidly turned into a threatening frown. Two inmates were wrestling with Cross, who was fighting a losing battle.

"What the fuck, Jingles!" he yelled out.

"You a good friend, Cross, but this is only business. I need the damn money for my kids."

Cross's eyes became wide with terror when he felt the cord tighten around his neck. He struggled for his life, but he was overpowered. He stared at Jingles while subdued on his knees, and the life started to fade from his eyes, as his attacker thrust his knee into his back and pulled brutally at the wire that was digging into his neck and cutting off circulation.

"Just die, Cross," Jingles uttered.

Cross slowly began to close his eyes, feeling his life being pulled from him. His killer was strong like an ox, his biceps the size of boulders, and he wasn't letting go of the wire gripped around his knuckles until every ounce of breath was gone from Cross' lungs. And then Cross' body went limp.

The killer released his powerful hold around Cross' neck, and his body dropped at Jingles' feet. It would be the first of many deaths to come in the months ahead.

EPILOGUE

After the black hood was removed from around Chico's face, he squinted up at his kidnappers. They had kept him in the dark for hours. And now he found himself restrained to a chair.

"Y'all niggas know who the fuck I am?"

"Shut the fuck up!" someone yelled.

Chico's remark warranted a pistol-whip by the Glock 17. He spewed blood from his mouth and glared at the men surrounding him in the dark room.

Chico's eyes darted in every direction. He tried to break free from his restraints, but they had him tied down really good. He continued to curse and threaten everyone in the room.

He shouted, "I'ma fuck y'all up. You fuckin' hear me? I'm fuckin' Chico. I run this shit!"

"Shut the fuck up!" the suited gangster replied. He struck Chico with the butt of his pistol several times, bruising his face and cracking some teeth. "I'm sick of your fuckin' mouth."

Chico coughed and spat up blood. He was the only one left. His crew was dead—Torrez, Bad and Rome, all gunned down by AK-47 as they exited a nightclub. Then he was beaten and pushed into a van and brought there.

"You a fuckin' cowboy, Chico . . . too fuckin' reckless out there. We can't have that going on in Harlem anymore," a man said.

"Fuck you!"

"No, fuck you!"

Chico instantly knew the voice and spun his head in the direction where it came from.

Apple came limping into the room, clutching her cane. She glared at Chico. Their eyes locked.

"You fuckin' bitch!" he spat.

"I told you, I was comin' for you, and you was going to hurt bad, and feel every bit of pain I felt."

"You always been a bitch, Apple. I should have killed you a long time ago."

"You did try, didn't you?"

Chico growled at her. He wanted to rip her apart.

Apple told him, "Oh, and I do have a surprise for you. You're not in this alone, muthafucka." She nodded to one of the thugs, and he went to retrieve the special gift she had for him.

A short moment later, the muscular thug pushed another captive into the room with Chico. It was obvious she was a female, by her curvy shape. She wore a hood over her head, and her wrists were tied in front of her.

Apple snatched the hood off Blythe's head.

"Nooo!" Chico screamed out. "Let her go!"

"Are you serious?" Apple shouted. "You love her over me? This bitch?"

"I don't wanna die. Please, I don't wanna die," Blythe pleaded, tears trickling down her face. "Please let me go."

"Apple, she ain't got shit to do wit' us. Just let her go, please."

"You love her, Chico?" Apple asked. "You fuckin' love this bitch? She took you away from me. I loved you."

"Apple, just let her go. I'm begging you."

"You're fuckin' beggin' me? Did you feel this torn up for me when I was in Mexico?"

"I searched everywhere for you! I paid everyone to try and find you. I did look for you! I LOOKED EVERYWHERE FOR YOU!" Chico screamed madly.

"Well, it's obvious you didn't look hard enough, because this dumb bitch had most of your time. Was it worth it, Chico? Huh? Was the pussy worth dying over?"

"You a sick bitch, Apple. You are. You took everything from me."

"So now you know how it fuckin' feels."

"I'm pregnant, Chico," Blythe uttered.

Apple was in pure rage. "Pregnant?" She put the gun to Blythe's head, her finger on the trigger, and then stared at Chico. "You know, I gave birth to a daughter in that hellhole."

"I know. Her name is Peaches, right?" Chico said.

Apple's face was fluttered with bewilderment. "How did you know?"

"The enemy of my enemy is now a friend. Me and Shaun, we suddenly had a lot in common. I've seen ya fuckin' daughter. She's pretty, but I know she ain't mines; the time frame doesn't add up."

"Where is she?"

"Fuck you! Just let her go first, and then we can talk,"

Now Apple was put into a difficult situation. She was furious that Chico had befriended Shaun. It was the ultimate treachery. But she yearned to know the whereabouts of her daughter. And it also infuriated her that Chico loved Blythe more than he'd loved her.

"You let her go, and then we can talk," Chico said.

It amazed Apple how Chico was still able to gain control of the situation he was in. Suddenly, Chico had the upper hand in the room.

"Let her fuckin' go, Apple," he roared.

It was a hard decision for Apple. She wanted to see them both dead.

Her plan was to kill Blythe in front of Chico and make him suffer.

She hated to do it, but she released Blythe and continued to torture Chico until he revealed where Shaun had her daughter. Afterwards, she personally put three rounds into his head, splattered his brain all over the walls and concrete.

Shortly thereafter, her goons got a hold of Blythe and strangled the life and that of her baby out of her. There wasn't any way Apple was going to allow her to live happily ever after with Chico's baby. This was the hood, where there were no happy endings.

*

When Apple got word that Eduardo's soldiers had caught up with Shaun in New Mexico, she put the word out that she wanted him alive. She and Kola flew out there immediately under their new identities, and under the darkened sky of the vast desert, the black SUV they rode in hastily moved toward the hole Shaun was being buried alive in.

When they arrived, Shaun was buried up to his neck in the cold desert, his face was badly beaten, and three armed thugs towering over him.

Apple rushed out of the truck and ran toward that muthafucka with a ferocious look of a lion. She wanted to tear him apart. Finding out he had her daughter made her insane.

"Where is she, you muthafucka?" Apple screamed out.

Shaun taunted her by laughing.

"Where is she?" Apple kicked him in the face with the bottom of her heels.

The pain was excruciating for Shaun, but he continued on with his mocking smile and laugh. "Fuck you, bitch!"

Apple was about to break his head off. She always thought she would enjoy this moment, but it flipped on her like a coin in the air. Her tears started to drop.

"You ain't gonna never find that little bitch. Fuck you, Apple! Fuck you and everything about you. What you did to my family, to me, bitch, rot in hell! 'Cause your daughter . . . you ain't gonna never see that little fuckin' bitch again. I made sure of that."

Apple couldn't hold her composure. She broke down in front of everyone. It wasn't fair. Even on the brink of death, Shaun still had the advantage over her. The pleasure of torturing and killing him wasn't there anymore.

Shaun continued to mock Apple, until Kola silenced him with four hot shots into his head. He wasn't going to talk. After that, the men buried him in the desert, but Apple was left with no closure.

Kola was shocked to find out that she was an aunt. "Why didn't you tell me?" she asked Apple.

"'Cause it was my fuckin' business."

Kola didn't push the issue because Apple was too distraught. Kola tried to console her, saying, "We'll find her."

But Apple didn't know anymore. Her life had been one big free fall of terror and anguish. Everything had been taken from her—Nichols, her mother, her daughter, her beauty, and even her dignity.

Now, the twins were being forced to leave the country because they had to repay a debt to Eduardo, and the feds were closing in on them with for murder, racketeering, tax evasion, and on and on, each charge carrying twenty to life sentences. The twins had to disappear, and Eduardo was ready to make it happen.

In two days, they were going to board a plane, with new identities and leave for the south of France, and then head for Colombia. Kola was ready to show her loyalty to Eduardo, but Apple wasn't so sure. But what choice did she have? If she chose to stay, then her freedom and her life would be in jeopardy.

*

Guy Tony walked into his penthouse suite in Houston wanting to relax. So far it had been a good day. He turned on the TV, and it was all over the news—The FBI had a nationwide manhunt out for the twins. He smiled.

Somehow, the twins had escaped capture and hadn't been seen in weeks. Guy Tony felt he could relax more. He figured he'd outsmarted Apple. Kola was just a bonus.

Guy walked into the bedroom to undress, but he felt a strange presence in the room with him. Before he could turn around and react, he felt the cold steel of a Desert Eagle pressed against the back of his head.

"Don't fuckin' move, muthafucka!" a voice growled in the dark.

"What is it that you want, nigga? Money, huh? I got plenty of it around. Help yourself."

"I don't want ya fuckin' money, Guy, I want ya life."

"Yo, we can work this shit out. I can give you whatever! Who's payin' you for this job? Huh, muthafucka? Who's payin' you for this shit?"

"Not a damn soul. This is pro bono," the man replied.

The man squeezed the trigger and unloaded a hot slug into the back of Guy's head, and Guy crumpled to the floor. The man continued to fire, shooting the body five more times.

Terri hated a snitch. He stepped over the body as it began pooling with blood. Now, it was time for him to leave the country too, and maybe link up with the twins and work for Eduardo's empire. He had nothing else left in Houston or New York.